EVERYTHING YOU'VE EVER WANTED

A HEARTWARMING STORY OF FRIENDSHIP, STARTING OVER, AND FINDING THE COURAGE TO BRING A LIFELONG DREAM TO LIFE

CLEARWATER DREAMS

BOOK 2

JESS AMES

This book is dedicated to the Schells.

Thank you for everything you've taught me. Through a lifetime of selfless giving of your time and love, you've proven that the bonds of true family are so much stronger than blood.

GIGI'S CHICKEN & DUMPLINGS

Chicken soup
2 rotisserie chickens or comparable
2 containers of chicken stock
2 packs country gravy mix
2 sticks butter (salted or unsalted)
3 tsp sea salt (divided/2)
¼ tsp ground sage (optional)
1 medium white onion
2 bags sliced carrots
1 pint half and half

Dumplings
3 cups flour
4 tsp baking powder
1 ½ cups milk
6 Tbsp parsley

Chop onion, cook in Dutch oven over low heat in 1 ½ sticks butter until translucent.

Add in the country gravy mix.

Pour in chicken stock and use a flat-end wooden spatula to scrape the bottom of the pot.

Add 1 ½ tsp salt (or measure with your heart)

Turn flame up to medium.

Use a whisk to mix

Add shredded chicken

Add carrots

Add half and half

Cover and turn heat down to medium-low. It will still boil a little. That's fine. If it sounds like two drunks are under the lid wrestling over the last Old Milwaukee, turn the heat down a little.

While all those flavors get acquainted, it's time to make the dumplings.

Put the last 4 Tbsp of butter in a mug and melt it in the microwave 15 seconds at a time.

Keep an eye on your Dutch oven. If it looks like it's trying to boil over, turn the flame down a teeeensy bit at a time until it behaves. Boiling—good. Volcanic eruptions in the kitchen—bad.

Put the flour, baking powder, 1 ½ tsp salt, milk, butter and parsley in a bowl. You can use a large mixing spoon or the paddle mixer on the kitchen aid.

Mix until blended.

Take a peek at your chicken soup. If it's boiling, it's time for the dumplings to head into the hot tub.

Start spooning the dumpling mixture into the Dutch oven one heaping tablespoon at a time. They can be anywhere from a golf ball to a racquetball size. Once they're all in there, close the lid AND DO NOT OPEN

IT FOR TWENTY MINUTES!!!

After twenty minutes, take the lid off and turn the flame off.

Serve as soon as it's not thermonuclear.

1

___

I was sifting powdered sugar over a just-cooled apple strudel when my husband called from county jail. Leaning over the tiny kitchen table in my tiny new apartment above the café where I worked, I was imagining myself with my apron-covered hip propped against a gleaming stainless steel table, putting the finishing touches on a last-minute order that had come in through my bakery's website. Back and forth with the sifter... downy, white flakes danced around each other as they floated and settled into their resting places.

B-r-r-r-r-t

The rumble of the phone against the white laminate broke me from my time-worn daydream. I reached up to adjust the white baker's cap that existed only in my mind, pressed pause on my dream, and shook my head to clear it. When I read the caller ID, my stomach folded in on itself.

'Collect call'

Craig.

I took a deep breath that settled in my chest and refused to return. I set the sifter down on a nearby dish and picked up my phone. For a moment, just a moment, I held it in my hand and considered letting him go to voicemail. But a lifetime of experience told me that ignoring a man who will not be ignored would only delay the inevitable.

"Hello?" I said, forcing the air from my lungs.

My husband's out-of-touch politician's voice poured through the phone. "Jenna, sweetheart. Are you busy?" Without waiting for me to answer, he continued. "I need you to do me a favor, baby. Can you please come down here and bail me out? I can't sit here for one more day."

I shifted the phone to my other ear and wrapped my free arm around my waist as I paced the twenty steps it took to reach the other end of my apartment and back. He wasn't going to like my reply. "Craig, I just don't think I can do that. I don't have the money for it right now. I'm sorry."

This was apparently not the answer he was expecting, because, as expected, his demeanor slipped from the fake, sticky sweetness of corn syrup to hot, burning rage faster than a falling soufflé. "You're sorry? You're *sorry?* Be sorry that you haven't already come down here to get me. I'm your husband, Jenna. Remember the vows you took? Love, honor, and *obey?*"

Recognizing the opening line to the endless refrain of our marriage, I pulled a chair away from my kitchen table and willed my shaky legs to deposit me safely into it.

"Yes, I *do* remember, Craig. But I still can't afford to come and bail you out right now. I have expenses I need to think about."

The sound of what I could only assume was the phone bashing against a hard surface assaulted my eardrum. "You have expenses because you decided to leave our home and go live above that — that *woman's* café."

"That woman is my *boss*, and my *friend*," I reminded him, "and she's been nice enough to let me stay here."

"You don't need to stay there," Craig argued back. "What you need to do is come and get me so we can go home together where we belong."

I'd prepared for this moment in therapy. We had role-played and rehearsed for weeks, and as I tilted the phone away from my ear in preparation of what I knew was coming next, I sent up a silent prayer that I could speak with the same resolve I'd finally achieved in my sessions.

"I'm just not so sure about that anymore, Craig. That's not *our* home anymore, and for the record, I like it here."

My therapist's voice floated through my head. *"Good. Very good. Keep going, Jenna. You've got this."* I focused on the tension in my shoulders and let them drop from somewhere near my earlobes.

"Oh, I'm sure you *do* like it there, living it up and doing whatever the hell you want, but you have to know it'll never last, Jenna. You need me. You'll never survive on your own. So, go down to the bank and get the money and get me the hell out of here," he volleyed back. I could almost see his confident sneer as he waited for his words to take shape in my soft, pliable mind.

But what Craig didn't know, and what I was finally learning, was that my mind could bend to *my* will, too.

I let the silence stretch long enough to gather up the scraps of my newly found strength, breathe in slowly through my nose, and look around to ground myself in the new life I was willing into existence, one bright white and navy throw pillow at a time. "Craig, I don't think it's a great idea for me to come bail you out right now," I began with all the confidence I could muster, "but I'm sure your attorney will be able to work something out."

"I don't have an attorney, Jenna. I have a *public defender*," he spit out.

"I know, Craig. But I —"

"Jenna, you're being ridiculous. Come down here right—"

Taking a page from his own book, I cut him off. Hung up the phone. For the first time, I didn't feel compelled to listen to him go on and on about all the ways I'd failed him, and all the ways he'd saved me. I no longer needed my subscription to his misguided savior program. It had become painfully clear who had been saving whom in our relationship, and I was no longer compelled to rescue him after what he'd done to land himself in jail. It was embarrassing enough to know that he had destroyed my friend's home, just as I was starting to get my feet under me and maybe forge my own path to a little bit of independence. I can't even imagine how Paige had felt to come home and find her kitchen and bedroom destroyed. And then to find out it was my husband who had done it out of anger and jealousy that she was offering me a chance to bake for her retreats—an opportunity to gain some independence (God forbid)... I'd been lucky that Paige was such an understanding friend and didn't hold Craig's actions against me.

Since then, I'd been working hard to plan out the pastries that would make up the breakfasts at her writers' retreats. After months of planning and prep, they were finally starting up the following weekend. The Sensational Six had jumped into action and helped Paige put the whole thing together in a matter of a few months. It was incredible, and I was honored to be a part of it.

I'd worked hard and had proven myself, and I wouldn't let Craig ruin that for me. I felt safer with him behind bars. Safer than I'd ever felt (outside of weekends with my grandma when I was a child).

I took a lap around the apartment, trying to cool myself down a little bit. I took in everything I'd done to make the place mine in the last few weeks. I had hung white sheers and topped them with sunshine-yellow valances. The cushion on the white rattan couch that came with the apartment had been re-covered with a yellow slipcover and bright white and navy throw pillows lounged along the back. The framed prints I had found in the local thrift stores surrounded it nicely, and complemented the Iceland landscape painting centered above it that Cat had bright back from her travels and gave me when I'd moved in. "To remind you of the great big world that's out there waiting for you," she'd said. As I stopped to look at it, vibrant green mountains complete with a waterfall flowing into an otherwise still pool. I doubted I'd ever be brave enough to travel that far, and I admired Cat even more because she was.

I smiled at the thought, then sat back down at the table and slid my grandmother's recipe book onto my lap. Thumbing the edges of pages I knew by heart, I flipped to one that held a memory that was equal parts fond and painful. Lavender cupcakes. The last thing we ever baked together.

Ten years had passed, and I was no less naïve than that young girl who had blown out eighteen white candles in the center of eighteen purple frosting swirls. Ten years had seen me cleaning up more broken glass from my parents' drunken battles, smiling through stony silences and words that left my wilted self-confidence in tatters. Ten years had shown me that you could escape from arms that held you at a distance while slowly crushing you... and wake up one morning to find your life with your new husband—the one you thought would be a refuge—looks and sounds and feels like more of the same.

I traced her outline, my fingers gliding over the photo we'd called her neighbor over to take that day. If we had known it would be the last we spent consuming copious amounts of sugar in her garden, would it have been as sweet? Would we have lingered a moment longer to soak in the last rays of the evening sun? Would I have rushed off to prepare a dinner that would be pushed aside to conserve space for the amber liquid that had stained my childhood memories? Would I have said thank you one more time for the many ways she wrapped me in her strength and peace?

Yes.

But I couldn't say I would go back to that day. I would never want to relive those ten years.

From deep inside that cherished memory, I heard the long, repeated buzz of my phone against the table. My reverie broken and my stomach again in knots, I flipped it over and smiled when I read the screen.

Swiping with one hand while the other lifted the recipe book onto the table, I marveled at my friends' ability to call or show up at exactly the right time. "Hi, Grace," I said as my phone reached my ear. "What are you up to?"

"Hey there, Sugar," rumbled over the line in Grace's trademark sultry tone. I'd never read any of her books, but often thought that if their tone matched hers, it was no wonder they were so popular. Even at sixty-five years young, her voice alone oozed sex. "What are you up to today?"

"Just going through some of my grandma's old recipes to see what I want to make this weekend."

"Darlin', Paige has talked about nothing else but this weekend and how excited she is to see what you're bringing. You're certainly keeping things under wraps, aren't you?"

"Well, she told me that she trusted my judgment, and I wanted to take a few days to think about it; try to find a few things that perhaps nobody had seen before. I've been baking up a storm all week, and I think I've nailed it down. My kitchen is covered in flour and butter, and—" I took a breath, realizing I was talking way too fast. "As you can probably tell, I'm excited too."

"I bet you are, and I can't wait to see what you come up with. From what I've heard of your grandma, she was an excellent baker, just like you. And everything is going to be just perfect."

"From your lips to God's ear, Grace," I said.

BAKED APPLE STRUDEL

1 medium Granny Smith apple coarsely shredded

2 medium Granny Smith apples cored and sliced

3/4 cup light brown sugar

2 tablespoons all purpose flour

2 sheets frozen puff pastry, thawed

1/2 teaspoon salt

1 large egg

1 tablespoon half and half

Preheat the oven to 400 degrees.

Line a large rimmed baking sheet with parchment paper.

Place shredded and chopped apples in a large bowl.

Stir in brown sugar, flour, and salt.

Place one puff pastry sheet on a lightly floured work surface.

Roll lightly with a rolling pin into a 10x12-inch rectangle.

Arrange 1/2 of the apple filling (about 3 cups) down one side of the puff pastry sheet lengthwise.

Fold the pastry sheet lengthwise over the apple mixture.

Dampen edges of pastry with water, then press edges to seal.

Repeat process with 2nd pastry sheet and remaining apple mixture.

Place on the prepared baking sheet, leaving at least 2 inches between each pastry.

Whisk egg and half and half together.

Brush on top of each pastry.

Cut 3 or 4 slits on top of each pastry to allow steam to escape.

Bake in the preheated oven until golden brown (30 to 35 minutes).

2

After hanging up with Grace, I continued flipping through my recipe book and decided on a cheddar jalapeno sourdough to have with my chicken and dumplings for dinner the next night. I finished chopping and de-seeding the peppers just as the intercom buzzed. Even though I knew he was in jail, my anxiety spiked. What if he'd gotten out without my knowledge. Would he come here?

"Hello? Who is it?" I asked through the intercom.

"Hey, it's me. I have something for you," came back in my friend's voice, followed by five solid seconds of ear-piercing static. It wasn't the most recent technology as far as intercoms went, but I was grateful for it nonetheless.

"Come on up, Paige," I replied, wondering what she had in store for me. A minute later, I heard a feather-light knock on the door and swung it open.

She walked in, dropped her black tote bag on the floor, and leaned over with her hands on her knees, her breath leaving in short bursts. "Every time I climb them, I feel like there are more stairs than the last time I was here."

"I understand," I said, rubbing her back and trying not to let my grin invade my voice. "But, I believe it's been the same this whole time."

She stood up and moved into the space between us for a hug. "Maybe my legs are getting shorter." Giving me a quick squeeze, she stepped back.

"Hopefully not," I replied. "How long would it take before you disappeared altogether?"

"Yeah, I don't have much to spare," said Paige with a laugh. Her ice-blue eyes zeroed in on my apron that had begun its day covered in mauve tea roses, but somewhere along the way, had become an artistic interpretation of a garden blooming inside of a cirrus cloud. "What are you up to?"

"Let me go wash my hands," I said, leading her to the kitchen. "I was just chopping jalapenos for my sourdough tomorrow."

"Well, that sounds interesting," she said, as she sat in the chair I'd recently vacated. The cookbook still lay open to the recipe I'd been daydreaming about earlier, and as I dried my hands, I saw her scan the page. I was tempted to cave and ask her if she thought lavender cupcakes were a little too out there for her retreat attendees, but I managed to hold back. I had told her it was going to be a surprise, and I knew I needed to learn how to have a little faith in my choices.

"I'm trying out some new recipes, and I came across a few things I want to consider for your retreat this weekend."

"I love it," she said. "I can't wait to see what you come up with. Whatever it is, I'm sure it will be wonderful."

"I appreciate your faith in me, Paige," I said, feeling the heat race up my neck. I was much better at baking than I was at taking compliments.

Paige reached across the table and lay her hand on top of mine. "We all have faith in you, Jenna."

"Well, I wish I could say the same for Craig."

"Oh boy," she said with an awkward smile. "I'm sorry. I know it's hard when you put your faith in someone, and they let you down. It can be hard to see them in a different light. You want to believe the best in the people you've committed yourself to. You expect them to love you and treat you the way you love and treat them, but sometimes that's just not the case. It's a hard lesson to learn as we go through life, isn't it? Not everybody turns out the way we hope."

"I'm disappointed, and a lot of how I'm feeling seems to come back to shock. I'm shocked at how things have turned out. I'm shocked at his behavior, and I'm shocked that he's still not ready to take accountability for himself. And it all hurts, it all just... I can't seem to wrap my mind around what's happened and everything that's changing for me."

"We'll come back to that in a second," said Paige, "because that feeling is something that I happen to know a lot about, as you know. But when was the last time you talked to Craig?"

I took a deep breath, relatively sure of how Paige was going to react. "Well, I actually just hung up with him a few minutes before you got here."

"Oh, yeah?" asked Paige, feigning indifference as she flipped through the recipe book.

"It didn't go very well. He's begging me to come bail him out of jail and find the money to hire a better lawyer. When I tell him that I'm not able to or I don't think it's a good idea, he immediately changes his tune and blames everything on my friendship with all of you."

Paige rolled her eyes, but remained silent. I continued.

"The whole reason he's there is because he can't seem to get a handle on his emotions. To prove my point, as soon as he didn't get his way, he turned into the Craig that I've come to know, and it's just not what I want in my life right now. I'm finally getting my feet under me. I'm living on my own for the first time. And I'm actually enjoying it." Pausing, I looked down at my apron and scratched at a lump of dried flour with my fingernail. "Even though it gets a little lonely sometimes."

"I understand that well," said Paige, squeezing my arm.

I looked up at my friend, focusing on the white stripe separating her short brown pixie cut right at the center of her forehead. "But at the same time, that loneliness passes, and I'm actually enjoying my own company. I'm reading more, and I've been having so much fun going through my grandma's recipe books." I set my hand on the one in front of us. "And I'm finding more and more handwritten recipes stashed in her historical fiction books that I had set aside, but now am *finally* putting on a bookshelf." My eyes wandered over to the corner of the living room where my recently thrifted treasure proudly bowed under the weight of them. To its right, my grandmother's rose pink guitar sat on its stand, a lady waiting. "So I've been trying out new recipes and redecorating after I get home from the café."

Paige looked around and took in everything I had done to make the apartment *mine*. I walked Paige back to the tiny bedroom I had turned into a big girl's paradise. The brass daybed was bursting with yellow and navy blue pillows painstakingly arranged along the back of the white eyelet coverlet.

She walked across the room and fiddled with the antique perfume bottles I had displayed on the white rattan dresser. "This place is absolutely adorable," she said, making eye contact with me. "I'm so happy to see you settling in here and putting your stamp on this place. And I'm enjoying getting to know you without the added pressure of you having to handle Craig and his behavior. Now that you know you have all of us to lean on, we're seeing a whole new Jenna come through, and it's a beautiful thing."

My throat began to close involuntarily, but I managed to choke down the emotions that had bubbled up out of nowhere. "I have all of you to thank for where I am right now. You have all helped me find the strength to stand on my own after seeing Craig's behavior through clear eyes. I was a lot like the frog in the pot of water. Things were getting worse and worse at home, but they were such small changes, I thought I could influence him to turn things around. Perhaps I never would have. And then what? But having all of your support and friendship has been invaluable to me at a time in my life when I thought I was alone in what was happening in my marriage."

Paige walked over from the dresser and wrapped her arms around me, and I set my head down on her shoulder. "You're never alone. You. Are. Never. Alone. You are an important part of the Sensational Six, and we aren't going anywhere." A few emotional moments later, we walked back out to the kitchen, where some of my experimental baking was cooling on racks. "And look at this, Jenna! Look at what you have done for your-self. You are blossoming into a whole new woman right before our eyes. We're all so proud of you and want to support you in every way we can."

She cleared her throat and shifted her weight to her other foot. "Can I give you a little bit of advice? I hesitate to ask because I never want to be that person who's just jamming my opinion down someone else's throat, but I feel like I've fallen into this big sister role with you."

Her declaration instantly warmed my heart. I had always wanted a sister—any sibling, really—and I'd grown to feel the same way about Paige in the short time she'd been a part of our group. "Of course. I value your opinion and your friendship, so whatever you have to say, I'm ready to hear it."

"Okay. I honestly feel like you need to give Craig time to consider his predicament and how he got there. It's not a bad idea to let him sit for a while; he really needs to have that time alone to think about what he's done and how he can maybe make himself a better person. I'm not telling you how to live your life, but in the short term, I would love to see you have a little peace as he works through what he needs to work through." Paige paused and reached out to rest her hand on my forearm, then continued. "And you can't do that if he's here knocking on your door, begging you to take him back. You can take advantage of this situation to learn more about *Jenna*." She spun back toward the counter where my strudel was resting. "The Jenna who decorated this beautiful apartment and baked this masterpiece here, and has contributed so much to our little group."

"I understand what you're saying, Paige, I really do, and I appreciate you sharing your opinion with me because I know other people's opinions are not always well received, but I know that you have way more life experience than I do."

I walked over to the table and gestured to the other chair before I sat. I had a feeling this was going to be a longer conversation. As Paige dropped into the chair across from me, I looked over her shoulder at the strudel she'd pointed to. It had been one of my grandmother's specialties, requested at every gathering she attended, and I could smell the cinnamon as it floated by in the air we'd disturbed when we sat. It was as comforting as a thick, heavy quilt on a chilly night.

"I've been fairly sheltered after going from my parents' house to my marital home with Craig, and the behaviors never changed. I never told you this, but a couple months ago when I came home from one of our Sensational Six meetings while we were planning your retreat, he had changed the locks on our apartment. I had to beg him through the door to let me in. Some of our neighbors heard me knocking on the door for over thirty minutes and came out to see what was happening. It was humiliating. I had to pretend like I had lost my keys and Craig was asleep, but I heard him in there moving around. I'm used to having someone tell me that I'd never survive on my own, that I'm not good enough and I never will be, and that I need someone else's guidance to make it through life. This is something that I've been listening to my entire life."

I'd been staring at my hands clasped in my lap, but looked up at Paige at this point. Her eyes were heavy with concern, but I wasn't finished. "But hearing all of you tell me that none of it is true and pointing out my strengths and holding them up to the light for me to examine and try to believe for myself..." I took a deep breath and shifted my chair a little more toward Paige. "I can't tell you what that has meant for me."

"Well," Paige said as she picked up her tote bag from the back of the chair and set it on her lap. "I have something for you. And when I put it in my bag this morning, I laughed to myself because I remember receiving one myself not too long ago, and I thought it was the most ridiculous thing I had ever seen." I was dying of curiosity. She opened her bag, peered into it, then stuffed her hand in and began rummaging around. "But it's turned out to be instrumental in helping me put—and keep —things in perspective when it was difficult to see anything but what was going wrong in my life."

She took out a book and set it on the table. The cover read, *Gratitude Journal*. I groaned inwardly, but for Paige's sake, put a smile on my face.

"Wow, Paige, thank you. I'm sure I will find so many things to write in here." I thumbed through the pages to give the illusion of excitement, but at that very moment, I was having a hard time thinking of more than a few.

"You absolutely will. And, Jenna, I was where you are right now; where it didn't feel like there was a whole lot in my life to be grateful for." A tinkle of laughter spilled from her lips as she shook her head. "In fact, I stuffed this book in a drawer and left town without it. When Kari visited for the first time, she brought it back to me, and I finally decided to give it a shot." She placed her hand on the cover and patted it twice. "I can say with absolute certainty that physically writing what was going *right* in my life worked for me. Now, to manage your expectations, I have to be honest that it might not work for you right away. I'm not promising you're going to use this one time and feel compelled to pen a self-help book, but sometimes it helps to write things down, just to get them out of our head. It also helps to go back and read what you wrote; a lot of times, you'll find that you process everything in a different way.

"And if you have things in your life that you can be grateful for, writing them down and reading them over can really help put everything in perspective. Yes, your life is changing, but it's changing for the better. Yes, you're living on your own now, but you have your independence, and you're finding that you are flourishing as an independent woman. You're coming into your own even though you haven't had the best role models for getting your feet under you and finding your true self.

"You're finding out who Jenna is without being told by someone else, without languishing in the shadow of someone who told you that you couldn't survive without them. You are establishing your own roots in a community that is here to support you. These are all blessings in your life right now that you can focus on when you feel alone, when you feel as if everything is changing in your life and nothing looks or feels familiar, and you start to spiral a little bit. You can come back and flip open the pages and read the things that you do have to be grateful for. You can focus on the blessings you have in your life. Even for right now, if you just write down our names, the rest will come to you later. That's okay; just start somewhere."

Her eyes searched mine as she patted my knee. "I know you are going to be a huge success, and I know the sense of self—of who Jenna *really* is—that you are going to find is going to be one of the most valuable gifts you've ever given yourself. And I'm just so grateful..." She squeezed my arm. "... that I get to be here to witness it."

"Well, I'm grateful that you're here as well, Paige. I'm so glad that you ended up in Dunedin, and I'm beyond thrilled about the opportunity you've given me to help with the retreat."

Paige slapped the cover of the book. "Let's talk about the retreat. I'm so excited to see what you're bringing this weekend."

"Are you sure you don't want me to give you a list?" I asked. While I appreciated her faith in me, I was a little nervous to know I would be showing up at her first retreat with trays full of surprises she hadn't actually ordered.

"Not a chance. I believe in you, and I know whatever you choose to make is going to be awesome. So, I'm fine with being surprised, and I look forward to what you bring on Friday if it looks anything like what you've got on the counter right now." She pointed over her shoulder with her thumb without breaking eye contact.

"Well, I'm proud of *you*," I said, "for having this dream. And while it wasn't necessarily your dream from the start, you've worked hard to get here. You've invested so much of your time and money into getting this retreat off the ground. I'm *so* grateful to you for giving me the opportunity to provide break-fast for your guests. I won't let you down."

"I know you won't, sweetheart. I know you won't." She flipped her phone over so it was face up on the table and glanced at the time. "Well, I need to run over to the bookstore and drop off new flyers for Elyse to put in the window for February's romance author retreat. Hey, do you have any idea what's been going on with her lately?"

"What do you mean?"

She picked up her phone and turned it over in her hand while she looked up at the ceiling. "She just seems so distracted lately. Always on her phone. I'm just hoping everything is ok."

"I've noticed, but I haven't asked. I bet Cat knows, though. They're pretty close."

"True. Well, it's none of my business, really. I'm just worried something is wrong." She paused for a moment, and then tapped her phone on her left palm. "Anyway, I'm sure every-thing is fine. But, I better get going so I can drop these flyers off, although I'm not sure how long she will need to have them up."

I took the ponytail holder off my wrist and pulled my hair back and secured it. "Why is that?"

"Well, I'm happy to say, the next retreat is sold out, and it looks like February might be sold out in the next couple weeks."

"Paige, that is incredible! I would say I can't believe it, but that would be a lie."

She dropped her phone into her bag and we stood at the same time. I pulled her in for a hug. "You've been such a good role model for me and I'm so glad that I've gotten to know you. Thank you for your friendship, and for believing in me."

"Thank *you* for believing in *me*," she retorted then heaved her tote bag over her shoulder. "Now let's hope I can keep the dog out of the pool while the ladies are swimming." We both laughed at that mental image. Her golden retriever, Roxy, was always getting into some kind of mischief. A lot like her owner, actually.

"Ok, I need to get going. Think about what I said. Craig is going to call again, and it wouldn't hurt to have what you're going to say to him prepared ahead of time to make it a little easier to get through. I'm not telling you what to do, but just consider giving him some time to reflect on his actions and behavior while you give yourself some time to heal." Halfway to the door, she spun back to face me, her thumb looped through the strap under her shoulder. Her eyes searched my face. "Are you still going to therapy?" she asked, naked concern in her voice.

"I am," I said. "I actually have a session coming up this week. We are going to have a lot to unpack, but I feel ready when I don't think about it too much."

"I know you'll get through this and come out the other side a stronger, more confident Jenna," said Paige, then turned and made her way to the door. She pointed at the journal she'd left on the table. "See what you can do with that, and I will see you in a couple days."

"Not if I see you first," I said with a wink. "Tell Elyse I said hello. Although, I'm sure I'll be seeing her in the café tomorrow."

"Oh, I'm sure you will. She might need some kind of twelve-step program for Cat's club sandwiches." We both laughed as she opened the door and stepped through it into the hallway at the top of the stairs. "Alright. Now I'm really leaving. I'll see you soon."

As I watched her walk down the stairs toward the street outside the café, a lightness filled my chest. For the first time in my life, I was experiencing the joy of true friendship. Of the family I had chosen and who had chosen *me*. That was surely something to be grateful for.

A FEW MINUTES after Paige left, the timer went off to remind me to stretch and fold my sourdough. After four rounds with each ball, I covered them with a few tea towels and left them to rest on the counter. I'd decided to make a cheesy potato casserole with my dinner, so I set the O-brien potatoes on a paper towel to dry.

I turned back to the tiny table mere steps away, and the cover of the journal Paige had left behind caught my eye. It was decorated in baby pink and moss-green flowers that could have been inspired by my grandmother's favorite apron. The apron I was wearing at that very moment. It felt like a sign, and a sigh escaped without notice until it slipped past my lips.

My grandmother's voice floated up from my stored memories. *"The first step is always the hardest, but if the journey is worth-while, it's a step in the right direction."*

"I hear you, Gigi," I said out loud in the hopes that if she were somewhere nearby, watching over me, she'd know I was still listening to her guidance.

I sat down at the table and began to flip through the gratitude journal in earnest and found there were many different sections in the book, but the one that captured my eye was a simple list. It seemed like a bridge too far to sit and write a journal entry at that moment, but a list felt like something I could do. So I began.

TODAY, I'm grateful for:

- *My friends, Grace, Paige, Elyse, Cat, Sarah, and Adam.*
- *My tiny apartment, that's all mine.*
- *The opportunity to work at Cat's Bites.*
- *The opportunity to bake for Paige's writing retreats.*
- *My grandma, who has gone too soon.*

AFTER ADDING those five simple lines, I thought about my grandma and how she tried my whole life to counteract the messages I was receiving from my dysfunctional parents.

One thing I did not add to my list but what I was very grateful for was my grandma looking out for my future. She'd set up an annuity for me that kicked in when I turned eighteen. Without it, I would never have been able to support Craig and my modest lifestyle while he failed to maintain employment. While we were struggling financially, there were so many times I had wanted to get a job, but he'd always resisted, telling me that it was a man's job to provide and a woman's job to take care of the home. When our electricity went out for the fourth time in a year, I'd had enough and decided the best way to take care of our home was to make sure the lights turned on. I had made my way down Main Street, filling out applications wherever I could, and struck gold when I'd made it to Cat's bites. I'd explained to her that I was looking for some independence and, even though I had freely admitted to having no experience, she'd hired me on the spot. Besides having Gigi as my grandma, it turned out to be the single greatest thing that had ever happened to me.

It was easy to see from the distance I'd gained that his actions had all been an attempt to keep me under his thumb. As I forged more independence in his absence, I had started to see the cracks in our marriage. He *must* have known that would happen.

I closed the gratitude journal and walked into my bedroom. On the dresser sat the modest jewelry box that my grandmother gave me upon her passing. I lifted up the tray that bowed under the weight of her costume jewelry and, underneath, found Gigi's birthstone ring and the brooch she had bought herself to celebrate having made it through forty years of marriage. It was a symbol of strength and perseverance. It made me feel closer to her to wear her ring, a symbol of love that was true.

Underneath the ring and brooch was a letter that my grandmother had written me before she passed. It was full of truths that at that time I was not ready to hear.

I sat on the bed and read the letter. It stressed that I should get away from my parents as soon as I was able. She talked about the annuity she had set up to ensure I could afford to move away from my parents and live on my own. Grandma told me that my heart had remained soft and loving despite my upbringing, and she wanted to make sure that whoever I eventually gave my heart to was worthy. She encouraged me to follow my dreams.

I considered my grandma's words and wondered what she would think of my choice in Craig. I wondered what she would think of my husband sitting in jail as I ignored his request to come and bail him out. Knowing my grandma and understanding her better as an adult now myself, I knew that Gigi would be proud of my recent decisions.

I gently refolded grandma's letter and laid it in the bottom of the jewelry box, set the engagement ring and brooch on top, and replaced the tray. I may not have had a great role model in my parents, and my father's parents drank themselves to death years before I was even born, but my grandmother's love had always stood out in my mind as something that I hoped for, longed for, and assumed that I would have in a partner. Unfortunately, I had followed the example of my parents' unhealthy relationship in choosing the partner I had. Although, I'll admit that "Craig, king of the acid-washed jabs" who sat in jail was far removed from the "biting-snark Craig" that I had pledged my life and loyalty to years ago. I didn't know what had happened to that Craig, or if he would ever be back, but at no point had he been an example of who I wanted as a partner for the rest of my life. I no longer trusted that he could be that person or that he would ever get to that place.

I was learning in therapy that you can't fix somebody. They have to do the work themselves, and I just didn't see Craig putting that work in.

CHEESY POTATO CASSEROLE

1 can condensed cream of mushroom (or chicken) soup

2 cups sour cream

1 teaspoon salt

¼ teaspoon ground black pepper

2 cups shredded cheddar cheese

½ cup white onion

1 (30 ounce) package O'brien Potatoes

2 cups crushed corn flakes

¼ cup melted butter

Preheat the oven to 350 degrees.

Spray a 9x13-inch baking dish with nonstick spray.

Mix sour cream, soup, salt, and pepper in a large bowl.

Stir in cheese, onions, and potatoes until mixed.

Spread evenly into a buttered baking dish.

Mix crushed cereal and melted butter together in a medium bowl.

Sprinkle evenly over the casserole.

Bake uncovered until bubbly (45 to 50 minutes).

Remove from the oven and let rest for 5 minutes before serving.

3

———

Tuesday was busier than normal at the café, and the bakery case was sold out by noon. Cat walked into a packed house when she returned at one o'clock from golfing with the ladies league, and when she saw the empty shelves that had been full to bursting mere hours before, she raised her eyebrows at me. "Sold out again, huh?" she asked as she slid a fresh yellow bandana over her close-cropped hair. I let her rhetorical question slide by. She had been making little comments here and there about me starting up my own bakery, but there had been enough recent changes in my life—and besides, I had no idea where to even start with something like that.

When I got home from work around four, I decided to work on the lavender cupcake recipe that had caught my eye the day before. I'd stopped off to pick up a few supplies from the grocery store and was eager to get started. I was looking forward to feeling like I was baking with Gigi again, and recreating the feelings of contentment and pride I'd had that day.

With the oven preheating, I mixed the dry ingredients, then began the next step. The familiar sensation of cracking the eggs, mixing wet ingredients into dry, turning the spoon, reaching the point when the resistance lessened. I took out my dried lavender from the freezer and chopped it up while I considered the conversation with Cat that had taken place earlier. The comforting aroma filled the room and took me back to Gigi's warm kitchen and all the loving memories it contained within its butter-yellow walls.

When I was younger, I would often pretend I was a baker in my very own bakery. Gigi would play along, turning from my assistant baker to my customer. Those were the memories I cherished the most. To be able to turn that beautiful memory into a reality was something I had never dreamed would actually happen, but after watching the bakery case empty out day after day, I was starting to see it as a distant possibility.

As I measured the batter into cupcake tins, I continued to daydream, putting together collections and themes and even a few bits of decor in my mind. Lavender and white striped walls, white tables and chairs, the case full of almond croissants, cupcakes, tarts, and muffins.

Thirty minutes later, the first batch was out of the oven, cooled, and ready to be frosted. As I held the piping bag over the first cupcake, I squeezed it, and a soothing, muted purple flowed down and swirled around until the entire top was covered. I sprinkled a bit of the lavender sugar mix over one-half of the top and set it aside.

As I held the piping bag over the second cupcake, I heard my phone ding. It was a text from Grace.

Grace: Are you free in about ten minutes?

I set the piping bag down so that I could type my reply.

Me: Yes, I'll buzz you up and prop the door open when you get here. I'm baking.

Grace: Perfect, I'll see you in ten

When Grace arrived. I buzzed her in with my elbow and was just putting the finishing touches on the first batch as a streak of Lilly Pulitzer flashed into my peripheral vision. I turned mid-swirl to smile at my friend, noticing she'd recently lightened her platinum spikes.

"Love the hair," I said, finishing the last cupcake.

I saw the tips of her Taos sneakers slide into view next to my bare feet. "Love all of this," she said, bumping my shoulder as I pulled the lid off a plastic storage container. "Jenna, these cupcakes are gorgeous! They could be in a magazine." She turned and set her bag down on the white rattan couch.

Not one to accept a compliment without feeling like I wanted to crawl under a table, I looked at the counter and shrugged. "Thanks. They're lavender cupcakes; would you like to try one? They don't get much fresher than this."

Grace wasted no time unwrapping a cupcake and taking a bite. "Jenna, this is really good. Are you going to have these at the café this week?" she asked.

"No, not yet. I used to make these with my grandmother and came across the recipe again yesterday. I was thinking of making them for Paige's retreat this weekend, but it's been years. These are my trial run."

"Well, they definitely have my vote. Maybe I'll have one more just to be sure." Grace took another cupcake from the rack, unwrapped one side, and took a bite. She closed her eyes as she chewed. "Has Paige tried these?" she asked after she'd finished.

I grabbed the towel hanging from my sink, wiped a few stray crumbs into my hand and deposited them into the garbage before rehanging the towel. "Not yet. I wanted to get the recipe just right before I committed to making them. Paige was here yesterday, actually. We talked about the retreat a little, but mostly she talked me through what she thinks I should do about Craig. He's been calling asking me to come bail him out."

"We'll get to that asshat, but first, let me say how happy I am to see you opening up and engaging more with us. We are getting to see a side of you that we haven't seen much of before and I can't say that I hate it," said Grace.

"You have all been so wonderful to me. I haven't felt judged or like any of you have befriended me because they have something to gain. I feel more like one of the gang."

Grace balled up her cupcake wrapper and threw it in the trash can next to the counter. She crossed the kitchen and sat at the table, then patted the chair next to hers. "Sugar, you are one of us. Part of our family," she said once I'd sat.

My throat began to close and tears threatened the backs of my eyes.

Grace sat back in her chair. "I want you to know how proud I am of you for pushing through all of these tough days. These are not easy changes that you're going through and you've been handling it all so well. Better than well, actually. You're flourishing, and it's so wonderful to see you come into your own. I believe that you can do anything that you want," She pointed at the counter. "as long as what you want to do is make more of those cupcakes."

Her candor drew a chuckle from me. "I'll pack up a few for you to take home with you."

"I was hoping you'd say that. Now, tell me what's going on with Craig."

"Well, he's still begging me to come bail him out."

Grace cleared her throat, then paused, likely putting her much-touted 'ten-second cool down' technique into effect. "Aaaaand?" she asked.

"And I have been saying 'no' again and again. I've told him I don't have the money for it, which is true. But it's more than that. I've never felt as free as I do since he's been in jail. Isn't that awful? Does that make me a terrible wife?"

"No, it does not make you a terrible wife. It makes you a wife who has been controlled and put down for way too long.

And now you're seeing who you are without all of that, Jenna. And I think it's simply *wonderful.*"

I rested my elbow on the table and twisted a wavy lock of my dark brown hair around my finger. "I just don't know how I'm going to get through the next couple of months with Craig calling me all the time to come bail him out."

"Well, one option you have," Grace replied, "is to just block that number and continue living your life until you decide what you're going to do. You're free to do whatever you want, but this is a good opportunity for you to get a little more perspective on who you are without him. Who Jenna is *on her own*. We can all see your potential, sweetheart. I worry that if you keep answering his calls, he's going to weasel his way back into your heart before you have the chance to experience the thrill of independence. I want that for you, Jenna. You've earned it. Everyone should have a chance to live alone at least once in their life and this is your opportunity. You're living on your own and you're doing just fine. Did you ever see that coming?"

"No," I replied. "When I went from my parents' house to Craig's apartment right after we were married, I figured that was going to be it for me; that was going to be my life."

"But it doesn't have to be," said Grace. "You are doing great, and you have all of us here to help support you. Speaking of which, when are you working next?"

"I'm in the café tomorrow."

"Oh good. I'll probably stop in tomorrow afternoon. Cat has something she wants to discuss with me. Any idea what that might be?"

I had a sneaky suspicion it had something to do with me, but I kept that to myself so as not to open up a whole new bag of flour, so to speak. "No clue," I lied.

"Well, I guess I'll find out tomorrow." She stood, walked over to the couch, and rifled through her large purse until she pulled out a paperback. "I finally received my advanced review copies of my new book from the publisher. Any chance you want to read this for me?"

She held the book up so I could see the cover. It was illustrated in a similar fashion as the rest of her books—a woman (this one was brunette) leaning against a burly lumberjack with a green, snow-capped mountain range in the distance.

"I would!" I said, then chuckled again. "No pun intended."

Grace's gravely laugh filled my apartment. "They're easy to come by with this series." She set the book on the kitchen table and hauled her purse strap over her shoulder. "And with that, I'm going to scoot. I've got a few errands to run before I meet with my writers' group tonight."

"One moment. I'll get together the cupcakes for you." When I turned around with the cupcake-packed plastic container, her face lit up.

"This is why I love you." She took the cupcakes and made her way to the door. "Oh, and Jenna?"

"Yes?" I asked pensively.

"Do yourself a favor. Block that number."

She hugged me tightly, and a moment later, she was hurrying down the stairs with a wave and a kiss blown over her shoulder.

After she left, I packed up the few cupcakes that were left, took a shower, and crawled into bed with my new book. I had a lot to think about, but it was time to escape into the mountains with a lumberjack. Afterall, Grace *had* asked for my help.

FRIDAY CAME, and I woke early in the morning to finish frosting and decorating pastries for Paige's first morning of her writing retreats. After typing out a quick text in our group chat, I loaded up and headed out to deliver everything before too many people were awake.

I pulled into the driveway behind the light pink Victorian Paige had 'inherited' from her Uncle Mike, and saw four other vehicles parked along the eight-foot privacy fence. Her retreats seemed to be off to a good start. A moment after putting my car in park, Paige's mentor, and today's tutor, Caleb, pulled in next to me. Paige was so lucky to have found Caleb. He'd been a great resource for her, first as a writer, and then as a business owner.

I opened my door and could hear them greeting one another down the walkway. "Today's the big day!"

"Can you believe it?" she said excitedly before opening the back door of my car and pulling out two of the trays that were sitting on the backseat. It was a sea of lavender. "*What are these?*" she nearly shouted.

"My grandma Gigi's famous lavender cupcakes. I've got some almond croissants in here as well, and a few other surprises," I said. Now that the secret was out, I felt more confident in my choice than I had for the previous couple days. I'd been second-guessing myself up to the very last minute, but, I had to admit, they were gorgeous. Grace was still raving about them, so I had high hopes they'd be well received.

Caleb walked around the back of my car with his bag slung over his shoulder. "It's so great to see you again, Jenna. Everything you brought to Paige's ribbon cutting went so fast I didn't have a chance to try a single thing. People were talking about it all night and I can't tell you how excited I am to experience it for myself. Here, let me help you with these. I'll just put this in my car right now," he said with a wink as he took a tray off my stack and headed back toward his Subaru.

"All right, all right, funny guy," said Paige. "Let's get these inside before people start waking up."

Caleb feigned defeat as he trudged back toward us with the tray.

Paige balanced her trays on her hip and swung the back door open, stepping aside so we could pass. The view that greeted me never got old. Dark hardwood floors stretched from the back door to the front, where the bay could be seen through the glass. A gleaming banister to my left lined the staircase up two more floors, with mosaic-covered walls all the way up. It had been hand-painted by a local artist and featured local foliage disguising every manner of native bird, lizard, and bug. I found something new every time I looked.

Across from the staircase, an arched doorway led to an expansive kitchen, quite literally straight from the pages of Elle Decor. They would be taking pictures for a spring feature in the coming weeks. I set the trays I'd carried in on the immaculate white quartz-topped island that Paige was nervously cleaning despite it shining like the sun, devoid of even a speck of dust.

I helped Paige get everything else set up while Caleb prepared the sitting room for his session. We pretended not to notice his plate heaped with cupcakes, croissants, and fruit tarts as he strolled out of the kitchen.

We opened the trays, and I polished a few utensils to set out with the plates before sliding onto one of the six pink and palm frond-covered bar stools along the counter. "You good?" I asked, even though Paige wasn't much of a poker player, and I couldn't miss her wide eyes and typical smile pulled tight into a straight line.

"I'm kind of freaking out, but I'm sure I'll feel better once things get started today."

"How did last night go? Did you get to know them at all?"

Paige came around the counter, pulled out the seat next to mine, and climbed into it. "I did," Paige replied, her index finger tracing the palm frond next to her leg. "They all seem pretty great. And unique. It'll be interesting to see how the weekend shakes out."

"And no matter what happens, one of us can be here in minutes, so try to relax and enjoy this weekend. It'll never be the first again."

Paige stuck her lower lip out and blew, rearranging the baby hairs that lay across her forehead. I was delighted to notice that even they grew in white along with the stripe above them. "You're right." She shook out her hands and wiped her palms on her linen shorts, then smoothed the front of her t-shirt. I had a feeling they wouldn't be white for long.

"I just can't believe the first weekend is here. I've been so excited for it to finally arrive, but now I'm a nervous wreck. You're a hundred percent right, though. What could go wrong that the Sensational Six can't handle?"

"Not a thing," I assured her. "And I'll be here a few times dropping off food, so if you need something, just text."

"You're a lifesaver, Jenna." She cocked her head to the side at the same time I heard shuffling on the stairs.

"It's go time," I said as we slid onto our feet.

We were just storing the last of the lids in the pantry when the first guest walked into the kitchen.

"This looks incredible," she said, rubbing her eyes, "but first —coffee." Paige pointed out the white flamingo pink coffee mugs on the counter next to the trays, and she ambled over toward them.

"I'm going to take off," I said, "but I'll be back later with lunch. Cat's got something special planned for you all."

"If it's anything like this," she gestured toward the counter, "we're in for a real treat!"

A minute later, I pulled out of Page's driveway and down the gravel road back out onto the main street that would take me into downtown Dunedin and Cat's Bites. It may sound cliché, but I felt as if I were floating on a cloud of happiness. My heart felt lighter than it had in years. I had a dream, and I was fulfilling it. My journey was just beginning, and I couldn't wait to see what came next.

4

______

A fter I returned from dropping off lunch at Paige's retreat on Friday afternoon, I spent some time going through my recipe book to make sure I was all set for the next morning. I knew what I was going to make, but I was feeling a little anxious over ensuring I was prepared. Paige was putting so much faith in me, and I didn't want to let her down, especially during the first weekend of her retreats.

As I completed my list of last-minute ingredients I needed to pick up from the store, my phone rang from the kitchen table. I check the caller ID.

'Collect Call'

My anxiety immediately skyrocketed.

"Hello," I said, bracing myself.

"Hi, sweetheart," Craig said with a joviality that was decidedly unusual for him.

"Hi, Craig."

"TGIF, am I right?" he said, which was something that I had actually never heard him say.

"Sure," I replied. "Did you need something, Craig?"

"Well, aren't you cranky?" Craig replied.

"I'm just busy getting ready for tomorrow," I told him.

"What's tomorrow?"

"Paige's first retreat is this weekend."

"Oh, that thing is still happening?" He barked out a laugh. "So, did you actually end up cooking for her?"

"Yes, I baked several things that I dropped off this morning, and I'm going back tomorrow. But what is it that you need, Craig?" I said, getting impatient. I had things to do, and I didn't have time to play his games at that moment.

Or ever, *come to think of it.*

"Well, I'm calling to see how much progress you've made on finding a better attorney, and coming up with bail money. Maybe you can ask your friends. Who's that one who's published all those books? It seems she's got all kinds of money for you when you need a car, but not when your husband needs to get bailed out of jail."

"It's not really her responsibility to bail you out, Craig," I replied, my exasperation clearly evident in my tone.

"Let me guess what you'll say next. It's not your job either," he said with a sneer I could almost see, his typical sarcastic tone beginning to replace his second attempt at forced civility.

"Actually, you're right. I don't really think it is. And as I've already told you, I don't have the money to bail you out. I'm sure there's a perfectly good public defender there that can help you."

"Yeah, that idiot's already been by, and he doesn't know jack shit about anything. He's not here to help me at all. He's just looking to make a quick buck."

"I don't think public defenders make a whole lot of money, Craig."

"Yeah, well, that shows. So when can you get me a real attorney?" His impatience was growing more and more evident.

"I don't think I'm going to be able to, Craig. Attorneys are a lot of money, and I have expenses now myself."

"Yeah, now that you're paying rent when you don't need to. I don't understand why you felt the need to move out of our apartment."

"Because I did, Craig, and that's not something that I really feel like I need to explain to you at this point."

"Well, what you do need to explain to me at this point," said Craig, his tone icy, "is why you have all that money sitting there from your grandmother, but you refuse to use it for your husband, whom you have vowed to be faithful and supportive to. I'm not really feeling your support right now, Jenna."

"Well, to be honest, Craig, I'm not feeling very supportive right now, so I guess we agree on that one."

"This is ridiculous, Jenna. I don't really care to see the person that you have become since getting hooked up with these women. You're all burning bras and female independence while your husband rots in jail."

"My husband is rotting in jail due to his own choices, not mine. Now, I'm sure you have a busy day ahead of you," I deadpanned, "as do I, and I'm going to let you go, but I would go ahead and make another appointment with the public defender and actually listen to what he has to say, Craig. Maybe he has some decent advice for you based on experience, and it would *behoove* you to pay attention to that. Are you doing any work on yourself while you're there?"

"I don't need to work on myself, Jenna. I need to get the hell out of here. I don't belong here. These people are criminals and beat their wives with table legs, and the guy that I'm sharing a cell with was part of a bank robbery scheme in the next town over. I'm not a bank robber, and I'm not a wife beater. I don't deserve to be here!"

"Well, the law says you do, Craig and I don't have much sway in that regard—"

"—But you *can* sway your ass down to the bank and get me money for—" and at that moment, I did something for only the second time in my life. I pressed the end button and hung up on my husband. I knew from past experience that the conversation was going nowhere. And as I had told him, I had things to do. I was looking forward and not back. And what I saw in that view was hopeful. And it made me feel better than I had in a very long time.

I clicked on the contact in my recent call log and blocked the number he had called from. Instantly, my anxiety decreased.

"Well, that takes care of that," I said to myself, "and now it's time to go to the store." I wiped down my counters one more time, straightened the throw pillows on my couch, grabbed my purse, put my phone inside, and walked out the door to get ready for the next day.

I was done living in the past. My future was waiting.

WHEN I ARRIVED at Paige's on Saturday morning to drop off breakfast, there were already a few people outside. I recognized a few of them, and it appeared they also recognized me. It almost seemed as if they were waiting for me. When I got out of my car, a woman in the pool and the two women who were sitting on the pool deck looked up and waved. I waved back and turned to my car to pull the trays out.

The woman who had waved to me from the pool deftly climbed from the water and picked up a hot pink and white striped towel from one of the teal lounge chairs. As she and the other women started heading in my direction, I noticed Paige's groundskeeper, Tom, wrapping each of her palm trees in white lights.

That is going to be gorgeous tonight!

By the time I made it to the door with the trays, there was a mob of women surrounding me. I was led into the kitchen and found myself in a circle of flannel and—*pink bunny rabbit?*—pajamas, everyone talking at the same time as they pulled trays from my hands.

"Let me help you with this. Are these the croissants?"

"I have been up since five waiting for you to get here. And I don't even like cupcakes."

"I had a dream that I was in downward dog eating a fruit tart!"

Everybody started laughing, and within two minutes, breakfast was set up on the counter. The freshly brewed coffee elevated my senses, and the room smelled divine.

"If Heaven has a bakery that makes stuff like this, I'm going to have to start acting right," said a woman in pink bunny rabbit pajamas before stuffing a generous hunk of raspberry coffee cake into her mouth and making sounds that were borderline lurid.

Another guest's eyes rolled back as she bit into a slice of spinach and feta quiche. "I think I'm already there."

One by one, the women generously doled out praise, and I felt like I grew taller with each word. By the time I walked back down the driveway to my car, I was at least twelve feet tall.

5

———————

Saturday afternoon came and went in a flurry of order pickups and dining ticket payments. By six o'clock that night, my entire body was humming with nervous energy... and excitement. The event I'd committed myself to weeks ago was mere hours away.

In the time I'd been a part of the Sensational Six, I'd been forced to share more about my life than I ever had in the past, but there were still parts of me that I'd kept to myself. For instance, I not only played guitar, I did a little songwriting as well, but I had never played in front of anyone. Once in a while, our local pub had an open mic night. After attending over a dozen of them, I had finally made a promise to myself (and the owner) to be brave and get up on the stage to perform at the next one. Which was, as luck would have it, that night.

At eight p.m., I packed Gigi's guitar into its battered black leather case and made my way down the block to Jeff's Pub, where the line was flowing out the door and down the side-walk. While the owner, Jeff, didn't claim to have a knack for creative business names, he was a dead ringer for Sam Elliott and the self-proclaimed local heartthrob for the fifty and older crowd (men and women) in Dunedin. He was standing outside in skin-tight jeans and a tattered red and blue flannel directing foot traffic. His bright white teeth shone from under the curtain of a handlebar mustache stained a light yellow from decades of heavy tobacco use. His smile always put me at ease, even while he pressured me mercilessly to get on stage and perform. Jeff had been my choir teacher in middle school and knew first-hand I had a love for songwriting and singing, and he never missed an opportunity to invite me to get on stage during open mic night. He might have retired from teaching, but he'd never lost his love for music and the people who created it.

"There you are," he said with visible relief as I walked up to the front of the line. "I was worried you weren't going to show up." He unhooked the rope blocking the entrance and held out his arm to welcome me through. "I already added your name to the list, so stop by the MC and let him know what time you want to go on."

I walked past him without a word, but nodded that I understood.

"Hey, Jenna," he said just before I stepped through the black velvet curtain and into the pub. I turned and paused long enough to hear him say, "I'm proud of you. Knock 'em dead."

I mustered up enough of a smile to show my appreciation, then made my way through the curtain. As soon as I pulled it back, I was enveloped in the cacophony of third-date after-shave and first-impression perfume.The lights were low; just bright enough to see what needed to be seen—a stage across the back with a runway that stretched halfway to the door. *I would not be using that.* The tall four-top tables jockeyed for space but were not hurting for occupants, and the place was buzzing with patrons, many of whom recognized me and smiled as I made my way to the stage. The MC was tapping his pen on his podium and staring off into space.

"I'm Jenna," I croaked, then cleared my throat. "Jeff said he added me to the list. Can I go first so I don't have to sit here in a puddle of sweat all night?" I followed it up with some nervous laughter that came out more like a rooster being strangled mid-crow.

He gave me his best pity smile, then ran one hooked index finger down a list of names. After slashing a checkmark next to mine, he looked up at me and smiled.

"You're in luck, Jenna Mitchell. No one who's checked in so far has wanted to be first, so have at it. Grab a seat anywhere and come up on stage after you hear me introduce you."

An empty high top in the back was waiting patiently with my name on it, so I leaned my guitar case against the wall behind it before sitting down. I was having trouble keeping my bouncing legs still, but I clasped my hands in front of me to try and control at least some of my body which was humming with nervous energy.

At the very least, I would like to have control of my bladder.

I wanted to pick up my guitar and run right back through the curtains, down the street, and up to my quiet, empty apartment. But I'd made a promise to myself and a commitment to Jeff, and I intended to honor them, even if I spent the entire time praying for a small kitchen fire or perhaps the apocalypse.

Within fifteen minutes, the room was even more full of patrons, and the MC was on stage. "Good evening, party people!" he yelled into the microphone.

Skreeeeeeeeeeeeeee, the microphone shrieked, which made an excellent attention-getter. The entire audience fell silent, their faces turned toward the stage.

"Well, wasn't *that* a bit dramatic?" he quipped, and everyone (but me) laughed. "Let's try this again. Thank you for joining us tonight. We've got a great lineup for you, including some poetry, a jazz performance, and some singer/songwriters, including a few first-timers. In fact, our first guest falls into both of those categories and is so excited to perform an original song for you tonight. Let's give Jenna a warm welcome."

I was aware the crowd was clapping, but I was so locked in on getting my guitar out of its case and making it onto the stage without falling on my face that I hadn't looked around at the audience until I was facing them with my guitar held firmly in front of me. I stared at them and froze. My vocal cords locked up, and my mouth became so dry that my tongue felt hermetically sealed to the roof of my mouth. My hand gripped the neck of the guitar so tightly, my fingers were locked in a claw position. I shook it out and took a deep, shaky breath in.

Just as I gained enough self-awareness to recognize that my time was ticking away as everyone waited, my therapist's voice popped into my head unannounced (but quite welcome). After I told her what I had planned, she'd loaded me up with some public speaking tricks at my last appointment.

"Find the person in the audience that most resembles your grandmother, then lock onto them. Pretend like she's the only one in the room, and let it all go."

I strummed my guitar once and searched the near-dark room, my gaze landing on a woman who looked more like Grace than Gigi. She would have to do.

"Thanks in advance for being patient with me," I said. "This is my first time."

The frog in my throat threatened to make an appearance and I washed it down with a swig from the water bottle that had been set on a stool to my left.

"This song came to me after I had a dream about my late grandmother. I walked straight into her outstretched arms and it was the first time in a long time I'd felt that lightness in their weight around me. She whispered something in my ear I must have left behind when I awoke, but in its place was this song... It's called, "Fate's Gift".

I strummed my guitar once more, closed my eyes, and

began to play. By the time I had finished playing the intro, I was fully immersed in the song, and when the first verse came, I was ready for it. My voice flowed from me, deep and strong and true.

Dressed to impress
*   You cast your line,*
*   Onto your hook I fled.*
*   The child I'd wanted*
*   To be someday,*
*   Packed up and left for dead.*

My name had changed,
*   But not my faults;*
*   You taught me right from wrong.*
*   You molded me*
*   The way my folks*
*   Had tried to all along.*

The single soul
*   That knew my heart,*
*   Went on to find her zen.*
*   But then, my friends,*
*   The light of love*
*   Shone down on me again.*

Every window
*   Painted black*
*   'Til fate knocked on my door.*

*Four winds of change
Came blowing in,
A page turn drew one more.*

THEY SHOWED *me things
That I could do
I'd heard could not be done.
To reach for more,
Hold on to less,
And be priority one.*

I TELL *you now
(But not to boast)
Life's sweeter every day.
I'm thankful for
The family
That fate has sent my way.*

THEY SHOWED *me things
That I could do
I'd heard could not be done.
To reach for more,
Hold on to less,
And be priority one.*

I'M *thankful for
The family
That knew I'd find my way.*

.   .   .

AFTER THE LAST note from my guitar floated away, I opened my eyes and looked out into the silent crowd. My eyes rested once again on Grace's doppelgänger and she smiled back at me.

"Thank you very much," I said in her direction.

The crowd erupted in applause. Their cheering followed me back across the stage, down the stairs, and all the way to my table, where a cold glass of soda sat waiting in a puddle of its own sweat. I knew exactly how it felt. I took a sip and washed down a bubble of relief as I looked down at the table.

"Wow. Wow. That's going to be a tough act to follow," I heard the MC say once the applause died down. "Let's hear it again for Jenna!"

The clapping and whistling began again in earnest, forcing me to look up and acknowledge the audience seated all around me. The people at the next table were smiling at me, and Grace's lookalike gave me a thumbs-up.

I sat back and enjoyed the rest of the evening with a huge smile on my face, and after the last performer finished and the patrons began to make their way to the bar, I gathered up my guitar, put twenty dollars on the table, and made my way to the door where Jeff sat on a bar stool scrolling through his phone.

He looked up as I approached and held up his hand, waiting for a high-five. As our hands made contact, he shouted, "Woo! Jenna! You brought down the house tonight! When will you be back? Can I put you down for next month?"

His eyes were wide and sparkled with excitement, and while I wasn't sure if I'd have the courage to get up there again, I didn't have the heart to disappoint him outright. "Maybe," I replied. "Let me think about it. Can I let you know?"

"Maybe? Did you hear your fans, Jenna? Man alive, you could get addicted to that. Yes, please let me know when you'll be back, and I'll add you to the schedule no matter what. You were incredible." People were beginning to flow around us to move through the door, so I smiled at him and nodded.

I was incredible.

6

Monday at four o'clock, five members of the Sensational Six filed into the café. I walked toward the back side by side with Sarah, who had bucked tradition and wore jeans and a t-shirt instead of her typical business casual uniform. I was happy to see one thing remained the same. The headband holding back her ash-blonde hair matched the pink in the lettering of her shirt down to the last hexadecimal.

She stopped mid-stride and spun ninety degrees away from me. "Is that new?" she asked, pointing at a large painting I'd never seen before.

"It's the one she sent back from Iceland last month."

"It looks great next to the black and white she took in Greenland."

I nodded in agreement. The walls of Cat's café were an ever-expanding scrapbook of her travels, and it set the tone for the entire place. It was cozy, inviting, and there was always something new to look at.

One by one, Grace, Sarah, Paige, Elyse, and I all slid across the red vinyl to sit in our usual spots in our usual booth. After we'd settled, Cat came out of the kitchen to join us. After setting five cups of water on the table, she sat across from Elyse and slid down. She put her feet up next to Elyse, took off her signature lemon yellow bandana, and rested her head on the back of the booth. My boss was the hardest-working woman I knew, and I rarely saw her take a break. A moment later, her pale green eyes fluttered shut, her long eyelashes nearly camouflaged against smooth dark skin.

"Time for a Cat nap," Paige joked. She was never one to pass up the opportunity for a well-placed pun. Her eyes flashed with amusement, then turned to settle on Elyse, seated at the other end of the booth. "So, Elyse, you've got to be getting excited," she said softly.

Two green eyes peered over Elyse's phone and blinked, her eyebrows furrowed in confusion.

Paige giggled. "You and that phone lately. Your trip to Jamaica? That's coming up soon, isn't it?"

Elyse's mane of cherry cola curls had fallen in front of her face like an inflatable curtain and she tucked it behind her ears when she looked up. She pulled at the neck of her faded Nirvana t-shirt. "Oh, yes, I'm super excited. Which reminds me; I still need to get a hold of the kennel to see if they can take Eden for me."

"Kennel?" Paige asked. "Why doesn't Eden just come and hang out with Roxy for the week?"

"Are you sure?" She set her phone down on the table in front of her. "She can be a handful. As you know. And the two of them together... I don't know. Are you sure?"

"Absolutely. Every golden retriever needs a big German Shepherd to play with, and they get along so well. Besides, it'd be nice to have an actual guard dog for a week instead of just a ball of fluff."

"Alright, we'll talk about that. Let's put a pin in it for now, but that could work. Thank you, Paige."

Cat cleared her throat. "And I believe somebody at this table has a bit of news to share."

We all looked around, confused.

Cat lightly tapped the table in front of Grace, seated to the right of her. "Don't you have something you wanted to tell us?"

Grace smoothed the front of her Lilly Pulitzer cardigan. "Oh! Yes, I wanted to remind you all about my book launch party at the bookstore in a couple of weeks. We've got some fun things planned. I'll be doing a reading," she pointed across the table at me, "and Jenna here is going to be providing some delicious lavender cupcakes."

Paige sat up straight in her booth and clapped her hands together. "We got to try out those cupcakes at the retreat this weekend, and they wouldn't shut up about them. They were amazing. Who would think that lavender in a cupcake would be so irresistible?"

Sarah put her hand up. "I would bet on anything Jenna baking being delicious," she said and then looked across the table to Grace. "You can count on all of us to be there, Mom. *Obviously.*" The last word was delivered with a kiss blown across the table.

"It's good to know I can always count on at least five people at my book launch parties," said Grace.

Elyse, who had been furiously tapping away on her phone again during the last exchange, looked up and scoffed. "You know full well your book signing is sold out. I had to draw up a plan for how we could fit everyone in." Elyse didn't just manage the independent bookstore down the block, she expertly planned and executed each of their local author events. She looked over at Paige. "Why don't you tell us how your first retreat weekend went?"

"Oh, you guys, it was incredible. First, let me say that Jenna knocked it out of the park both days. On the first day, everyone was excited to try everything. The second day, everyone woke up early so they could stalk the kitchen and be ready when she got there."

"Yes, they were waiting outside for me when I pulled up on Saturday."

"They practically carried her in on their shoulders like that scene in Rudy," added Paige, holding her arms up to demonstrate.

Cat slapped the table in front of her. "Well, there you have it. You're an instant success. I *knew* you would be."

I could feel the blush creeping up my neck and was powerless to stop it. I shifted in my seat and tucked the edges of my skirt underneath my legs. "It was a lot of fun," I said. "Thank you for the opportunity, Paige."

"Thank you for putting so much work into it." She turned to address the rest of the group. "Caleb's session on plotting out your story was a huge hit. Everyone went home with a link to his presentation, some links to videos he likes, and a coupon for the platform he uses to plot out *his* books. He did a live demo that morning. It was *so good*."

"And what about yoga? Did you end up having the yoga instructor come by?" asked Cat.

Paige's face seemed to light up from within. "Oh yes, Estelle came in, and everyone loved it. The sunroom worked out perfectly, and I had enough mats and blocks for everyone. Estelle was a big hit and definitely got everyone's creative juices flowing. Right after she left, everyone ran and got their laptops and notebooks and I was finding them all over the property, even down on the boat dock."

"Oh, I bet that would be a great place to write. Don't be surprised if you look out your front window and find me there one of these days," said Grace with a wink.

Paige laughed. "Come by anytime. Yeah, the weekend went really well, and I already got tagged in a few reviews on Facebook, and I saw one on Yelp. So I think we're off to a good start."

Everyone took turns congratulating Paige, whose face grew redder with each word. She cleared her throat and broke into the melee. "That reminds me, I also want to invite everyone over to a pool party on Wednesday."

Elyse swiped across her phone, and a moment later, looked up. "Looks like I'm off Wednesday! I'll be there. What time?"

"I'm thinking four o'clock, so everyone can come. Sarah, I know your schedule is the least flexible. Does Wednesday at four work for you?"

Sarah reached into her tote bag to retrieve her phone, and a moment later said, "Yes, I'm available. You already know what I'm bringing." Sarah was the reigning queen of charcuterie boards.

"So it's set. I'll see you all Wednesday at four. Bring whatever you want to share as a snack, but I'll provide lunch," she said, then looked at Cat. "I'm going to order food from the café."

"I'll deliver, no tip required," said Cat with a chuckle. "What else is going on with everyone? Sarah, anything interesting happening at school lately?"

Sarah's face brightened. "Actually, a student from years ago stopped in to see me this week. I was in a meeting at the time and missed her. She didn't leave her name, but the secretary relayed the message that she would stop in again soon. I've never had a former student visit me!" She straightened her headband, and a flash of something crossed her face. "Unlike you, Cat. This café has a revolving door of your proteges stopping by for a visit. Oh that reminds me. I keep meaning to ask if there's any movement on the storefront next door. It's been empty for a while now."

Cat sighed and shook her head. "When the owners of the pizza place couldn't reach an agreement about the lease, they moved across the street but left all their equipment behind, so maybe it'll end up being another pizza place. Who knows? But I sure hope they find someone soon."

"Yeah, it's not a good look having empty storefronts on Main Street," Elyse commented.

"No kidding," said Cat. "The more storefronts we have in operation, the better business is for everyone."

We all continued to chat for another half hour or so. After everybody left, I went into the kitchen to do a quick inventory of the ingredients I had on hand so Cat could order what I needed for that week's baking. When I handed her the list ten minutes later, she put a business card in my hand.

"I'm not telling you what you should and shouldn't do or how to live your life, but I want you to know that you have options. You don't have to stay married just because you took a vow. A vow is for two people to uphold, not just one."

I looked at the card and was shocked at Cat's forwardness. It was for her son's attorney practice. She didn't usually interject in my personal life, so if Cat was bringing it up to me, I knew I needed to take note.

"When you call, make sure you tell him who you are. I've already prepped him, just in case."

"Thanks, Cat, but I don't think I can afford your son or any other attorney at this point."

"Is that what's holding you back?"

"Well, attorneys are notoriously expensive," I said, "and I'm so, so grateful for you letting me live in the apartment above the café, but money is still a concern. I'm getting by on my income from the café and some money that my grandmother left behind for me, but I have to be careful with it because it's not a lot."

"I don't want you to feel that you have to stay in this marriage due to lack of finances either, Jenna. I want you to know that my son works pro bono for victims of domestic abuse." As she said this, she dropped her head slowly, then looked back up at me and made eye contact. I looked away.

Domestic abuse?

I tucked the card into my purse and thanked Cat. Before going up to my apartment, I took a walk around downtown Dunedin to take in the decorations that were popping up everywhere. I passed the bandshell wrapped in warm white lights, then the library with pillars covered in spirals of greenery and red bows. I made a loop, coming all the way back to the café before going up. The whole time, Cat's words spun through my head.

Was I a victim of domestic abuse? What was abuse anyway? He never hit me. He was just a little controlling and had anger management issues.

In the end, I decided it was coming up often enough in conversations with my friends that I needed to know what it was so I could make that determination for myself. There was one person who I knew for sure could answer those questions, and luckily, I was going to see her that afternoon.

HONEY LAVENDER CUPCAKES

Lavender Milk

1 ⅔ cup milk

3 teaspoon dried lavender

Cupcakes

¼ cup salted butter, room temperature

⅔ cup honey

1 egg white, room temperature

1 ½ teaspoon vanilla extract

¼ cup dairy-free yogurt, room temperature

¾ cup all-purpose flour

1 teaspoon baking powder

½ teaspoon fine sea salt

½ cup lavender milk (recipe below)

Honey Lavender Buttercream

½ cup salted butter, room temperature

2 tablespoons honey

1 ⅔ cups powdered sugar

¼ teaspoon fine sea salt

3 tablespoons lavender milk
Purple food coloring *optional

Lavender Milk

In a small pot, combine the milk and dried lavender and bring to a boil over high heat.

Remove from the heat as soon as it starts to boil and allow the milk to cool to room temperature.

Strain the lavender from the milk and discard the lavender. Set the lavender milk aside.

Cupcakes

Preheat the oven to 350 degrees and place 8 cupcake liners in a cupcake pan.

In the bowl of a stand mixer with the whisk attachment, combine the butter and creamed honey and beat together on high until light and fluffy (approximately 5 minutes.)

Add in the egg white, vanilla extract, and yogurt and mix on high for 1 minute.

Add in the flour, baking powder, and salt and begin to mix on low.

With the mixer on low, slowly pour in the lavender milk and mix until just combined. Be careful to not overmix the batter or it will cause the cupcakes to be gummy in texture.

Fill each cupcake liner approximately ¾ full with the cupcake batter and bake for 15-17 minutes or until a toothpick inserted in the center comes out clean.

Remove the cupcakes from the oven and allow them to cool for 10 minutes. Gently remove each cupcake from the pan and place them on a cooling rack to fully cool.

Honey Lavender Buttercream

In the bowl of a stand mixer with the paddle attachment, cream the butter and honey together on high for 5 minutes until light and fluffy.

Add in the powdered sugar and salt and mix on low until combined.

Add in the lavender milk and purple food coloring and mix on low until combined.

Turn the mixer to high and beat for 5 minutes until light and fluffy.

Top the cupcakes with the frosting and enjoy

Store leftover cupcakes in an airtight container in the fridge for up to 7 days.

7

———

I had my appointment with my therapist Tuesday morning after Cat got back from golfing with her Ladies League, and it couldn't have come at a better time. I had so many questions swirling around in my mind about my relationship with Craig and how to handle the way he spoke to me.

So much of that relationship mirrored the one I had with my parents, who had always had very strong opinions about what I should do with my life and why. They told me constantly that their 'why' was out of concern for me and my ability to survive on my own. So many of my doubts were based on having been told for so long that I couldn't.

If only they could see me now...

I sat on the plush navy blue couch across from Leslie's brown leather chair that looked as if it had been around for more problems than I had seen in my lifetime. I always felt at peace there. Pale yellow walls held up framed prints of coastal scenes that weren't too different in style from the ones on my own walls. A dark wood coffee table held a waiting box of tissues. One of a half dozen pure white fluffy throw pillows tipped over against me, and I left it there, its presence oddly comforting.

I'd been seeing Leslie since Grace had handed me her card months before, and for the first time since I lost my grandmother, I felt seen. Understood. Uninhibited in what I shared. Maybe it was her signature pantsuit or the puffy cloud of white hair that looked so much like my Grandma Gigi's.

At the beginning of the session, we mostly chatted about the previous week and what I had going on in my life. Surface-level stuff. Luckily, she was already aware that Craig was in jail and why, but I felt as if I needed to catch her up on some of the conversations I had been having with my friends lately.

"Am I a victim of domestic abuse?" I asked outright.

She looked taken aback, sat up in her chair, and set her pen and notebook down on the table. "Do you feel like you're a victim, Jenna?"

"I don't feel as if I'm a victim, per se, but that's what's been alluded to during conversations with my friends."

"Well, I think that term is being used in the right context, but in the wrong way, Jenna. I don't see you as a victim of domestic abuse."

While I was instantly relieved, that relief was quickly replaced by confusion. "So, why do my friends seem to think I am?"

"It's not the term 'abuse' that is the problem with what they're telling you, Jenna. It's that you're not a victim at all. You're a *survivor*."

Tears instantly sprang to my eyes. I had never thought of myself in those terms. I knew that I had been controlled. I knew I had been told for a very long time that I would not be enough, but to think of where I stood now in those terms—as a survivor —meant I had to reframe so much of my thinking.

"I can see the confusion written all over your face, Jenna. Let me explain. What you have been told for so long is that you could not survive on your own. And you were being held in place by this belief so that your parents — and then Craig — could continue to control and abuse you. But what you have proven to them and everyone around you is that you're not a victim. You're a survivor, and you're proving every day that you *can* survive on your own.

"What I would expect from Craig from here on out is for him to double down on his attempts to control you, even from jail. He is going to continue with the rhetoric that you're not going to survive on your own. You'll have to keep things together until he gets out of jail. He will use that fear against you in order to get you to help him improve his situation, all so he can get back to his leisurely life."

I sat quietly for a moment. It was like she'd be listening to our phone calls. "He starts out nicer than he's ever been and as soon as I don't jump to his will, he becomes hostile. How can he possibly be surprised?"

"Narcissistic people find every way possible to justify their control, so they are shocked when it's not well received—especially after years of getting excellent results."

I nodded my head. What she said made sense, but I had no idea how to break out of the cycle I'd allowed and find the strength to continue standing on my own, even after he was released from jail. Again, she seemed to read my mind.

"I understand what must be going through your mind right now. These are lifelong patterns that you have come to expect and they've all been turned on their side, spilled out, and you're left to sift through them to find what's true and untrue.

"You're going to have to go against everything you have ever been told and everything that you believe to be true to find the truth about yourself. What *is* true from where I'm sitting as a professional is that you are *proving yourself to be a survivor.* You are proving yourself to be a strong, independent woman. You are proving yourself to be resourceful and strong. You are surviving on your own, and you have an excellent support system to make sure you continue to thrive. Lean into that support system and allow your friends to demonstrate their belief in you."

I pictured my new family all circled around me, holding me up when life ripped the rug out from under me. They'd never failed me. Never turned their back on me or asked for more than I was willing or able to give. They simply offered their support and a soft place to land.

"Sometimes when we're told something throughout our entire life, it can be difficult to change that belief on our own. When we are met with a positive message on a consistent basis, it can start to become true for us, just as the wrong thing can become true in our minds. So listen to your friends when they tell you that you are strong and capable, because they are right. And only in listening to those messages on a consistent basis, will you begin to believe them. You've done the hard part and broken the cycle of abuse. The first time you said no you broke free and stepped onto a new path. A path that has bought you happiness and showed you that not only can you survive, but you are thriving."

I sat quietly, weighing her words. Trying them on for size.

Realizing I wasn't going to contribute just yet, she continued. "Let me ask you something. Do you believe that Craig supports you and lifts you up as a partner should, or does he drag you down?"

I remained quiet as I contemplated her question. My mouth opened, then quickly closed. I didn't know if I was ready to say it out loud.

Again, reading my mind, she reassured me, "It's okay if you're not ready to answer me today. But what I would like you to do is to go home and sit in the quiet and ask yourself if you feel more at peace than you are lonely. If you feel supported by the people closest to you and if that feeling is one you got from your life with Craig."

"I can do that." I paused and took a breath, then found the words I needed. "I do," I said softly, while looking down at my hands folded in my lap. "I feel at peace in my new apartment."

"That's great, Jenna. What does that tell you?"

Mere weeks before, when Cat had walked me up to the apartment and offered it as a refuge from the life I was trying to escape, I'd been terrified. I'd never been able to imagine life on my own. It hadn't felt possible for me to be self-sufficient. But I'd come to realize that over dozens of trips up those stairs, every turn of my key in the door that was mine and mine alone, I was doing just fine. Better than fine. I was happy. "That it's right for me? Being on my own?" I sniffed, the hesitant admission bringing up emotions I didn't realize I had until then.

Her smile reached her eyes, and she reached for a Kleenex.

"For now, yes," she said as she handed it to me. "But the goal is for you to expect more. Respect is earned, sure, but it should also be expected in a long-term relationship. Especially when that relationship is with a family member, friend, or partner. It's not something you're used to demanding, but just because a choice makes you uncomfortable doesn't mean it's wrong."

We talked a bit more about how to handle Craig's calls, and she sided with Grace, agreeing that I had no reason to continue answering for—or to—him if the only purpose was to try to control, gaslight, and manipulate me. It felt good to hear her confirm what I'd already started to believe, but only time would tell how I'd feel when I put it into practice.

After our session, I knew I had a lot to consider. There was so much to think about that I was finding the cracks in everything I thought to be whole — or at least mostly whole. So, when I got home, I did exactly as the therapist had requested.

After 30 minutes of sitting in the quiet, I found that I was not waiting.

I was not waiting anxiously for Craig to come home.

I was not waiting to find out what his mood would be.

I was not waiting to find ways to make his life easier.

I was not waiting to find out what I had possibly done wrong that day.

I was enjoying the peace that surrounded me, just as the therapist had suggested. I didn't feel lonely at all. In fact, for the first time in my life I felt like I was worth more than what I could do for someone else.

And my time was my own.

SARAH STOPPED by after work on Wednesday, just as the café was getting ready to close. I was wiping down the glass on the bakery case when the bells chimed. When I turned around and saw Sarah, my whole mood lightened.

"Hey there," she said with a smile and a wave. "I came in to place an order for some muffins for the staff break room, but I have an ulterior motive."

"Okay," I said, drawing out the end of the word.

"It's nothing bad. I just wanted to catch up with you. How long until you're done here?"

I tilted my head, curious. "Maybe fifteen minutes."

"Perfect," she said, ignoring my obvious confusion. "I'm going to sit over there in the corner. *After* I get this order in with you, of course," she said with a laugh. "I'm going to get a little paperwork done while I wait. I won't bother you. Promise." She placed her order and left for the booth in the corner where the Sensational Six always sat.

Fifteen minutes later, we were off.

"You want to head to Clearwater Beach?" Sarah asked as we stepped out of the café into the hot afternoon sun.

"That sounds fabulous," I said. Walking on the beach sounded like a great idea after a whole day in the café.

Twenty-five minutes later, we were set up on beach chairs in front of Frenchie's with baskets of fries in our laps. I slipped off my work shoes, pulled up the bottom of my skirt, and let my fish-belly white legs see the sun for the first time in weeks.

After paying the attendants for our chairs when they came by, Sarah turned to me with a smile. "I was so happy to hear how well things went for you with Paige's retreat. We all knew that it would be a big hit, but to hear how excited everyone was to see you on Saturday says everything, don't you think?" she asked.

"I don't know," I said, stumbling over three short words. "I didn't even know what to say when I saw some of them sitting outside waiting for me when I got there."

"That's incredible, Jenna, and a huge testament to your talent. I hope you can see how your hard work has paid off and how you continue to grow and flourish. How are things at the apartment? I love what you've done there, by the way. It's so calming and peaceful now. I could take a nap on the couch every time I walk through the door. On second thought, it might be the fact I have two young kids at home."

I laughed. "Well, I have spent a few dollars at HomeGoods lately. But the place is starting to feel more like home than any place I've lived before. And it's just an apartment above the café."

"That says a lot, all on its own, doesn't it?" said Sarah.

"Yeah, I guess so."

"And what else have you been up to?"

"Well..." I started, and then hesitated. I didn't know how much I wanted to share about my conversation with the therapist or the card that Cat had shared with me. But I suspected

Sarah might already know. "Cat gave me a business card for her son's law firm."

"Oh really? How do you feel about that?" she said, her social worker training making its appearance in our conversation. "I'm sorry, that sounded very social worker-y of me. Sometimes, I can't seem to help myself."

"It's okay," I said. "It's a normal question. I'm not really sure how I feel about it. I know I needed a change, and I've never felt as free as I have since I moved into that apartment when Craig went to jail."

"I can imagine it's a huge change for you. Are you settling in through other means that don't involve throw pillows and dust covers?"

I laughed. "I have been." I decided to share a little bit about my conversation with the therapist after all. "In fact, I went to therapy yesterday and she had some interesting things to say." Sarah raised her eyebrows but remained silent, patiently waiting for me to continue. "She is of the same mindset that all of you are, that I was living in an abusive environment. I never really saw it that way because it was just what I was used to. I got the same messages from Craig that I had gotten from my parents my whole life and assumed that they knew me best. Craig just reinforced what my parents had been telling me all along. But she said that I'm not a victim of domestic abuse."

Sarah's eyebrows shot up again, and she set her empty basket on the sand in front of her and clenched her hands in her lap. "What do you mean?" she asked, anger evident in her voice. "What kind of crackpot therapist is this? Let me get you another referral."

"No, no, no," I said. "Sarah, Sarah, take a breath. She said I'm not a *victim* of abuse. I'm a survivor."

Sarah sat back in her chair, visibly relieved. "Phew! I almost went over there myself to have a little chat." She fanned herself with her hand. "I forgot my ten-second rule." We both laughed.

"That's true, Jenna. And you're right. We should be more careful with how we word things like this. You're not a victim. You're thriving in your new living environment, and we're all so proud of you. But what you have survived is in fact abuse, and I'm glad to hear that you are starting to recognize that. It means that you're healing, and this is such an important step. Do you have any questions for me that maybe I could answer that you've thought of since your appointment with the therapist?"

"Well, I do. I wonder what's next for me. I guess that's not really a question for you. It's more of a rhetorical question, but it's one that's been bouncing around in my head quite a bit. I don't know what comes next. I know that I'm very appreciative of my job at Cat's café, but I know it's not forever. And I know the opportunity she gave me is waiting for the next person in line. So where does that leave me? I know I'm capable of surviving on my own, but I'm not sure what it takes to get there."

"Let's take this one step at a time," urged Sarah. "You've had a major revelation this week. I think it's important that you let that sink in a bit and sit with it for a moment. See how it makes you feel. See how it affects your day-to-day life and how you want to move forward. The possibilities are endless! You can fulfill a lifelong dream. You can travel. You can house sit a villa in Tuscany. You can go back to school. This is the first day of the rest of your life. What do you want to do with it?"

I had dreams like anyone else, but they had always seemed far-fetched, destined to remain dreams, but as each day passed, I was growing stronger and more confident in my independence.

Sarah stretched her legs out in front of her and raised her arms above her head, then spun in her chair and pointed back toward Frenchy's. "I need to move my body a bit. What do you say we get out of these chairs? Have you ever played volleyball in the sand courts up by the restaurant?"

I spun around in my chair and looked to where she was pointing. Volleyballs were flying over five of the six nets set up in the sand outside the door. "Never. I haven't touched a volleyball since high school, but I enjoyed playing in gym class."

"Want to give it a go? Looks like there are a few games in progress now, but we might be able to jump into one."

I looked back at Sarah and nodded my head.

"Let's go," she said. We stood and started collecting our food baskets and drinks, then made our way over toward the games in progress. Nervous excitement filled my belly as we dropped our bags into the sand and undressed down to our one-piece bathing suits. She gave me an expectant look as one of the players motioned us over.

"Ready?" she asked.

"Ready."

The rest of the day was a blur of sand and spikes, serves and dives. It was the most fun I'd had in years, and as I rinsed as much sand off my body as I could at the nearby rinsing station, I thought about how different life could have been if Sarah had been my social worker when I was in middle school.

She could have made a difference sooner, but I was grateful to have her in my life right then.

8

―――――

On the day I was scheduled to see the attorney, I woke up with a sick, heavy feeling in the pit of my stomach. Nobody goes into a marriage expecting to fail, but it was time for me to admit that even *I* couldn't figure out how to make things work with Craig. Maybe somewhere deep inside of him was a kind, patient, and respectful man, but the longer I knew him, the more I doubted that man even existed, and no special dinner, no clean home, no amount of bending to his will would change that.

I made myself a spinach and feta frittata because cooking always calmed my nerves, and left with enough time to give myself a little bit of a cushion.

I pulled into the parking lot, and the feeling in my stomach intensified to the point I thought I might be sick, so I sat behind the wheel, took a few deep breaths, and then let them out slowly. It helped a little, but my anxiety was still sitting on my chest like an anvil.

I figured I might as well rip off the bandaid, so I turned the car off and headed inside. Sitting in the parking lot wasn't going to do me any good.

Sam met me at the door and shook my hand. His kind eyes looked so much like Cat's, I was immediately at ease, even though I was seeing him at his office instead of the café. "Jenna, it's nice to see you," he said and turned to retrieve a folder from the small desk in the brightly lit reception area I'd stepped into.

I nodded. "Nice to see you, Sam. Thank you for seeing me today."

"It's truly my pleasure. You mean a ton to my mom. In fact, between you and me, you're nearly fifty percent of what she ever talks about. She's so proud of you."

I didn't know what to say, so I nodded my head and studied the pattern in the deep navy carpet. The yellow specks looked like stars, giving the impression that I was floating in the night sky. His voice broke in.

"She also told me that you wouldn't be able to take a compliment," he smiled warmly. "Come with me. We're going to sit in the conference room."

I followed him to the back of the office through a set of double doors. They opened into a room about ten by twenty with a long dark laminate table stretching from one end to the other, and it was surrounded by the most cushy-looking black leather office chairs I had ever seen. Floor-to-ceiling windows lined one whole side.

"Is this entire place yours?" It seemed like a lot of space for one person.

"For the most part. I share with an insurance agent to save on expenses, but he's almost never here. He comes in once in a while and has meetings here in the conference room, but on a day-to-day basis, I really don't see him all that much."

"I bet it's nice to have the place mostly to yourself," I said, trying to make small talk to delay the inevitable. Knowing why I was there was hard enough, but the fact that he was helping me for free made me more than a little uncomfortable.

"Yes, and it definitely puts my clients at ease. Sometimes,

we're talking about sensitive subjects and it helps them to know there isn't anybody listening in. Now, why don't we have a chat about what's been going on in your world? My mom gave me a little bit of background, but why don't you tell me what you're hoping to accomplish? You don't have to go into any personal details that will make you uncomfortable. Just the basics is fine, so we can get started on what we need to do."

On the drive over, I wasn't sure what I would share with him, but once I opened my mouth... it all came tumbling out. The way Craig spoke to me, the control, and a little bit about what the other women had spoken to me about: following me, tracking my phone, the outburst in the café. "So, as you can imagine," I explained, "I didn't really recognize what was going on as it was happening, but now that I'm on my own, I can see it much more clearly."

"I know this is a difficult decision," he said, setting his pen down on his yellow notepad. "I want you to take some time and really think about what it is you want. I don't want you to make any permanent decisions based on other people's opinions."

I took a moment to absorb his words.

"I can understand why you would say that, and I do appreciate it, but I've made my decision. I've put a lot of thought into it. I've been living over your mom's café for about a month now. It's the happiest I've felt in a really long time, maybe forever, and I want to do whatever it takes to make this feeling last.

"I don't need Craig. I wanted him, and I wanted him to get better; I wanted us to have something that lasted forever, but our relationship has become something that isn't sustainable in a lifelong commitment. It's made me doubt myself more than anything, and I don't feel that that's how a marriage or relationship should be."

He picked up his pen and tapped it on the table.

"You're right about that, Jenna. It sounds to me like you *have* put a lot of thought into this."

"Yeah, well, therapy, your mom, and our other friends have helped, but this is a decision I have made on my own. I promise you."

"Well then, let's get started." The click of his pen clattered against my eardrums.

This is it. The beginning of the end.

"I have some questions for you, if you don't mind. We'll be getting into some personal information, so if you need to stop at any point, please let me know. Can I get you some water?"

"No thank you," I said, then hesitated for a moment. "What kind of information?"

He flipped the first page to reveal a list on a piece of printer paper. "Let's go through these questions. First things first: Are your finances combined?"

"Well, at this point, I'm the only one who's working. He's been having some trouble holding down a job, so I work at your mom's café, and I have an annuity from my grandmother. I don't have to give him any of that, right? Do I have to pay spousal support or anything?"

"No, anything that you're getting as part of an annuity or an inheritance is yours and yours alone, so you don't have to worry about that. Do you have those figures for me?"

I was prepared. "This is my income for the last two months," I said as I pulled a folded piece of notebook paper from my tote bag and slid it across the table, "and my projected income for the next six months, including the annuity from my grandmother."

He looked over my figures and jotted down notes.

I cleared my throat, trying to figure out the best way to word my one and only question. "What are we looking at here as far as the timeline?"

He looked up from what he was writing and smiled. "The good news is that Florida is a no-fault state, and no waiting period is required. So, theoretically, as soon as we have our paperwork in order, we can dissolve your marriage."

I sat back in my chair. I'd never thought about it like that. My marriage dissolved. Just the word alone gave thoughts of destruction and burning and pain. "I never expected it would be this... easy," I said.

"Well, it's definitely made easier by the fact that he's in jail. And while I'm sure it was a traumatic experience for you, from what it sounds like, it's been a blessing in disguise because it's given you a little space to make a decision and an opportunity to see what life would be like on your own. And from where I sit, it looks like you've got that nailed down. Are you enjoying your newfound peace?"

"More than I ever thought I would," I said. "I'd never lived alone, so this is a new experience for me. But I've been going home after work and doing some research on recipes for cooking for both the café and for Paige's retreats and I..."

How much am I going to share?

"...sometimes I write songs."

He set his pen down again and looked at me closely. "I had no idea. My mom never mentioned that you were a songwriter."

"I've never actually told them. It's just something I do when things are quiet, and everything else is done."

"Well, I'd love to hear something you've written someday, Jenna. From where I sit, you are a wildly talented woman with so much to offer the world. I'm looking forward to seeing how far you go without someone holding you down."

I felt embarrassment creeping up my neck. "Thank you" was all I could manage.

"You don't need to thank me Jenna. I'm just so grateful for your friendship with my mom and everything you do to help her. She works so hard, and it's nice to know that she has someone at the café she can trust to take over so she can enjoy a little time for herself."

"I feel honored that she puts so much faith in me," I said. "Your mom has done so much for me, and if I can help her by giving her a little peace of mind while she's away, that makes me feel like I've somewhat repaid the favor."

"I know my mom is grateful for you, Jenna, and I really would love to hear more about your writing. If you're ever looking for something to run past somebody, let me know. I'm a bit of a music buff myself. Do you play any instruments?"

"Yes, I play my grandma's guitar from when she was a teenager. She traveled around and played in a folk band for a bit before she met my grandfather and got married. Her life would have looked a lot different had she just stayed on the road."

He looked intrigued while trying to keep his face neutral. "What happened?"

"She met my grandfather, who was less than kind. It didn't change who she was, but it definitely changed the course of all of our lives. Maybe I wouldn't be here right now if she hadn't met him, but there would have been a lot less pain in the world."

"I'm sorry to hear that, Jenna, but it sounds like your grandma was a remarkable person and you were lucky to have her."

"I was," I said, feeling tears about to fall. "I miss her, and I know she would be proud of me now. So, I just tried to remain grateful that I had her in my life and that she believed that I could be something more."

"Well, if she believed it, then you should believe it, Jenna. Everything I've heard about you has been positive. And I'm glad that I can be a small part of helping you find your independence. It's an important time in your life, and one that everyone should get to enjoy. And it may have come for you a little later than some, but it's never *too* late. You're going to learn a lot about yourself over the next few months, and some of it is going to come as a shock. But be kind to yourself, take things slow, and just remember to give yourself some grace while you learn this new way of life. And you always have my mom and the rest of your group to support you if you're feeling lonely or can't find your way."

"That's the one thing that's kept me going through all of this. Knowing that my friends believe in me and think I will be ok. *Their* belief is what's helping *me* believe."

"Sometimes that's all you need to get started," Sam said, "and once this paperwork is filed, you'll be able to close this painful chapter in your life and begin a new one. And what that chapter contains from this point forward is completely up to you to write."

"I can't thank you enough. I never would have been able to do this without your generosity. I know you must be so busy, and you are taking time out of your life to do this for me... well, it means so much."

"This is my way of giving back," he said. "My mom does so much for our community through the café, and she's inspired me to do the same. So I want to be here to help shepherd you into *your* fresh start, Jenna, and it makes me happy to be able to do so."

He stood and came around the table and held his hand out to pull me up, and once I was standing, he shook the hand he was holding. "I mean it, Jenna. I'm looking forward to seeing what you do with your independence. From everything I've seen and heard, it's going to be remarkable."

I looked down at the floor and then back up at him. "Would it be okay if I hugged you real quick?" I asked, shocked by my bold words. It's not often that I initiate physical contact or affection. It feels foreign to me under most circumstances, but knowing what he was giving me out of the kindness of his heart made a handshake feel less than adequate.

"You sure can, Jenna." He held his arms out, and I quickly squeezed him and stepped back.

"Well, I better be going. I'm going to help your mom get the café closed down for the day and then I'm headed home to make some sourdough chocolate chip cookies. Thank you again for everything, and please let me know if there is anything else I need to do." I turned and retrieved my bag from the chair next to the one I'd been sitting in.

"Nothing at all that I can think of, but if anything comes up, I know where to find you... unless you want to drop off some of those cookies once they're done," he said, and then chuckled.

He walked me out, and as he waved and closed the door behind me, the click of the latch echoed in my ears. Endings are always sad, but it wasn't just sadness that I felt. It felt like the beginning of something. My independence, yes, but I knew that I was meant for more, and I was starting to feel like I had the strength to find it.

SOURDOUGH BROWN BUTTER CHOCOLATE CHIP COOKIES

½ cup melted butter

2 large eggs

1 cup brown sugar

1 cup white sugar

1 tsp baking soda

½ tsp salt

1 cup sourdough starter or discard

1-¼ cup flour

1-½ cup chocolate chips (or measure with your heart)

Preheat the oven to 350 degrees.

Combine dry ingredients in a separate bowl.

Melt butter in a saucepan. It's ready when it gives off a "nutty" aroma while boiling.

Combine the butter and sugars in a bowl or stand mixer.

Add in eggs one at a time.

Blend completely.

Add sourdough starter.

Add dry ingredients.

Add chocolate chips.

Drop 2 tablespoons of batter onto a greased cookie sheet 2" apart.

Bake for 9-11 minutes or until the bottom of the cookie is golden brown around the edges.

Remove the baking sheet from the oven and let sit for one minute.

Remove cookies from baking sheet and let cool on wire rack.

9

Once I was back at the café, Cat and I worked quickly to get everything cleaned up so we could leave by four. I enjoyed cleaning and the process of getting everything ready for the next day.

After my areas were cleaned and prepped, I went through the cooler to see if there was anything that we needed for the next week's baking. I had just finished checking on how much butter was left from the last order when I turned around to find Cat standing behind me, her bag over her shoulder.

"Do you have a minute?" she asked, and my curiosity was piqued. Typically, Cat raced out of there to make it to one community development meeting or another on time.

"Sure, what did you have in mind?"

"Let's take a walk next door. I really want to see what they've got going on over there. Who knows, maybe I'll expand."

I laughed, thinking the last thing Cat needed was double the responsibility when she already had so much on her plate. But I wasn't there to judge her ambitions. I was just there to bake, run the register during the day, and be her friend.

"Sure, let's go," I said. "I'm going to leave this order on your desk." On the way out of Cat's office, I grabbed my tote bag, checked for my phone and keys, and walked out behind Cat, who locked up behind us. The empty storefront was only steps past the door leading to my apartment, quite literally right next door. Cat reached into her pocket and pulled out a separate key ring.

"Elizabeth Wells, the leasing agent, stopped by earlier and dropped this off for me. I know her from school, and the Chamber of Commerce meetings, and we've gotten pretty close. She knows I won't come in here and trash the place."

I laughed knowing that that would never be a concern with Cat. She unlocked the door, pushed it open, and the smell of old cooking oil met us at the door.

"Whooey!" she said. "Based on the smell, this place is going to be a hard sell."

I looked around, and once I was past the initial sensory overload, I could see that the space itself was in good shape. It had exposed brick walls, and a counter with a case at the end, where I could only assume they had once stored their cannolis and tiramisu.

"Look at this place," exclaimed Cat. "It's actually pretty nice. I had come in here a few times to pick up pizza when they were open, but it looks different without people in here and the usual chaos of a business during working hours."

"What kind of equipment do they have in back?" I asked.

"Let's go check it out."

We walked around the counter and pushed through the swinging doors that led into the kitchen, similarly to Cat's. There was a giant commercial mixer, a long stainless steel table for prep, a large walk-in cooler, and two ovens, not including what looked like a wood-fire oven in the corner. I wondered if another pizza place might end up moving in there.

It would be nice to have the smell of freshly baked pizza dough wafting into my home.

I paused for a moment. That was the first time I'd really thought of the apartment as my *home*.

I smiled at the thought, then looked over to where Cat was obviously waiting for my reaction. "Looks pretty good. Are you thinking of opening a pizza place, Cat?"

"Not exactly, but I'm keeping my options open." She spun in place, her face clearly showing her delight. "Look at all this equipment. This oven looks just like mine. And this mixer looks pretty familiar too, doesn't it?"

"Yep, looks like the one I use every morning," I agreed.

"Interesting," said Cat. "Don't you think that all this equipment would be great if someone were to open a bakery here?"

I looked at Cat, and suddenly, the pieces clicked into place. Of course there was an ulterior motive for her bringing me over there. My anxiety quickly rose as I tried to figure out how to address her question. I certainly wasn't in a position to start my own business.

"A bakery could definitely be running this space, but by whom? Are you going to open a bakery?"

"No, Jenna, but you could."

I swallowed hard and looked down at the floor as I wrung my hands. "I don't know how I could ever make that work yet. I'm barely getting by. And while I'm appreciative of my bargain basement living expenses, there's no way that I could afford to rent this space on top of it. It takes years to get a business in the black, and I don't know if I'd be able to raise the funds to ever even dream of stepping foot in this place. Besides, how would Craig feel about me owning my own business?" Despite the time I'd recently spent building up my confidence, I'd been conditioned to accept his unreasonable demands over my own wants and needs.

Cat turned me around so I was facing her, and kept her hands on my shoulders. "Jenna. I want you to remember that you're free to forge your own path. The question you need to ask yourself is, 'How do *I* feel about owning my own business?' You have a lot of hard decisions coming up, but this one is worth thinking about. This is exactly what you've *always* talked about, and the opportunity is here... and I think it's here for a reason. I know you're going to be just fine, and maybe, just maybe, this place right here could be the doorway to fine. Just think about it. Now tell me what my son had to say. You don't have to share anything personal. Just the basics. He's pretty great, right?"

I nodded my head, still mute. But I knew that Cat was genuinely invested in my survival and success. "He's great, Cat. Really great, and you did such a wonderful job with him. What a fabulous human being you've raised. He's getting the paperwork together and will have it delivered to Craig at the jail." What I didn't say was that I was starting to have second thoughts. I was doing fine during the day, getting stronger on my own and enjoying my own company, but when night fell, my thoughts of the future were as dark as the sky outside my windows. I couldn't see what was ahead, and it terrified me.

Cat pumped her fist and then dropped her arm, looking contrite. "Did he say how long the process would take?"

We were still standing in the middle of the space. The smell had faded and when I looked around me again, I started to see things in the light that Cat had shone.

"He said everything could be finished pretty quickly. I think the word he used was dissolve, and I'm not sure how I feel about that, but I'm grateful that I won't have to endure a long drawn-out process. There isn't anything to divide, and thankfully, we didn't end up having any kids, so it's basically just a tragic end to what I thought was my beginning."

Cat stepped into the space between us and wrapped me in her arms, as she so often did. "You're going to be just fine, Jenna. Better than fine. And you have all of us to make sure of that. I don't want to pressure you with this, but I want you to consider what it could look like. Why don't you think first about whether it's something that you would want to do? Then let us help you figure out how to make it happen. We've done it before," she sighed and winked, and I chuckled. It wasn't long ago that we dragged Paige—nearly kicking and screaming—through the plans to open her writing retreat.

"And look how that turned out," Cat reminded me, as if she could read my mind.

"I'll give it some thought," I promised. "It seems I have a lot to think about these days."

"And that's a beautiful thing," said Cat. "Now, let's get out of here. I've got things to do, and I need to have a little chat with Elyse."

Her last words were thrown over her shoulder in the same tone as the one that greeted my ears when her motorcycle kicked to life outside a minute later.

***

The weekend sped by, and it had been peaceful since I blocked the jail's number. I was able to focus on putting the finishing touches on the apartment, and I really loved how everything came together. The clean, crisp white with the splashes of yellow and blue felt like the coastal decor I had always longed for. I had found a few prints of local beaches at the thrift store on Sunday and spent the day hanging them, dreaming of what was next.

Every time the idea of the bakery popped into my head, I pushed it aside. Dreams that big were meant for someone else. Although I hated to disappoint Cat.

After the café closed on Monday, Cat walked up and leaned against the bakery case. "Busy day today," she said. "Looks like we sold out of everything..." She paused. "...again. You're going to have to start coming in an hour earlier just to make more. Everyone loves your pastries." I knew what she was doing, but I let her have fun.

"Yep, it must be magic. I doubled the sugar in this week's recipes, so that's probably what it is."

"No, you did not, and you know that wouldn't be what it is anyway. You have something really special, Jenna. Which is evidenced by the constant dinging of the door, and they're not here for the club sandwiches."

"No, they're here for the Eggs Benedict," I shot back. Eggs Benedict was the specialty at Cat's Bites, and we had regulars that came in nearly every day to order it. Aside from them, many diners let us know they were there on a referral from a friend or an online review.

"You might have to open that bakery just so that my Eggs Benedict can be the star of the show around here again," she said with a laugh. "But I do want to talk to you about that. There's been a development." Her face twisted into a grimace, a rarity for Cat. The bottom of my stomach dropped out. People telling you they want to talk to you is seldom followed by good news.

"Elizabeth texted me. The landlord wants to have a signed lease within the next thirty days."

My throat closed up. That was the pressure I was afraid of. I didn't know what to do. I'd never had the opportunity to make decisions for myself, and now I was being met with important decisions that needed to be made left and right.

Cat waved a hand in front of my face to break me from my internal spiral. "Are you okay, Jenna? Don't panic. I just wanted to give you all the information."

The nighttime doubts that I fought so hard to ignore during the day forced their way to the surface. "I've been having second thoughts about divorcing Craig," I blurted. "I don't know that the finances would be solid if I opened a store. And it seems like a lot of stress. Right now, I'm just wishing I could get a sneak peek of what my life looks like in six months."

"Follow me," she said, and walked toward the swinging

doors that led to the seating area of the café. When she reached the booth where the Sensational Six usually sat, she slid into her normal spot and gestured to mine along the left side of the curve.

Once I was seated and settled, she spoke. "I want to share something with you that I don't often talk about." She took a deep breath in and let it out slowly. She pulled her bandana off her head and used it to mop her face, then folded it and set it on the table in front of her. I could recognize avoidance when I saw it.

"You probably don't know this," she began, "but I lost my parents when I was young, and no one from my family came forward to take me in. I spent a couple of years in foster care, but was finally adopted by a wonderful couple who were thrilled to have the opportunity to raise a child. They had tried for years, but it had not been in the cards for them, so they were as happy to have me as I was to have them.

"Although it took me some time to fully trust the situation. Would the bottom come out from underneath my feet as it had in the past? That kind of trauma doesn't just go away. A lot of times, when the people we trust are no longer there for one reason or another, or when the people we are supposed to trust the most betray us, it can be difficult to overcome. But I have learned through my experience that the people you draw into your life, the ones who see the best and the worst in you and choose to stay; those are your true family." She bent over the table to catch my eye before continuing. "I ask that you put some faith in the family you trust, the people you've drawn into your life. The five of us will *always* be your family, and will *always* have your best interests in mind."

I shifted in my seat.

"Now, I can't make your decision about your future with Craig, but we will be here to support you no matter what. I want you to think about your life decisions in the context of what's best for Jenna. Ask yourself where you want to see your-self in six months, what it would take to get there, and who would support you versus standing in the way of that goal. Knowing that, you can move forward confidently and with the faith that your true family will be there to cheer you on and support you the whole way."

When Cat stopped talking, she looked at me, not as if to pressure me into a reply, but to let her message sink in. And it had. It was beginning to anyway. But I did have another concern.

"You've done so much for me, and I would feel terrible about leaving the café."

Cat reached forward and enveloped my hands in her own. "Jenna, my ultimate goal at the café is never to have the women I hire work for me forever. My mission here is to give the women without experience, and those who just need someone to believe in them, a chance. I like building up your skills and confidence and sending you all to the next step in your fabu-lous lives. This is what I feel I'm meant to do, and your next step will not leave me in a bad position. It leaves me in the posi-tion to help the next person in line.

"You're a part of my legacy, and I want you to achieve your dreams. How about this? If we can find a way to make the bakery work, you can help me decide who to choose next, and that person will become a part of *both* of our legacies."

At this point, the tears were streaming down my face. I'd never known such love since I lost my grandmother, especially from people who were not related to me by blood. I thought about what she said about my true family, and realized she was right. At every moment in the past year—good, bad, and other-wise—those five women were there for me, and I had no choice but to put my faith in Cat's words in the hopes that they were true.

"Well, I can't obviously make a decision at this very moment without knowing all the information, but I will think about it. I promise."

"Don't let any of us pressure you into making any decision one way or another, Jenna. I just want to make sure that you're looking at your options through clear eyes, unclouded by all the bullshit that's been piled on top of you for so many years. We'll be here to support you no matter what you decide, and if this opportunity," she pointed at the wall toward the space next door, "isn't right for you, then the one that is right for you will come along and you'll be ready for it.

"You're meant to do great things, Jenna. That's why you've remained largely unjaded through everything you've endured. I have so much respect for you, and I'm looking forward to cheering you on through your next steps, regardless of where they might take you.

"I'm your family, Jenna. We all are. And we want you to be happy. Now, let's get out of here so we can enjoy the rest of our night."

We slid out of the booth and started making our way toward the door. When we reached the hostess stand, Cat put her hand out and touched my arm. "You've got some things to think about, but you don't have to make the decisions alone. The Sensational Six is sensational for a reason."

I laughed, knowing she was right.

We walked out the door, and Cat turned to lock it. "Before you go upstairs, take a moment and peek through the window. See what feelings it brings up. Besides, of course, anxiety." And with that, she walked around the side and disappeared, throwing a "toodles!" over her shoulder. A moment later, the roar of her bike came around the side of the building.

I stood in front of the previous pizza place and did as Cat had requested. I put my hands against the window and peered through them into the space.

Could this be my future?

I couldn't see how, but Cat had asked me to put my faith in them, so I could only do what she requested. I pictured myself standing next to the dusty bakery case, flour in my hair and butter on my cheek. I pictured myself behind the counter as people streamed in to pick up their orders or sit for a cup of coffee and dessert. I pictured people working quietly on their computers, plates of croissants waiting beyond their screens.

Could someone like me dare to have such lofty goals?

I didn't know. But I knew that all I could do was take the steps to find out.

10

On the afternoon of Paige's pool party, I dug out a cute one-piece bathing suit with open sides that had been sitting in a drawer since I'd bought it months before. I took it out and put it back several times before I decided to be brave and wear what *I* wanted to wear for once. I didn't get many opportunities to swim other than at Paige's and I'd been so busy at the café and getting settled into the apartment that I hadn't done much of anything else. The irony of living in a beach community and not having time to go to the beach did not escape me.

When I got to Paige's, she waved to me from where she was relaxing on one of the teal lounge chairs surrounding the pool and hot tub area. And Kari, Paige's best friend from Madison, sat on the pool lounger to her right. This was a nice surprise as everyone loved Kari and she fit right in with our group. Roxy was running back and forth across the lawn, chasing something, her nose down and tail in the air (which was pretty much how I saw her every single time I was there). All three of them seemed very happy. Content even.

It looked like I had beaten everybody else there, but that

was to be expected; I have always been early everywhere I go. I pulled my bag with my beach towel, sunglasses, sunscreen, and the bag of food from the café out of the back seat and headed toward the others.

"It's so great to see you, Jenna," Kari said.

I gave as much of a wave as I could and smiled as I stood there in my bathing suit cover-up, balancing a large paper bag from the café under one arm and a Pyrex dish in the other hand like Lady Liberty headed to a potluck on the beach. "Great to see you, too!" I replied.

I made my way across the yard to where Kari and her mass of blonde curls (Yes, they were a separate entity. They should have their own zip code.) were heading toward me. My arms were loaded, but she leaned in to embrace me and then stepped back, pushing a curl out of her face. "Here, give me that dish. What is this? Is that cheese on top? You sure know the way to our hearts. Paige, this woman is a wonder."

Paige had already made her way to Kari's side and was waiting for a hug of her own, which I happily provided.

"Do you need to change? You didn't need to bring a towel. I have everything, even sunscreen."

I looked down to where my tattered beach towel was hanging out of my bag and felt momentarily embarrassed.

"I don't need to change. I have my suit underneath my cover-up."

I followed Paige, Kari, and my Pyrex dish inside after setting my phone down on the chair to the left of Paige's. There were already a few dishes on the counter, along with hot pink cups and small white plates with flamingos all over them.

"Cat texted; she's on her way. Grace and Sarah are driving together and stopped to pick up a bag of ice because my ice machine is on the fritz again, and we can't have frozen margaritas without ice."

"Definitely not," I said.

"And happy hour is starting soon," added Kari.

I wasn't big on happy hour. Having grown up with two alcoholics, I wasn't much of a drinker, but I wasn't there to begrudge anyone else their good time.

"We have pink lemonade," said Paige, as if reading my mind. "So help yourself to anything you want to drink. Flavored seltzer is in the fridge, and there's some wild cherry Pepsi in there for you as well."

Kari took the plastic lid off the Pyrex dish and stared down into it. "What delicious treat do we have here?"

"It's a Mexican corn dip," I replied, pulling a bag of tortilla chips out of my beach bag and setting it on the counter.

"Yes, please," said Kari, picking up a plate and spoon. She heaped a generous portion onto her flamingo plate and opened the bag of chips.

"What have you been up to, Jenna? Paige has told me all about the retreat and what a big hit breakfast was for everyone. Anything else exciting on the horizon for you?"

"Well, my life sure looks a lot different than the last time you were here."

Kari waited patiently for me to continue as she piled chips onto her plate.

"I'm separated from my husband and living above the café for now. Cat has generously offered to let me stay there while I figure out my next steps."

Kari gave me a sympathetic smile, then walked around the counter and pulled a large serving bowl down from the white glass-front cabinets lining the wall. "And what, pray tell, might these next steps be for you? Do you have anything in mind? Because if not, this group will make short work of getting a list ready for you."

I laughed. "Don't I know it. I was part of that whole process for Paige's retreats."

When we stepped out into the backyard, Grace and Sarah were pulling up in Grace's white Range Rover.

"Hey there, you two," said Grace, stepping down in a teal and pink kaftan and white Tory Burch sandals. Colorful casual was Grace's signature style.

Sarah came around from the passenger side and greeted Kari heartily, followed by Grace. "Who's ready for a pool party?" Sarah asked.

"I definitely am," said Paige. "I've been so busy this week. I've walked past this pool fifty times and didn't have a spare moment to get in. I'm probably going to spend most of the day floating on a raft, but you all know your way around here, and I don't need to entertain you. Just help yourself to whatever you need. Food and drinks are in the house."

"We brought ice," said Sarah, holding it above her head as she pulled her beach bag higher on her other shoulder.

"Perfect. I made some room for it in the freezer. I'll go inside and make margaritas in a little bit."

"I'm happy to put myself to work if it means that the margaritas come out sooner," said Grace.

Paige laughed. "If you want to whip up a batch, I'm not going to stand in your way. In fact, I'm not going to stand at all." And with that, she slipped into the pool.

I was ready for a swim as well and followed her in.

"Kari, Jenna, can we get you anything?" asked Grace.

"No, I have my soda and a plate full of snacks, so I'm good to go. Thank you."

Kari lifted her Yeti. "I'm good with lemonade for now, thanks."

Sarah ran back to the Range Rover. "I almost forgot," she said, opening the back driver's side door and pulling out a large, rectangular plastic container with a lid. "You know I don't go into any social function without a charcuterie board."

"And that's why we're friends," said Paige. "You're just trying to catch my eye. Are you sure you don't want me to come in and help you?"

"No way, you stay in there. We're more than capable of getting things set up in the kitchen. We'll be out in a minute."

Grace and Sarah disappeared inside just as the roar of Cat's motorcycle reached our ears. She pulled into the driveway and parked, swung her leg over the side, and turned our way. She flipped up the visor, looking confused, and said, "What's everybody looking at?"

"You, silly," said Paige. "We're looking to see if Elyse was maybe on the back of your bike. Have you heard from her?"

Cat turned, removed her helmet, and set it on her bike seat. She opened up the saddlebag and pulled out a string backpack. It almost seemed like she was stalling.

"So have you heard from Elyse?" Paige asked again.

"Don't get me started," said Cat as she stalked over.

Paige and I shared a look. She shrugged her shoulders, and I made a "yikes" face.

Somebody's in trouble.

"I'm sure she'll be here soon," said Paige, trying to snuff out the fuse she'd inadvertently lit.

"Mm-hmm," said Cat. "I'm gonna go inside and change."

"Alright, you know where everything is. Sarah is in there setting up the charcuterie board and Grace is making margaritas, if that is of interest to you. Otherwise, there's pop and flavored seltzer water in the fridge, and pink lemonade on the counter."

Cat seemed distracted as she walked past us toward the back door. "Thanks. I'll be out in a minute." With that, she disappeared inside.

"There's something going on with those two," Paige said to me after the back door had closed.

"Yeah, I've picked up on that, but I figured it's none of my business, so I'm not going to ask." I hesitated before saying, "But I will admit, I'm a little curious."

"Right? This has been going on for a month now."

"I'm sure they'll work it out; they've been friends for such a long time."

"I'm sure you're right," said Paige.

A moment later, Grace and Sarah walked out. Grace was holding two margarita glasses, and Sarah was holding one margarita glass and a white flamingo plate heaped with cheese and sausage.

"We come bearing snacks and drinks," said Sarah. "Paige, this is for you." Paige paddled over and Sarah leaned down and handed her a Yeti, its straw tipped with tajin. "Cat's inside making her own. And from the look on her face, I'm not sure if we should be trusting her with that bottle of tequila. So be fore-warned if you accept a glass from her."

"Noted," said Kari.

I was suddenly very glad I didn't drink. "I'm probably going to just stick with my soda," I said as I climbed the steps to exit the pool.

A stony-faced Cat came out a moment later with a glass in her hand.

"Does anyone want a margarita?"

"I think we're good, Cat," said Paige, "but thank you." She looked at Grace with the same "yikes" face I'd given her moments before.

"Good to see you again, Kari," she said, then fell silent again.

As Cat was getting settled by the pool, Elyse's Audi pulled into the driveway.

"Well, look who decided to join us," said Cat in a sarcastic tone.

I was hoping they wouldn't be sniping at each other all day. I needed a bit of peace and tranquility.

After Elyse went in and changed, we all gathered around the pool to make it easier to talk to Paige and Kari, who were slowly ping-ponging off the sides and each other.

Thirty minutes later, everyone was full of snacks, margaritas, pink lemonade, seltzer water, and, for me, my favorite soda. The conversation flowed naturally (other than between Cat and Elyse), and after everybody had finished catching up with Kari, the attention turned to me.

Sarah sat on my left, dangling her legs into the pool and swishing the water back and forth.

"How are things *really* going for you, Jenna? It seems like you're settling into your apartment nicely."

"Yes, I love what you've done with the place," said Cat. "It looks like a beach retreat up there."

"It really does," said Grace. "You've done an excellent job. I'm so happy to see it."

"Just walking in there when I get home makes me happier. Being surrounded by that resort motif almost makes it feel like an escape."

"Well, I think it looks beautiful," said Cat.

"I'd love to stop by and see what you've done," said Kari. "Paige and I will be in the café over the next few days if you have time for us."

"Stop by in the evening sometime. I'd love to show it to you," I said, feeling a little embarrassed from all the attention being directed my way. Lately, it had happened a lot, and it hadn't gotten any easier to sit through. I took the barrette out of my hair and put it back in, feeling for strays and repeating the process several times.

"Any word about Craig? How is that situation playing out?" Paige asked from her raft.

I finally got it perfect and dropped my hands down into my lap. "Well, I do have some news on that front," I told the group. "I was planning on telling you today anyway. I went to see Cat's son last week, and we actually got the paperwork started. Craig will be served at the county jail." Cat's head shot up, and she gave me a quick nod. "And, in my conversations with his public defender, it sounds like he will likely get a year in county jail, but be out in six months. This means that by the time he gets out, we should be legally divorced."

"How do you feel about that?" asked Sarah.

"I do have to admit that even though I feel some relief that this part of my life will improve, I am still sad. Because, while I have always had mixed feelings about motherhood after not having had the best role models as parents, it's something I have always pictured for myself. I've always wanted to be a mom and give a child all the love I never had." I paused for a moment to collect my thoughts and decide how much of my fears I wanted to share. I took a breath, then continued. "But I'm scared. What if I'm like *them?*"

Sarah put her arm around my shoulder. "I know that you have some reservations, Jenna, but there is some proof here that you are breaking that generational cycle. Going to therapy has been so good for you, and once you do have kids, you'll have the tools to be a loving mother. When you know better you do better, right?

"I can see the kind of person you are, Jenna. You're very loving and very patient, compassionate, and empathetic, and I think that any child would be lucky to have you as a mom. And I believe that having children will be very healing for you. But to put a more positive spin on things, you have an opportunity to raise a child in a loving environment instead of the same one you grew up in. And you're only twenty-eight."

You're still a *baby,*" said Elyse, "and you have plenty of time to find the right person..." she paused to take a sip of her margarita. "...or have a baby *without* the right person. It's completely up to you. There is still plenty of time to decide what's best. For *you.*"

"I do still have some things that I want to accomplish in the meantime," I said. "I know that I want big things for myself. I want something that I can be proud of. Something that's mine."

Grace laughed, "These are all very reasonable wants and desires, Jenna, but I'm going to echo Sarah's sentiment. You are still in your twenties and have plenty of time to realize your dreams. Hell, look at me, I was in my fifties before I ever published my first book, and I'm still expanding my dreams every day. So don't look at the passage of time as a wasted opportunity. Look back on all of your experiences so far. All the steps you took in order to get where you are and know what you know. These are all necessary to build who we become as we continue to grow."

"That makes sense," I said. "I guess I'm forgetting that even though I feel like I put all my eggs in one basket, there are plenty of good eggs out there."

"Yeah, like a certain security technician," said Cat with a smirk. While I was happy to see she was loosening up and getting her sense of humor back, I was ready to point it in a different direction. It was time to change the subject.

"So, Sarah, anything interesting going on at school?"

Sarah stood up from where she was sitting on the side of the pool and wrapped herself in a towel, then flopped down onto a lounge chair. "Do you all remember I told you about that student of mine that stopped in? She came back while I was in the office, and we had a chance to talk for a little while. She had moved out of town, got married young, had a baby, and was recently widowed, so she moved back to Clearwater. She said she wanted to come in and talk to me because I had made such an impact on her when she was a young child, and she thought about me often. How sweet is that? I have never had any of my students come back after so many years. I mean, the last time I ever see them is eighth grade. And who cares about a social worker they had when they were in eighth grade? Anyway, her name is Allison, and she has a four-year-old son named Noah. She wants to go back to school to become a grief counselor and was asking if I had any resources for her. How awesome is that?"

Cat set her margarita glass on the pool deck next to her and stretched her arms over her head, visibly more relaxed than she was when she arrived. "That's incredible, Sarah. Hopefully, she stays in contact with you so you can keep track of her journey."

"I hope so, too," said Sarah.

"So, Paige," said Grace. "It sounds like your retreat went well. Did anything noteworthy happen?"

"Well, breakfast was all anyone could talk about after Friday morning."

Oh boy. Here we go. This reeks of a setup.

"With good reason," said Elyse.

Grace asked, "Did you make the lavender cupcakes?"

"She did, and they were a big hit," said Paige before I had a chance to answer, "as was everything else. In fact, I checked some of the reviews online last night. Three out of four mentioned breakfast. Not the session, not the yoga, not the comfortable beds. *Pastries.*" She looked at me pointedly. "Jenna, you have a real talent."

"I just really enjoy baking," I said, trying desperately to think of another distraction.

Could I slip under the water and hold my breath long enough for them to grow bored of trying to convince each other of my guaranteed success—something they already seem so sure of?

"While we're on the subject," said Cat, and my stomach clenched up. I knew where the conversation was headed.

"Jenna and I went and took a look at the open space next to the café the other day. It has all the same equipment that she's currently using in my kitchen." She looked at me and winked, "and I really think she ought to take a run at it. I know she could make it work. What do you all think?"

"Well, just judging by the reaction from my retreaters, Jenna, you'd probably be able to retire in a year."

I laughed, but inside, my stomach was churning with anxiety.

Sarah stretched out her arms and examined them, then applied more sunscreen as she spoke. "You could really have something there, Jenna. Something that's yours. Something that you have built into a success. Something that *nobody* can take away from you, or tell you that you're not capable of. We all believe this could be a good idea for you, but what do *you* think?"

"I don't really know what to think. The space is perfect and has a lot of potential to be beautiful, plus all the right equipment is there. I just don't know if it's something that I can make happen. I need the first month's rent, security deposit, and money to buy all of my ingredients before I even step foot in the place. Is the equipment working? We don't know. What's involved in starting a business? I have no idea." I could feel myself starting to spiral.

"I have some of those figures for you," said Cat. "I can tell you what my monthly bills are down to the penny, any month of the year for the past seven years."

"Well, *I guarantee* it's more money than I have right now. Even with the little bit I have set aside."

"Well, that's nothing that can't be fixed, Jenna. They give out small business loans every day at the bank. I can help you get your paperwork done and just see what they say."

"I'm not really sure. Can I think on it?" I looked down at my feet dangling in the water. Paige bumped me with her toe as she floated by and gave me an encouraging smile when I looked up.

"Absolutely," said Elyse. "Elizabeth is a friend of mine. Cat and I both know her from the Chamber of Commerce, and she's a good person."

Cat tapped her chin thoughtfully. "Let me see if she knows if the rent is negotiable and what the landlord is looking for. But now that the landlord wants a signed lease in hand within thirty days, Jenna's feet are in the fire."

"I think it's an excellent idea," said Kari. "Look at all the success you've had already without even having your own space."

"Word of mouth is invaluable in this town," said Sarah. "And if people knew that the muffins that I've been bringing into the break room at school were available at a bakery right downtown, you would have people beating down your door."

"You could continue to provide pastries for a lot of different events," added Grace. "My book launch party is coming up fast, and I think you should leave some business cards out on the table with your phone number and...," she looked over at Elyse, "Raina could help her set up a Facebook page." Then she looked at Cat sitting next to her. "Are you okay with Jenna increasing her business while she's in your space?"

"Of course," Cat said, "the more business she gets outside of the café, the more she will believe that this is more than just a possibility."

"You've got a real gift, Jenna," said Elyse, "and I would love to see you make this a reality. But we aren't going to pressure you." She looked around at the rest of the group, one by one. "I feel like Paige is still recovering from the way we dragged her through the planning of her writers' retreats."

"But look at what a wild success those have become," crowed Grace proudly.

"Well, one has been successful so far," said Paige with a smile, "but yes, there is promise, and yes, I'm still recovering from being dragged around by my ankles for months."

"So what do you need in order to make a decision, Jenna?" asked Sarah.

"For starters, I have no idea what it would cost to furnish the place so that people can actually sit down, which I think would be a nice touch."

Kari chuckled. "And maybe some additional equipment. A decent coffee machine would be nice. People can sit down and have a cup of coffee and a muffin. And maybe they would end up getting something additional to take home for their family or friends. You could offer them a discount on an extra pastry to go."

"Or they could donate a pastry to the shelter in Clearwater," added Sarah.

Elyse's head whipped around toward her. "Ooh, that would work."

"I think we're getting into the weeds here, ladies," said Grace, "but these are all good ideas. So what other kinds of expenses can you think of? It seems like we have most everything accounted for."

"You would need some kind of marketing," said Elyse, "and I'm sure Raina can help with that for a reasonable price if you just need a few things set up and nothing super involved. Besides, I'm betting that word of mouth would be enough to get you started."

"Okay, so your next step would be what?" asked Paige. "Getting a business loan?"

"Yes, I suppose so," I agreed. "Although I don't really know much about those or what would be required. I'm just learning how to balance my own checking account; I'm in my baby steps era here."

"Luckily, you have all of us to help support you," said Elyse, "and many of us have a lot of experience with small businesses."

"I think this is a fantastic time for you to take a step toward your dreams, Jenna," said Sarah. "Not only will it eventually give you some financial stability, but it will be great for your self-esteem as well. Think how proud you're going to feel when you're celebrating your first year in business, and your fifth year in business, and then your tenth year. Sure, it's going to be hard sometimes, but you'll learn from that, too. I know you can make this work, and you have all of us here to help make sure that it does."

"I wonder," said Grace, tapping her chin with a hot pink manicured nail, "who would take Jenna's place at the café?"

Sarah nodded her head. "And how will the Cat's Bites experience change *that* woman's life? Think about that, Jenna. You fulfilling your dreams means that somebody else is right behind you in line to discover theirs."

"I wonder who it will be," said Elyse.

Sarah stood from the lounge chair and sat next to Cat. "I have a sneaky suspicion that the universe will lead her straight to your door."

MEXICAN CORN DIP

(2) 11 oz can of corn (drained)
(2) 4.5 oz. can of green chiles
(2) cups grated monterey jack cheese
¾ cup grated parmesan cheese
1 cup mayonnaise

Preheat the oven to 350 degrees.
Grease a 9x13x2 casserole dish or use a large cast iron pan.
Mix the ingredients and spread into the dish.
Bake uncovered for 30 to 40 minutes or until bubbly around the edges.

Serve with tortilla chips or scooping-style corn chips.

11

As soon as I got home from work the next day, I grabbed my new gratitude journal from the table in the kitchen and brought it over to the couch. I propped my feet up on the coffee table and set the journal on my lap. Snuggling into the throw Sarah had bought me as a housewarming present, I opened the journal and read what I'd written, then dated the top of the page that followed.

NOVEMBER 10, 2023

WELL, here I'm, making my second entry in a week. That seems like a good sign, right? What I'm most grateful for has changed in the last few days. Today, I'm most grateful for the friends I've made. They are constantly lifting me up, encouraging me, and supporting me. They seem to know when I need them. It's so nice to have people who have my best interests in mind instead of their own. It's not something that I'm used to, but I'm growing to like it.

It's so comforting to know that I can depend on these women no matter what, and they've proven that time and time again. I'm also grateful for the wonderful people in the world who help people like me when we need it most. Cat's son has been a godsend to me. There's no way I would have ever known how to get through all the legal hoops to separate from Craig. And I never would have been able to afford his services without him being so generous. Even though the reason why he's helping me for free certainly sucks.

I'm grateful for the people who have reached out to me to place orders. It's really making me wonder whether I could maybe get this thing off the ground and be successful. I can picture it. The bakery, people standing in line, picking up orders, big smiles on their faces. It's funny how a few weeks ago, I didn't even know I wanted this. And now it's suddenly all I can think about.

It would be nice to have something to hopefully keep my head above water. It would also be really nice to have something that I've created that's successful. I've never had that before. And especially considering the state of my marriage, I'm not feeling very successful at all lately. But maybe that will change now. I hate getting my hopes up about it. I worry about the rug getting ripped out from under me. It seems like so much of my life has been waiting for that moment, bracing for it instead of enjoying all the good that was around me.

Now I feel like I have the space to do that, and instead of worrying about the rug, I'm able to put my faith in the people around me to hold me up when I falter. Life is certainly different these days, but I'm finding that as each day passes, I do, in fact, have more and more to be grateful for.

As I CLOSED the journal and set it on the coffee table, the buzzer for the front door sounded. I stood and walked over to the intercom. "Hello?"

"It's Grace. Can you buzz me up?" came back in a husky rasp. I pressed the button to let her in and opened my door as she climbed the steps.

"Hey there, darlin'," she said as she closed the door behind her and turned to wrap me in a hug. "I just stopped by for a chat. I know I just saw you at Paige's, but I wanted to talk to you one-on-one about what we were discussing... you know... about the bakery. I wanted to make sure you weren't too overwhelmed. I know this is all a lot for you to wrap your mind around."

I spun on my heel and started walking toward the kitchen table, motioning with my arm to follow me. "Let's sit at the table. I'll make you some coffee."

As I busied myself in the kitchen, measuring grounds, pouring water, and taking out coffee cups, Grace wasted no time. "I know you have some reservations, and that is completely normal. You *should* have reservations because it's a big decision, but I want you to make sure that you consider all sides of this."

I lifted my grandmother's recipe book off the table and set it on my lap, thumbing the corners of the pages absentmindedly. "I'm trying, but I don't know what I don't know, and that's scary. I've never run a business before. I've never even run my own life before."

"I completely understand, Jenna, and I wouldn't be here right now if I didn't think you could handle it. You have everything you need, including a good support system and a community that wants to see you succeed, so between those three things, you are nearly guaranteed success." She paused and looked at me pointedly. "But it has to begin with *you*. *You* have to believe that you'll be successful in order for it to happen. It doesn't happen in a vacuum or because other people tell you that it will. Success steps into the space that doubt leaves behind. Let go of your doubt. Have faith in your community and your family; the rest will work itself out."

"If only it were that simple," I said, returning the book to the table. "I have been thinking about it, but the same concern always bubbles up no matter how positive I'm feeling in the moment or what someone is telling me. It all comes down to: what about all the logistics? I don't know the first thing about running a business. It just seems like so much to think about all at once, and the funding is a major concern."

Grace squeezed my hand. "Sweetheart, I understand how this could all feel very overwhelming, but let me remind you about a certain sister from the North who blew into this town with a dog, a heavy dose of 'what the hell do I do next', and a whole lot of baggage. And this past weekend, you provided breakfast for the writing retreat that she didn't think was possible."

She paused to give me time to marinate in her observation. "I don't want you to feel pressured to do anything, but if you're holding back based on fear of the logistics, let me remind you that your friends are willing and capable of helping to carry you to the finish line here. Especially your big sister, Grace. I've got plenty of resources to help you with any problem you come up against. Every single one of us believes that you can do this, Jenna. But it's up to *you* to believe it as well."

"I can definitely see how you managed to convince Paige, but that's not all I worry about. I feel... guilty thinking about leaving Cat in a bind at the café. I know it's what she wants, but... I'm conflicted."

"Remember, Jenna, you're just the most recent of a long line of women Cat has helped find better opportunities, and you will not be the last. This is what Cat wants. She doesn't want you to work at the café forever. She wants you to *use* your experience at the café to make you stronger as you take your next step." She leaned forward to pat my hand. "She believes in you just as much as I do. This is what she wants, Jenna, I promise you. And if you're concerned, you can always help her find or choose the next person. The best way to honor Cat's commitment to you right now is to follow in your predecessor's path and take the next right step. And if your hesitation is based on fear of what comes next, we'll be here to help you. No matter what."

I stood and leaned over next to Grace to put my arms around her. She would hate that I said this, but sometimes she felt so much like having my grandmother around again. Being in her presence made me feel more comfortable, no matter the subject at hand.

"Thank you for having faith in me, and thank you for being positive about this. I'm not trying to be negative, but I *am* hoping that this could be something that could work out for me, but let me just think about it for a little bit longer. I just need to see how the pieces could come together."

"Take your time, but don't take too long." Her rumbly chuckle filled the apartment. "We'll be here for you either way."

I straightened back up and walked to the kitchen to make two cups of coffee. When I carried them over to the table, I saw Grace slip something under the recipe book.

We spent the rest of our visit chatting about her book launch, Paige's retreat, and Sarah's children, and the bakery didn't come up again. Grace was persistent, but she knew when to back off and let her message do the work.

After she left, I lifted the recipe book and found a slip of paper. On it, she had written, "Give yourself permission to have the life that was meant for you. The rest will work itself out. I promise."

But how? I wondered. *How do I get from here to there?*

"Faith, Jenna. You need to have faith," said Gigi's voice in my head.

Faith or not, I was going to have to start giving this some serious consideration.

12

———————

I was back in the café bright and early Thursday morning, preparing everything that was to go in the bakery case that day. Croissants were something that I made every day, and I typically switched out the cupcake theme based on the season and local events. It was nearly winter, so I'd settled on cream cheese cupcakes with a pumpkin chiffon filling and a whipped cream topping. I also planned to make berry tarts, some cannoli, and apple fritters, which were a big hit in any season. I had even stopped by our local craft store to pick up a few things to decorate the case for winter. While it was true that our colors didn't change to vibrant then muted hues, nor did we get that crisp weather the northern states enjoy, I thought it would be nice to bring a little holiday flair into the café, regardless.

Early mornings at the café were my favorite. It was still quiet in the kitchen, which gave me a little bit of time to think without the distraction of anyone else around or people coming in and out once the café opened, and I moved out to cover the register. That was what I was initially hired for until the baker who had been here when I started moved on to work as a chef at the local golf club. Cat often came back from lunch at the club after ladies' league on Tuesdays and told me how proud she was of her and what she'd added to the menu. She was always so proud of the people who have worked here and moved on. I knew I was a part of that, and I was grateful that Cat put her faith in me when I walked in on that fateful day.

What I was looking for that day was some financial independence from Craig, and what I got were five friends, a brand new life, and the possibility of a future that I could be proud of.

Maybe someday I'll be one of those people Cat talks about with pride.

The more I considered the idea of the bakery, the more excited I got about the possibility. But it was still very hard to shake all the self-doubt that had been a part of me my entire life. It wasn't easy to change my way of thinking at the drop of a hat, or just because the other women said it would work. It seemed like a lot of risk to take for something that wasn't guaranteed to be successful.

I could see where the other women were coming from. I had seen an increase in orders coming through the café, and I had people contacting me from the reviews posted about Paige's retreat. That made me feel really good, but it wasn't likely those people were going to be stopping by the bakery *every day*. And as much as I loved the business that my friends gave me, they weren't going to be able to keep me afloat on their own. Although, it was true that whatever our group set their intentions on seemed to come up smelling of roses. Paige's retreat, especially.

I had finished baking and was moving everything out to the bakery case when Cat came in at six-thirty to start prepping for the breakfast rush.

It was a busy morning, and within two hours of being open, half the case had emptied out. Around eleven, as we prepared for the lunch rush, two familiar faces popped into the window at the front of the café. As Paige opened the door and stepped through with Kari at her heels, I could see a mischievous look in her eye. She was either planning some elaborate prank, which was her specialty, or she had some good news to share.

"Hey there, stranger," she said as she and Kari walked up to the counter and stood looking inside the case. "These are all so beautiful. I know I sound like I'm beating a dead horse, but people are still talking about the croissants."

"Yeah, they're popular here at the café as well. I have to make them every day because there are people who come in daily expecting them to be here."

"They're outrageously good," said Kari. "Paige had a few that she picked up before I arrived, and I've been eating them with breakfast *and* lunch every day since I got here. In fact, I ate the last one this morning." She turned to Paige. "Sorry."

Paige chuckled. "No worries. We're here to clean you out, Jenna," said Paige.

I smiled at their enthusiasm while making a mental note to double the next day's croissant batch. "No need to apologize, that's why I make them. Although Peggy from the library is going to be upset. She comes in for one on her lunch break every day. Do you mind if I hold one back for her?"

"How about you put a couple in a bag and I'll drop them off to her on our way out? We could stand to walk a few steps today."

"We've done nothing but float in the pool drinking piña coladas and eating croissants for three days," Kari explained.

I laughed, picturing the two of them floating around Paige's gorgeous pool with drinks in one hand and croissants in the other. "That makes perfect sense," I said with a wink. "Just let me know when you're almost ready to leave, and I'll get them ready for you. Are you staying for lunch?"

"Not today, so you can bag them up now. We just stopped in to get more croissants—"

"— and see you, of course," Kari cut in.

"We're coming from a Dash of Flair. We stopped in to see my Uncle Mike and Chris. Their new window display is... incredible. For once, I didn't have words."

I laughed as I took out a bakery box and started loading it with most of what I had left. "I have been hearing about it from customers. It seems like he took what could have been a very basic Great Gatsby theme and turned it into something exceptional. As usual. I need to stop over there and take a look. He's so creative!"

"Yeah, everyone gets a kick out of him matching his window display to whatever they're putting on at Ruth Eckerd Hall. He's kind of making a name for himself," Paige said.

"He's so talented with his design work. You can see it everywhere in his haberdashery. I wonder, is he still doing interior design on the side?" Kari asked.

"I don't think so," said Paige. "I know he misses it, but he's been so busy getting the store up and running and everything that entails. I don't know that he's had a whole lot of time for design projects other than his own, but I know he'd love to get back into it in some form or another."

"Well, your house is a showstopper, and Dash of Flair is literally a work of art. Maybe he'll find some time to fit in some side projects here and there just to keep that part of him happy."

"I hope he does, but who knows? We'll see what he does next; it's always a surprise."

I finished ringing them up for the croissants and packing up the two she would take over to Peggy at the library two doors down. After they left, I ran to the cooler in the back to pull out the extra cupcakes I had made that morning. I needed to fill the empty bakery case.

~

As I was pushing through the swinging doors to come back out with the third tray to continue refilling the case, I heard the ding of the bell, indicating that someone had walked in. When I looked up from the tray I was holding, I saw it was Paige's Uncle Mike and his partner, Chris. Even in the Florida weather, they certainly dressed the part of men's clothing store owners.

Paige's uncle was wearing a navy pinstripe suit that fit his tall, thin frame so well, it was obviously custom-tailored. His look was complete with a pocket square, but he was tie-free, and the top button of the light blue dress shirt that matched his eyes was left undone. Chris's attire was similar in style, albeit shorter in length, complete with a bowtie that seemed to mirror his bushy brown mustache and twinkling brown eyes just above it.

The window displays at their store were legendary and had garnered them quite a bit of business for men's apparel. And being huge supporters of local businesses, they referred lots of women to the dress shop next door to them. From what I could tell, their efforts were paying off after only a year in business. The men in our community (and surrounding communities) flocked to them for their formal and business attire.

They were standing there gaping at the half-filled bakery case, and Paige's uncle had stars in his eyes. He had a notorious sweet tooth.

"I think you're going to like what I just brought out, Mr. Turner."

He looked up at me and shook his head. "Mr. Turner, Mr. Turner. How long is this going to go on, Jenna? Please call me Mike. In fact, if you're Paige's friend, that makes you family. So you can call me Uncle Mike. And I want you to consider me family as well."

"Same goes for me," said Chris, pointing his finger at me. He then pointed at something inside the case. "Especially if you have more of these fruit tarts here."

"I believe I have a half dozen more in the back."

"We'll take two," said Uncle Mike, winking at Chris.

"You got it. Anything else for you today?"

Paige's uncle turned around and looked behind him to make sure he wasn't holding up a line. "I did actually want to talk to you about something else."

"You did?" I asked, my curiosity piqued. "What about?"

Chris nudged him and said, "I'm going to walk over to the bookstore to pick up my order. Elyse called yesterday to tell me it was in. Meet me over there when you're finished up here. Don't forget the fruit tarts." He looked back at me. "Everything looks delicious as always, Jenna. You should be very proud of yourself. We hear about the things in this case every day at a Dash of Flair. In fact, we're going to have to start checking people for powdered sugar and frosting when they walk in because half of them are covered in it."

That made me chuckle. "Maybe each purchase should come with a single-use hand wipe."

"Now you're talking. Or we can hand them out at the door. Kind of like the holy water in church." We both laughed, his loud wheezing exhale drawing attention from some of the other patrons. He looked around and saw a few sets of eyes turned his way and shrugged. Uncle Mike was unapologetically Uncle Mike.

Chris stepped around the counter and put his arms out for a hug, which I accepted. "Jenna, it was great to see you, and I'll be seeing you again soon," he said as we embraced. "Stop by the haberdashery for a chat anytime."

After he released me, I excused myself and headed back to the cooler to pull out the fruit tarts I'd promised them. I suddenly felt a little anxious about the mystery topic Uncle Mike (that was going to take some getting used to) wanted to discuss with me. I would have put money on it being something about the bakery.

"Paige and Kari stopped by the store this morning," he said as soon as I'd walked back out with a tray.

Bingo.

"Oh, they mentioned that," I replied, mentally scrolling through a list of ways I could divert the topic as I assembled a bakery box for their order. "I have walked past your most recent window display several times and always find something new and surprising."

Uncle Mike pointed at the cupcakes I'd just loaded in. "Four of those, please. Yeah, I've decided to put some Easter eggs in there. Before I switch it out at the end of the month, I'm going to do a contest to see how many people have found."

"Oh, I love that idea. It will get you a little more foot traffic, at the very least. Even if they're just staring through the window, they're there, right? Maybe they will see something they like and come in. You have such creative ideas," I said. I wanted to finish with "Uncle Mike," but I just wasn't there yet.

"That's what I wanted to talk to you about," he said. "Paige mentioned that you're thinking about opening up a bakery in the open spot next door."

I looked down at the counter and straightened the pens in the pen cup. "Yes, it's something I have been considering since Cat brought it up and then told the whole group."

Uncle Mike laughed. "It does seem that they're relentless when they put their mind to something, but if they think it's going to be a success, it might be worth thinking about, Jenna. Paige mentioned that it has all the equipment that you would need in order to run a bakery. So, it sounds like a win-win to me."

"Well, I still have a few things that I need to figure out before I can decide if it's feasible." I added the two fruit tarts Chris had ordered, then taped the lid of the box down.

"You mean, like, money? That's the easy part," said Uncle Mike with a flip of his hand. "Where there's a will, there's a way.

That's always been my motto, and it's served me well. I think if this is something that you decide you want to do and it's meant to be, the opportunity will present itself."

I rang him up and recited the total. As he took out his wallet, he continued. "And if you decide this is the route you want to go, I want to offer my services. I'd love to redecorate the place for you. I've always loved the interior, even when it was a pizza place. And that exposed brick wall keeps me up at night. It adds to the charm of that entire place."

"But...," I trailed off, dumbfounded. "You're so busy and have so much going on at your store." But he was right; there was so much to consider, and that was one thing that hadn't even been on my radar.

He looked around again to make sure he wasn't holding up a line. "Things are going well there, and between you and me, I get really tired of suiting up and folding socks and sweaters all day. I've been itching to get into another design project for a while, but don't have the time to do an entire home, which is what everybody wants from me. But to have the opportunity in a space like that would be the perfect project for me. It's across the street from the store, so if Chris needed me, I could just pop right back there. Plus, it would be one less thing that you would have to worry about. And I would give you the friends and family discount." He held his hand up, his fingers forming the shape of a zero, and raised his eyebrows at me to drive the point home.

I felt my mouth hanging open and snapped it shut, but I couldn't find the appropriate words to respond.

Is he for real? A famous interior designer wants to design a space for me? Me?

"Just say you'll consider it, Jenna," he said in response to my silence.

"I will and thank you so much; that is such a generous offer."

"It's not just an offer, Jenna. We're family now, so it's a promise. I hate to brag, but I'm pretty good at what I do." He jokingly blew on his nails and pretended to buff them on his suit coat in an 'I'm kind of a big deal' way. "And I'd love the opportunity to bring that space to life for you. I have some ideas, if you ever want to talk about them. When do you need to have an answer about whether you're going to move forward?"

I finally managed to form a coherent thought. "Cat said the leasing agent stopped in a few days ago and told her that the landlord wants a signed lease within thirty days, which doesn't give me a lot of time. I need to figure out if I can get a business loan before I can make any decision like that."

"Psshh...." He waved his hand around the café. "Your mentor here is a whiz with business finances. She helped Chris and I so much when we were opening the haberdashery. And since we started, she's had some absolutely incredible advice for us. If you have her on your side, you have everything you need in order to get the paperwork together for a business loan. So you can cross that off your list."

This didn't come as a surprise to me; I knew that Cat was great at managing her business. But, I hadn't considered the ongoing financial aspect of owning a bakery until that very moment; I'd been focused on how to get the initial funding and hadn't even gotten as far as learning how to do all the bookkeeping that would be involved. Just the thought of trying to keep track of all that made my throat close up.

Uncle Mike chuckled again. "Well, I can see that I have maybe put a little too much information into your head, but try to have a little faith that it can work out. From what it sounds like, everyone has faith in you to make this a success, so that tells me that you should put a little faith in your friends. They believe in you, so *I* believe in you, and we would all love to help you get this off the ground, Jenna. Let me know what you think, and if you decide to do this, I would love to be on your team."

"Thank you... *Uncle Mike*," I squeaked out, the words falling from my mouth like a first attempt at a foreign language. "I do appreciate it. It just all feels so overwhelming right now, but it's all I think about at the moment. I plan on sitting down with Cat to talk about the financial part of this. She's getting some numbers together to show me her expenses so we'll see what happens, I guess."

"I'm excited to see where this goes," said Uncle Mike. "And having even more of this," he swept his hand across the bakery case, "at my disposal every day could be dangerous, but it's worth it."

He came around the counter and put his arms out for a hug. "Now give Uncle Mike a hug, and I'll get out of your hair."

As people stepped up to the counter, he put up his index finger to tell them, 'one moment', then hugged me and stepped aside. "See you soon, Jenna," he said as he walked back around the counter and picked up his box.

"Thank you, Uncle Mike," I said. With the warm comfort of his hug still lingering, saying it that time felt a little more natural.

EASY PEASY FRUIT TARTS

Tart Shell
16 oz sugar cookie dough
OR
2 ¾ cups all-purpose flour
1 teaspoon baking soda
½ teaspoon baking powder
1 cup butter, softened
1 ⅔ cups white sugar
1 egg
1 ½ teaspoon vanilla extract

No-Bake Cheesecake Filling
8 ounces cream cheese, softened
½ cup granulated sugar
1 teaspoon vanilla extract

Topping
6 ounces limeade concentrate
1 tablespoon cornstarch

¼ cup sugar
Fresh fruit berries, etc

Prepare the sugar cookie dough (if making homemade)
Preheat the oven to 350°F.
Stir flour, baking soda, and baking powder together in a small bowl.
Beat sugar and butter together in a large bowl with an electric mixer until smooth.
Beat in egg and vanilla.
Gradually blend in flour mixture.
Spray mini muffin pans with nonstick cooking spray.
Place 1 tablespoon cookie dough (or one premade square) into each muffin pan cavity.
Bake for 12–16 minutes, or until the cookies are baked through.
Cool completely before removing from the pan.

Tip: for easy removal use a butter knife and run it around the edge of each cookie.

Use your finger or the back of a wooden spoon to make an indentation in each cookie to make room for some filling.

Glaze
In a small skillet or saucepan, add the concentrate, cornstarch, and sugar. Whisk to dissolve the cornstarch and sugar and cook until it boils and thickens, just a few minutes.
Remove from heat to cool.

Filling
Beat the cream cheese with sugar and vanilla until smooth.

Assemble the tarts
Spoon about a tablespoon of filling into each cookie cup.
Top with some fresh berries or other chopped fruit.
Brush with the lime glaze.

Serve within 3 hours of topping with fruit. Once assembled, these are best eaten the day they're made.

Note: You can make all the components of this up to 24 hours ahead and assemble right before serving, if desired. Store filling and glaze in the refrigerator and cookie cups in an airtight container.

13

———

When I returned home from the café that day, my mind was spinning. I immediately spied the gratitude journal on my coffee table and thought writing down how I was feeling would help me sort through some of it.

November 14, 2023
Dear Grandma,

Kari and Paige and then Uncle Mike and Chris came by the café today. Everybody cleared out the bakery case, which was great, but at the same time, left a lot more questions in my mind.

It makes me feel like this might be a feasible idea, but to be honest, I've had enough change to last a lifetime, and I'm only twenty-eight. But knowing that I have less than thirty days to decide and see if I can even get a business loan makes me very anxious.

The decision is bearing down on me. I can somewhat understand how Paige felt just a few months ago, when she was dragged into the writer's retreat idea. My friends keep saying that anything I put my mind to is possible, but getting from here to there feels like an impossible undertaking.

I've never even had a credit card or a car loan. How would I ever get approved for a business loan? Everyone seems to think it's possible, so I'm just putting one foot in front of the other at this point. And I guess we'll see what happens.

Paige's retreat has certainly taken off, and she seems so happy and fulfilled since she arrived in town. And while I know that our friendship has contributed to that, I'm sure quite a bit is coming from the success of her retreat.

I wouldn't mind feeling like that myself, but I have no idea how to navigate through all these decisions or if this is something that would even succeed. It is good to know that I would have Raina at my disposal for marketing, and she's done an excellent job between the bookstore and Paige's retreat. That makes me feel a little more hopeful.

I can visualize myself behind the counter in a baker's cap and apron. Isn't that silly? But I just don't know the steps to get from here to there. The path is there in front of me, but it's covered by brambles and bushes, and I can't see my way through. I don't want to have to depend on my friends for everything right now. They've put a roof over my head, and I have a car to drive and a job, so how can I reasonably expect them to help lead me through opening an entire business? That seems too much to allow them to take on, even if they are offering.

And I can't help but feel bad about Craig sitting in jail. I know he is receiving his paperwork for the divorce today, and it makes me feel sad. No one goes into a marriage expecting it to fail. I always thought I would make a good wife because I love to bake, and I'm a pretty patient person, and it makes me sad to know that I couldn't make this work. Plus, knowing that Craig is alone in jail, realizing that our marriage is over, makes me feel very sad for him. I hope I'm making the right decision.

I know this is a gratitude journal, and I haven't really written much in the way of gratitude today, so I should probably focus on those things.

1. I'm grateful for my friends who have put a roof over my head, and have so much faith in me.
2. I'm grateful for my job at the café, and the opportunity to make others happy through my baking.
3. I'm grateful for all the time I've been given to learn about myself and gain independence.
4. I'm grateful that Uncle Mike — See? I did it! — came in and offered to do the design for the inside of the bakery should I decide to go in that direction.
5. I'm grateful for you. Your voice is in my head just as often as mine, and your messages to me are definitely more positive than my own, but I'm starting to catch up.
6. I'm grateful for all the recipes that you left behind for me that have allowed me to contribute more at the café, and who knows, maybe start my own business.

ON THAT THOUGHT, I closed the journal and set it down with my pen on the coffee table. I had a little bit of work ahead of me today, coming up with a few new recipes for the café and a few more for Paige's next retreat.

I walked into the kitchen, sat at the small table, and then

opened the recipe book. Just as I picked up my notebook, my phone rang.

'Collect call'

Craig? How?

~

I KNEW what was coming and braced myself. I considered not picking up at all, but I'd only be delaying the inevitable at that point. I figured I might as well just get it over with. He'd gone so far as to call from a different number.

"Hello?" I began, grateful I was already sitting down. My knees suddenly felt like they were made of wet tissue paper.

"Hey there, darlin'," he said. His sweet-as-pie tone was surprising, but a lifetime of experience had shown me that people can hide a lot under the veneer of civility, especially if it's dressed in affection. "How are you doing?"

"I'm doing fine, Craig. How are you doing?" It seemed a ridiculous question, considering he was sitting in jail and most likely had received divorce papers that day, but it was only polite to ask.

"Well, Jenna, as I'm sure you know, I received some paperwork from an attorney today, and I have to say I'm confused. I thought you believed in the vows that we took at the courthouse." His tone faltered at the end, slipping into the biting sarcasm that was his love language.

"I do believe in those vows," I replied.

"Well, these papers here say otherwise, Jenna. I thought you were a good wife who would stand by your man 'til death do us part."

"I have been a good wife to you, Craig," I replied. Then, taking a deep breath while reaching down to find the courage I'd started to develop in therapy, I finally said what was on my mind. "But can you say the same? Have you been a good husband? Can you honestly say that you have?"

"Jenna," he said, with irritation no longer veiled. "I understand that you're *emotional* right now." I could feel the barely veiled anger in his choice of words. I was emotional, but not the emotion he was insinuating. I was sad, yes... but more so, I was beginning to feel anger for having wasted so many years trying to put the pieces of my husband back together with glue made from my own tears.

He continued. "But I know that you'll come to your senses. I *have* been a good husband. I *have* been supportive of you and have shown you the ropes of being a good wife. Some things you seem to have forgotten in the last few months, but don't worry, we can put all this behind us once I'm out of here and we can get back to the way things used to be."

"That's just it, Craig," I said, my confidence slowly growing. "I don't want to go back to the way things used to be. Our relationship wasn't healthy. You controlling my every move and telling me how things need to be isn't the way a marriage works."

"Well, it worked for as long as we were married, so why fix what isn't broken?"

"It was broken, Craig. I believe I've finally come to my senses, and I'm pretty sure that I have done what's best for me for once. And I bet if you can sit and think about things logically and be honest with yourself, you'll see that I'm right."

He scoffed, clearly agitated. "'Pretty sure' isn't good enough to back out of the commitment that you made, Jenna. You didn't start acting like this until you started hanging around with *those women*. And if you're going to continue to be influenced by other people who have nothing to do with our relationship and make decisions that aren't in line with the woman I married, I'm going to contest this divorce until you fall in line.

You will eventually run out of money and need to come back to me, anyway."

I felt myself getting emotional and refused to let Craig hear that, especially after all the progress I had made. I mustered as much strength in my voice as I could and said, "I guess we'll just have to see," and I hung up.

Craig instantly called back and I sent him to voicemail. I then pulled up the new number he'd called from and blocked it. I knew I needed some peace while I made a decision.

As I clicked 'Block number,' my phone buzzed in my hand. I switched over to my texts and saw that the Sensational Six group chat was heating up. The last text I could see on my screen was from Cat that said, "I'll be finishing up around three if you all want to come in around three-thirty."

With my curiosity piqued, I clicked into the chat and saw that the texts were coming in faster than I could read them. I scrolled up a bit and saw that there were some plans being made.

Me: What's going on?

Grace: We wanted to see if you could meet up at the café tomorrow after closing.

Sarah: We'll all be there.

I let them know that I could meet them after work. I didn't have much else going on other than looking for and practicing new recipes. I knew they were up to no good, but I was still looking forward to being in their company.

14

When Paige walked in at three-thirty the next afternoon, Cat popped her head up from where she was cleaning in the back and nodded to the right to let her know she should head to the booth and wait for us. We had met like this enough times that her body language shorthand was enough.

"Oh boy," I said. "What am I in for?"

"Just a little bit of karma headed your way," said Paige, with a laugh. "I believe you're owed a few planning sessions of payback."

There were a few times where we came prepared for a planning session that Paige wasn't even aware was about to happen. I knew I was in for it that day. By the time I got to the booth in the back corner, Sarah, Grace, Paige, and Elyse were already waiting with their notebooks out in front of them.

"This is going to be so much fun," said Paige.

"Paige, you must be so happy that she's in the hot seat instead of you," said Elyse. She waited for Jenna and Sarah to slide in, then set her trademark orange backpack on the seat and sat next to it. I slid in on the other side and sat next to Jenna, followed by Grace who sat across from Sarah.

Paige looked up from her phone. "Cat texted a few minutes ago and told us that she would be out shortly. It sounds like the lunch rush ran over a bit today, but she said she would be done soon, and we should start without her."

"Okay," I said, "tell me what I'm going to lose sleep over later."

"Oh, Jenna," said Sarah. "It's not like you to be dramatic."

"Yeah, but having your life planned around you is not a comfortable feeling, guys," said Paige and then winked at me. "But I'm glad it's you instead of me this time." She took her own notebook out of her tote bag, set it on the table, and flipped it open with a flourish. "Well, shall we begin?" she said.

I had a sneaky suspicion that I would need it, so I took the notebook I'd brought out of my bag and set it on the table. "Alright, where do we start? I'm assuming Sarah already has a spreadsheet prepared."

Sarah's notebook was open on the table, but she reached into her tote bag, pulled out six stapled packets, handed one to each of us, and left one in front of Cat's open seat next to Grace. The front said, "Jenna's Bakery."

"Obviously, we're going to need a better name than that," said Sarah. "But this is what we're working with." We flipped it open and there was a list of things to consider, number one being the name of the bakery.

"We'll leave that one up to your discretion," said Grace as she sent a wink in my direction. "But if you need any help, you know who to call. I've become an expert at coming up with titles."

"Let's see how far we get with this scheme of yours, and then we'll decide if it needs a name or not," I said as Cat slid into her seat next to Grace.

Sarah wrote "Jenna" next to that item on her list. "Okay, so we'll leave the name for last. "The next item on the list is funding."

My stomach clenched hard at that word.

"Now," Sarah said, "if you turn to the next page, I have created a spreadsheet to help you figure out what your regular monthly expenses are going to be."

Cat picked up her pen and chewed the cap, deep in thought. "I pulled out my utilities for the last year and have everything piled up in my office. We know what the rent is going to be, and I was able to separate all of the grocery items that I have purchased just for what you've been making for me, Jenna, so we know exactly what those expenses are. Now, that's obviously on a much smaller scale than having to plan ingredients for an entire bakery. So those expenses are going to change, but we could probably come up with a rough estimate."

"Okay, so it all comes down to how to get our hands on that money," said Sarah.

I had been silent for most of this, and I was really starting to get a feel for what Paige had been going through only months before. A wave of sympathy washed over me as I realized how helpless I was feeling about something that was supposed to help me feel empowered.

As if she could read my thoughts, Sarah reached over and grabbed the hand that was holding the pen frozen above the paper next to the word 'funding.' "I can see your panic, Jenna. But we've all got you. No one is going to throw you into the deep end and expect you to swim. You have all of us here to help you."

"And we know what we're doing," said Paige. "Or at least they do. I know how to follow directions."

"That's all you need," added Grace.

"Knowing how much everything is going to cost is half the battle," said Cat, "and we've got a very good idea of what that's going to be. If you have Raina doing marketing, and Uncle

Mike is going to work on the interior design of the space, then all you really need to do, Jenna, is figure out what you are going to make and apply for a loan from the bank."

"I don't know how any......" I trailed off and looked down at the table.

"Tell us what you're thinking," said Sarah, switching into social worker mode. "What are you most worried about?"

"I just don't know how I'm going to get a loan from the bank when I've never... I don't even have any credit history. I didn't even have a checking account until a few years ago. I have never had a credit card. I have never had a home loan. I have never had even so much as a car loan. I don't know how a bank is going to approve a loan for me."

"I can understand why you would be concerned, Jenna, but all you can do is try, right? And if you apply, and they turn you down, then we just figure out what's next."

"Well, I only have two kidneys," I joked, trying to inject some levity into the conversation.

"Luckily, you only need one," joked Elyse, "so we can always look and see what your other one is worth. How will you choose?"

"Ha ha," said Cat. "Jenna's keeping both of her kidneys, but we will find a way to make this work, Jenna. And think of it this way. This is something that you've always known that you wanted." She paused and chuckled. "Unlike Paige, who didn't know what she wanted until she got here and we told her. And look how happy she is."

Paige grinned like a Cheshire cat in her sarcastic 'oh boy, look how happy I am' way. But I knew that she was ecstatic about the direction her life had taken since she'd arrived. And one thing that I knew I wanted was to feel like that. Like my life had purpose and direction. At that point, it had neither.

Grace looked at me with sympathy in her eyes. "We will figure it out. If this is something that you really want, you have all of our support behind you, and we will help you make it happen."

"I think I do, but I'm unsure of the steps I need to take. All of this is foreign to me."

"Well, sure, those are normal concerns," she said. "But that's why we have this list." Grace lifted her spreadsheet and shook it gently. "You worry about the things that *you* need to worry about, and let *us* help you with the rest."

"So next up would be to apply for a loan from the bank. Time is ticking down," said Cat. "It might take a while. And we only have two weeks before the landlord wants a signed lease in hand. I don't know how long he's going to go without showing the space to other interested parties, so we kind of need to get a move on it with the loan application. I would like to sit down with you and work on a business plan. They're not hard to put together, but the bank is going to expect it. And luckily we already have all the information we need, we just need to put it all together into one document."

Sarah tapped her spreadsheet with her pen. "Next up: We are going to need some marketing."

Elyse raised her hand. "I'm going to reach out to Raina to see if she'd be available to put some marketing ideas together if this moves forward."

"Great idea," said Cat. "She's done a phenomenal job with everything she's worked on for us. I have her working on some new graphics for our Facebook page, and she's going to put together a video for TikTok."

"Oh, that would be so much fun," said Sarah. "I can't wait to see what she comes up with."

"She is so creative," added Grace.

Paige looked up from her list. "Raina did such a fabulous job with the retreats. Remind me to come back to that later. But I know she would have people beating down your door here, Jenna."

"I'm open to hearing whatever she has to say. She did a beautiful job with your website and all your graphics. I would definitely put my faith in her for this, but I would have to pay her in muffins."

"We'll work all that out later," said Grace. "So you would need some furniture."

"Uncle Mike mentioned that he talked to you about decorating the space," said Paige.

"Yes, he came in and let me know that he had a bunch of ideas and that if this plan were to move forward, I should reach out to him, and he would share them with me. So, I would probably leave that part up to him. Although it kind of terrifies me to think about the cost that would be associated with that. From the looks of Paige's house and A Dash of Flair, he has expensive taste."

"He does," agreed Paige, "but the good news is that he can sniff out a deal. My dad and uncle did not grow up with a lot of disposable income, so he has learned to be a bargain shopper, and most of what you've seen, he's either found a way to make it himself or hired a local craftsman to put things together based on something he saw as inspiration in a magazine. So, much of what is in his shop is handcrafted for a fraction of the cost of what it would be to buy it in a specialty store."

"Think about all of the shelving he has in there," said Sarah. "It's absolutely gorgeous. That long table that goes through the entire length of the store would probably have cost tens of thousands of dollars."

"Yeah, I asked him about that table and he didn't disclose the cost, but he did say it was a lot less expensive to have it made by someone local," said Paige.

Sarah tapped her pen on her paper again. "Okay, so we have Raina covering marketing and Uncle Mike covering the interior design and probably choosing furniture. I'm sure he could find some cute tables at flea markets, so I wouldn't worry too much about him getting out of control with the expenses. He understands that you would be on a tight budget so let's just trust that he will keep that in mind while he is putting his touch on the design."

"Okay, next up, you would need recipes, but from what I have seen, you have no shortage of inspiration there," said Elyse. "What else is on the list?"

Sarah ran her finger down the list. "Equipment is covered. Everything is already in place to run a bakery."

Cat nodded. "Assuming that everything works, I'll talk to Elizabeth later today and ask if we can get in there and test it all out before we get much further. Whatever we need to do to make this happen, she's going to bend over backward for us. I have talked to her about the bakery and how much we want to make this work and she is trying to hold off the landlord for as long as possible. Since working equipment might be the deciding factor in all of this, I'm sure she won't have a problem with it."

"Alright, so equipment we're going to assign to Cat," said Sarah, and wrote Cat's name next to that line item on her list.

"Thank you." Warmth filled my heart as my eyes traveled from one person to the next. These women who at one point had all been strangers to me and now were my family. I felt emotion strangling me and my vocal cords seized up. I wanted to say thank you but the best I could do was croak out an "okay."

"And this is still all in your control, Jenna," said Cat. "We do not want to force you to do anything. We just want you to know that you're supported and that we're here to help you. So if you think that you want to see about getting a loan from the bank, then you let me know and we will work on a business plan this week."

"Oh, okay," I said, my voice slowly coming back. "I will."

"Let's let Jenna take a breath now," said Paige. "Because I

wanted to talk to you guys about the writers' retreat. Which, by the way, I know I've said it before, but I wouldn't have that writers' retreat if not for all of you, and I'm eternally grateful. I'm having the time of my life and have you all to thank for it. In fact..." she reached back into her bag and pulled out a piece of paper, "...here are a few of the reviews posted in the last couple weeks from my first retreat weekend." She passed the paper across the table, and Elyse read the first one out loud.

"Come for the writing. Stay for the croissants. Ha! That's pretty good." She passed it to Grace.

"This one says, 'I had the best writing retreat experience ever. And the scones were out of this world.' Are they all like this?"

"Pretty much," said Paige. "Keep reading."

Grace passed the paper to her right, and Sarah's eyes scanned the page. "I can't believe this. Oh, here's a mention of Caleb. He'll be thrilled. 'The writing session on Friday morning was some of the best advice I have ever gotten.'"

Grace scoffed. "Where was Caleb when I was struggling to write my first book?"

"Did you write that one, Paige?" asked Elyse with a laugh.

"I could have, but I didn't. I've been hearing a lot about how great Caleb's session was, but keep reading that one."

"'The only thing better than learning about plotting a book is learning how to plot a book with a cupcake, and those were in high demand at this retreat weekend.'"

Paige looked over at me. "They all look like that, Jenna. Every single one mentions your baked goods. But my point is that the first weekend went extremely well, and I know things are going to happen, and we're going to have bad weekends, and I'm going to have bad reviews. But Raina has done such an amazing job helping me get the word out about these. I'm booked up until mid-January."

"Paige, that is amazing," said Sarah. Everyone else nodded

their heads and continued passing the reviews around the table.

"I have decided that throughout spring I will be increasing my retreats to two weekends a month and see how that goes. Do you think you can handle that, Jenna?"

"Look at that," said Sarah. "Jenna, you just doubled your business with Paige. That has to be encouraging."

"I'm so happy for you, Paige," I said. "I'm glad that everything was so well received. That makes me really happy."

"Yes, and I have you to thank for helping to make my retreat a success. So thank you." She looked around the table. "Thank *all* of you. This has been one of the greatest experiences of my life. After struggling for so long when my kids went to school, having this sense of belonging and purpose in my life has been invaluable."

"So when is Kari moving down here?" asked Elyse.

"Believe me, we talk about that all the time. Nick travels so much for work it really wouldn't make a difference where they live. I wouldn't be surprised if she pulled up here next week behind the wheel of a moving truck."

"We would have to change our name," I said, grateful I was finally out of the hot seat.

"Well, at least the Sensational Seven still works," said Grace.

We continued to chat for a bit until Sarah needed to leave to start dinner, and everyone had something going on that evening, but we agreed that we would all see each other again soon at book club, and one by one, the women all started to leave.

"Jenna, could you hang out here for a minute?" said Cat as she scooted out of the booth to let Sarah and Paige out. "I just wanted to talk to you about tomorrow."

The rest of the ladies said their goodbyes and filed out, after which Cat and I walked back to her office. "Your favorite security tech is coming in tomorrow to check on a few of the camera feeds, and I didn't want you to be surprised when someone knocked on the door at six a.m. I would have told you out there that Adam was coming, but you know how some of those women can be."

"Thank you. I can just hear their giggles and ooh-la-las."

"Exactly. Some of them are so immature," she joked, knowing she was typically lumped in with 'some of them.'

We went through what I'd be baking over the next few days, including a new recipe for chocolate pecan-filled cupcakes, and a few minutes later, I was unlocking the door to head up to my apartment. I realized that instead of feeling anxious about what I'd face once I arrived home (or of going home to be alone), I was looking forward to my own company.

CHOCOLATE PECAN-FILLED CUPCAKES

Chocolate Cupcakes

1 ½ cups all-purpose flour

1 cup granulated sugar

½ cup Dutch-process cocoa powder

1 ¼ tsp. baking powder

¼ tsp. kosher salt

⅔ cup canola or vegetable oil

½ cup whole milk, at room temperature

1 large egg plus 1 yolk (room temperature)

1 tsp. vanilla extract

⅓ cup boiling water

Chocolate-Pecan Filling

⅓ cup packed light brown sugar

¼ cup light corn syrup

3 Tbsp. unsalted butter

½ tsp. kosher salt

1 Tbsp. cornstarch

1 cup chopped toasted pecans, plus more for topping

1 Tbsp. bourbon (optional) or 1/2 teaspoon pure vanilla extract

1 ½ oz. bittersweet chocolate, chopped

Cream Cheese Frosting

8 oz. room temperature cream cheese

1 stick unsalted room temperature butter

Pinch of salt

3 ½ cups confectioners' sugar

1 ½ tsp. pure vanilla extract

Heat oven to 350°F and line 12-cup muffin pan with paper liners.

In a large bowl, whisk together flour, granulated sugar, cocoa powder, baking powder, and salt. In a medium bowl, whisk together oil, milk, egg, yolk, and vanilla.

Make a well in the dry ingredients and gradually add wet ingredients to the bowl, whisking to combine.

Add boiling water and gently whisk until the batter is smooth.

Fill each cup about two-thirds full.

Bake until the toothpick inserted in the center comes out clean (20 to 22) minutes.

Let cool.

Filling

In a small saucepan, heat brown sugar, corn syrup, butter, and salt on medium until melted.

In a small bowl, whisk cornstarch with 2 teaspoons of water, then add slurry to the pot and bring to a simmer.

Simmer for 2 minutes. Remove from heat and stir in pecans, bourbon and chocolate.

Let cool for 10 to 15 minutes before using.

Frosting
Beat cream cheese, butter, and a pinch of salt in a large bowl until smooth.

Add confectioners' sugar, 1 cup at a time, mixing after each addition.

Mix in vanilla.
Transfer cream cheese frosting to a piping bag.

Cupcakes
Using a paring knife, carve an 1-1/2-inch-diameter cavity in each cupcake, leaving the bottom intact.

Fill each cavity with about 1 tablespoon Chocolate-Pecan Filling

Pipe Cream Cheese Frosting on top and sprinkle with chopped pecans.

15

The next day, I went in a little early to get some orders prepared for a few upcoming events. I had to get some apple tarts ready for a book fair, some custom cookies, and a matching cake made for a birthday party being thrown by a friend of one of the women from Paige's first retreat, and the rest of the day's baking for the café.

About an hour before the café was due to open, I heard a knock at the door. When I got to the front, Adam's bright smile greeted me as he waved through the window. He was wearing his typical baseball cap with a pen tucked behind his ear. His dark blonde hair spilled out from under the rim and curled up over the edges. He had always had longer hair than any of the other boys at our school, and it seemed to suit him just fine because he had never changed it. On anyone else, it would look unkempt, but on him, it just looked like Adam. I mostly saw him in jeans and t-shirts or a flannel shirt on cooler days, and always sporting kind blue eyes. The girls in Clearwater and Dunedin fell all over him, but he never dated much. Not that I saw, anyway.

I went and unlocked the door to let him in, then locked it behind us after he walked past.

"How's it going, Adam?" I asked.

"Not too bad. How's it going with you?" he replied.

"Doing a lot of baking. Cat told me you were coming in, so I set aside a blueberry muffin for you. They just came out of the oven, and I have some Irish butter warming on the table if you want to head back and have a quick bite to eat before you get started."

His eyes lit up. "You take such good care of me, Jenna," he said as we walked past the front counter and into the kitchen.

While we chatted about our mutual friends, Adam wolfed down his muffin, finishing it in record time. He then headed back to Cat's office while I finished whipping up the frosting for the cookie order. A few minutes later, he was back, leaning his hip on the counter next to me. He set his clipboard down, tucked his pencil behind his ear, and scratched his neck. I had known Adam since grade school, and his nervous tics stuck out like a sore thumb.

"Everything okay?" I asked. I looked up from the mixer and saw him staring at me. "Did you want to say something?" I asked, turning my attention back to the mixer. I turned off the motor and flipped up the beater.

"My mom always let me lick the beater," he said.

"Well, let me get this one scraped off, and then you're more than welcome to it," I said.

"Really?" he asked, as excited as a four-year-old.

I laughed. "Of course. If I licked the beater every time, I'd need a much better fitness plan."

"I'd just love to know what you put in your frosting," said Adam. "It's the best I've ever had."

"Well, thank you," I said, ducking my head. I dismantled the mixer, slid the bowl off, and started scooping the frosting into piping bags. "Hey, since you're here, could you do me a favor?

Would you open the oven door so I can take a look and see how much longer the cookies have?"

Adam spun and opened the door.

"Alright. Looks like a minute and a half left," I said.

Adam looked at the cookies, which were still pretty soft in the center and mostly white. "How can you even tell that? If I had to guess, I would say they had another hour left."

I chuckled, "I don't think you'd want to eat those cookies. No frosting in the world would be enough to make up for a char-coal hockey puck."

"Well, if you ever decide to test that theory, you know who to call."

"So, did you find the problem with the camera feeds?"

Adam scratched his neck again. "Nope, I didn't find anything. It looks like everything is recording, so I don't know. Maybe the problem is on Cat's end. I'll stop back in later. Do you know when she's going to be in?"

"She'll be in after Ladies' League, so maybe one o'clock."

"Okay. I'll stop in after that. I have a few more appointments to get to."

I sometimes wished there was someone here in the morn-ings. Most of the time, I enjoyed the quiet, but it was nice to have a change of pace and actually have someone to talk to while I worked. He must have seen the disappointment on my face, because he quickly added, "But I don't have to leave just yet. I have a little time. I want to hear how you're doing."

He looked at me pointedly, and I knew right away what he was referring to.

"You mean with Craig?" I asked.

"Well, yeah, and everything else. I know you've had a lot of changes recently, and you and I have been friends for a long time. I worry about you, and I just want to make sure you're okay."

"That's really sweet, Adam. You're a good friend. And as for Craig, he's still in county jail, and I don't think he's getting out anytime soon."

I hesitated, not wanting to admit to my friend that my marriage had failed. But I knew it was going to come out eventually, and I might as well start practicing now. "I filed for a divorce. Craig is less than happy about it and has promised to contest it. But my attorney has assured me that he doesn't have a leg to stand on. We don't have any children or shared assets, so the whole process should take a few weeks, tops."

I stopped there because I could feel a lump forming in my throat. Adam saw me struggling and jumped in to save me.

"Jenna," he said, "I'm so proud of you and I know that this has been very difficult for you, but you don't need anyone in order to feel happy. And Craig was certainly not doing that for you anyways." He paused. "I never thought he was good enough for you." He looked down at the floor, then back up at me.

I nodded my head in agreement as I took the cookies out of the oven, then stood staring at the bags of frosting lined up on the stainless steel counter.

"I'm mostly confident that I will be happy as a single woman. It's different, but it's growing on me. I feel a lot more freedom now. I can go out and do the things that I need or want to do without having somebody checking on me or tracking my every move."

I could see Adam's hand clench on the counter where it was resting, and the muscle in his jaw flexed with tension, but he remained silent. "I'm sad my marriage is ending. Though it's not what I had hoped for and certainly not what I had pictured for myself when I took my vows." I sighed and looked down at the floor, pushing some rogue swirls of flour around with my toe. "I can't help but feel guilty for not trying hard enough."

Adam put his hand up to stop me. "Jenna, you tried a lot

longer than most women would have — or *should* have. I don't want to turn this into a husband-bashing session because that's not the point. But you put up with a lot in your marriage. Anyone could see that he was having trouble. And I know that divorcing him isn't necessarily a punishment, but it might make him open his eyes and maybe be a better person for anyone else that comes into his life later." He swallowed and then scanned my face. "I'm sorry," he said. "I didn't mean to say that. Does it bother you to think that he will date again someday?"

I scoffed and then put my hand on his arm. "You don't need to apologize, Adam. You can say pretty much anything. To be honest, I hadn't even thought that far ahead. I mean, I'm sure it's going to happen. And yes, maybe the experience in our marriage will make him think twice about how he treats the next person."

"What about you?" he asked. "Have you thought about your next steps? How have things been going? Living here?" he asked, pointing at the ceiling toward my apartment above.

"What's next for me is kind of up in the air. No pun intended. But the rest of the ladies have been trying to talk me into opening a bakery in that empty space next door that used to be the pizza place."

"Oh, man. That place is awesome inside. I can totally see a bakery there. What are you thinking?"

"Well, all the equipment is there. In fact, everything I would need besides the ingredients and the customers is already there. It's got a stove and walk-in cooler and even a brick pizza oven." I paused and considered the possibilities. "I bet I could do something fun with that. Maybe some sourdough pizza."

"That sounds amazing. So where does it stand now? Do you think that you're going to do it?"

"I don't know. Cat and I are going to go over some numbers and figure out what it would cost per month. And then try to see how much business I would have to do in order to just keep the lights on."

"That's a smart place to start. I know when I opened up my security company, there were so many expenses that I never expected. Luckily, I was prepared for them financially. But if I hadn't been, it would have made things very difficult for me. It's good that you have Cat to guide you on what to expect. It will help you make a more educated decision. Which way are you leaning?"

I folded my arms and leaned back on the edge of the counter across from him. "I haven't really wanted to tell the other ladies because they will immediately get completely out of control, and I still want a little bit of time and space to make sure that I'm making the best decision for my future. But between you and me, Adam, this is something that I have always wanted. As a little girl baking with my grandma Gigi, I would pretend that we were running a bakery. And after I lost her, it didn't really seem like there was anyone left to share my dreams with who didn't think that they were silly or impossible for me. But to hear the other ladies talk, it makes me think maybe I could do it. I have to admit though, I have no idea how I would even get started. Obviously, I would need to get a loan. But I don't have so much as a credit card. So, I have no idea how that would play out."

"All you can do is just keep taking the next right step, Jenna."

I looked up at him. "That's so funny you said that. It sounds to me like Paige is rubbing off on all of us, isn't she? I've heard her say that a dozen times."

"That must be where I heard it," said Adam, "because I don't remember having ever said that before." He chuckled.

He took his phone out of his pocket and checked the time. "I better get going, but I'm going to see you soon. Keep me updated on the bakery, and let me know what you decide. I promise I will keep it to myself."

He started walking toward the door to exit the kitchen, but put his hand on it and turned back to me. "If you decide to do this, I can help you out with some security equipment. I have a bunch at the office that I have kept after swapping them out for newer units at some of my customers' homes and businesses, so I can easily get you set up on the cheap."

"That sounds good, Adam; I really appreciate it, and I will definitely let you know what I decide. In fact, you'll probably be the first to know, just so I can tell someone without ear-piercing shrieks in reply."

"I mean, I still might..."

"Just don't," I said with a laugh.

Adam grinned, then walked back over and gave me a quick side hug. "I'm so proud of you, Jenna, and I'm so happy to see you so happy. I know that you are going to be a success, no matter what you decide. And I will be here to support you."

"Thank you, Adam. Do you want to take a muffin for the road?"

"What kind of question is that?" he said as I handed him a paper bag I had ready.

"You know me too well," he said as he tucked the bag into the backpack.

After he left, it struck me how many people I had rooting for me, how many people believed in me that I hadn't even realized, all while I was busy protecting the one person who should have believed in me the most.

~

JUST AS I was reloading the croissants into the bakery case, I saw Paige walk through the door, followed by Ben Alcott, the police officer who had responded to the call when Craig had broken into Paige's home the previous month and destroyed it.

Interesting.

I gave her a wink and made a 'pick anywhere' signal with my hand, and then opened my eyes wide as if to say, *"What the heck?"* Paige gave me the *"What can you do?"* shoulder shrug, then turned and followed Ben as he led them over to a table, sliding his aviators onto his head as he walked. The cherry on top of this surprise sundae came when he held the chair out for Paige before she sat. Every now and then, I would look over at them, and I couldn't help but notice how happy she looked. Her laugh could be heard throughout the whole restaurant, and every time I looked at her, she was smiling. Everything I saw, every giggle, every sparkle-eyed smile, was in stark contrast to the shell of a woman who had rolled into town mere months before.

I didn't have any kids, but I had tried to sympathize with how Paige had felt when she first arrived in our little town. She was missing her grown children so badly, and she couldn't even see the steps she needed to take in front of her.

But now her life had so much purpose. I was so happy for her, and grateful that she had found her way here. Not only had she become one of my best friends, it was like she said... she was like a sister to me. She was also an example of someone who had worked hard and watched her dreams come true. It was something I wanted so badly for myself, and having witnessed her transformation firsthand made me want to put my faith in my friends to help me see it through.

Again and again, Paige's laughter tinkled over to where I stood at the counter. When I stole another look at her, it thrilled me to see her eyes were closed, her head thrown back in genuine laughter. Ben's arm was thrown over the back of his chair, loafers crossed at the end of his outstretched legs, obviously at ease in their friendship. I was happy to see them there, enjoying one another's company. It made me feel hopeful.

I wondered if happiness like that was in the cards for me, but that was an entirely different leap of faith, and not one I was in a position to make at that time.

Maybe one day. But until that day, I'm looking forward to spending time getting to know Jenna.

SOURDOUGH PIZZA CRUST

50g active sourdough starter
250g water
360g bread flour (I use King Arthur)

Combine the ingredients and cover with plastic wrap or a tea towel (I use a plastic shower cap).
Let rest for 30 minutes.
Fold the dough over itself several times to create a rough ball.
Transfer the ball to a well-oiled bowl and cover.
Let it rest for 10-12 hours. It's ready when it's doubled in size.
Note: I have used this dough well before the 10 hour mark, but individual results may vary.
Coat a 9x13 baking pan with 1 tablespoon olive oil.
Pour the dough into the pan and use your fingers to carefully stretch the dough to the corners of the pan.
Cover and let rest for 30 minutes. (It's exhausted!)

Preheat the oven to 450 degrees.

Bake the dough for 15-18 minutes or until the surface is set and the bottom is a light golden brown.

Cover with toppings. (Use fresh mozzarella or burrata and top with basil for a real treat!)

Bake until the cheese is your desired color of "doneness".

16

November 18, 2023

Walking through town and seeing all the Christmas decorations makes me feel festive, but I sometimes wish I had someone who I could share the magic of this joyful season with. Craig was never much for driving around looking at Christmas lights, but Grace and Sarah always drove a little out of their way to make sure I got to see a few of the best houses. I always got such a kick out of the palm trees wrapped in white lights. I'd seen pictures of houses in the North under a foot of snow around the holidays, but I'd never seen a white Christmas in person, and palm trees with white lights winding up their trunks and green St. Augustine grass-covered front yards are the norm for me. I think they're absolutely beautiful.

Now that I have my own car, I can drive around and look at the lights any time I want, but it's not the same when I'm alone. Every time I think about hopping into the car to visit the houses I used to go to with the other women, it just makes me sad. I never pictured myself doing all these things alone. I wonder where I went so wrong.

When grandma Gigi and I talked about the man I'd marry someday, she always warned me about choosing too quickly. "People can only be on their best behavior for six months, tops," she'd said, "and then you need to live with them for at least a year before you decide to marry them. At *least* a year. Because the man you date is *not* the man you live with."

Spoiler alert: I did not listen to Gigi. I was in such a hurry to escape my parents' house that I ignored every red flag and accepted Craig's proposal after four months of dating. When he showed up late, drunk, I chalked it up to a bad day at work. I'd offer to drive, and he would tell me that boys drove and girls sat in the passenger seat and looked pretty. I'd never been told that I was pretty before, so I disregarded everything that came before it.

When he told me he wanted to marry me so I could run things around the house, I was so excited. This was my chance to break free of the control and caustic barbs of my parents. What I didn't realize was that what I would be 'running' around the house would be the vacuum cleaner, blender, oven, and washing machine. But enough about that clown.

At night, when I'm lying in bed trying to fall asleep to the tick of the clock above the kitchen sink, I wonder about what comes next.

Will I open a bakery?

Will I make my friends proud?

Would my grandma be proud if she could see me?

Will I have someone special in my life who will cherish and respect me?

Will I have children of my own to love?

Grace tells me that I'm doing well on my own and Paige continues to encourage me to take the next right step, but where will all these steps lead? How long will it be before I trust myself to make a good decision about a partner? Grace and Cat seem to be doing fine on their own and I'm in no hurry... but it doesn't stop me from wondering if the kind of happiness Elyse eventually found when she reconnected with Drew is something that's in the cards for me. I guess, if I'm being honest, she did go through a lot with her first husband. Cheating, lying, verbal abuse. I should be grateful Craig was too lazy to cheat on me. Now that I think about it, I should be amazed that Elyse is as trusting as she is.

Anyway, I'm going to focus on what I do have instead of what I don't.

WHAT I'M grateful for today:

1. My friends
2. My job at the café
3. This apartment
4. My grandma's recipe book
5. This time to find out who I'm on my own
6. Thrift stores that allowed me to decorate the way I want
7. The Christmas lights in downtown Dunedin

WELL, that's it for now. I'm sure there's more I'm grateful for, but it's time for me to get to bed. It's baking day tomorrow and I'm making lavender shortbread!

LAVENDER SHORTBREAD

For shortbread
¾ cup unsalted room temperature butter
⅓ cup granulated sugar
2 tsp. finely grated lemon zest
1 tsp. finely grated orange zest
½ tsp. pure vanilla extract
1 ½ cups all-purpose flour, plus more for dusting
¼ tsp. kosher salt
For glaze
1 ¼ cups confectioners' sugar
1 Tbsp. fresh lemon juice
1 Tbsp. milk
½ tsp. pure vanilla extract
Dried lavender, for topping
Orange zest, for topping

Heat oven to 325°F.

Butter a 9-inch round cake pan, then line the bottom with parchment paper.

In a stand mixer, beat butter on medium until smooth and creamy.

Add granulated sugar, citrus zests and vanilla and beat, scraping down the bowl halfway through, until combined, about 2 minutes.

Gradually add flour and salt and mix on low just until dough comes together.

Using lightly floured hands, press dough into the prepared pan in an even layer and poke the dough with a fork several times.

Bake until the edges are light golden brown, 30 to 35 minutes.

Let cool in the pan for 30 minutes, then loosen edges with small offset spatula.

Very carefully (shortbread will be delicate) turn out onto a wire rack lined with parchment paper.

Let cool completely.

Make glaze
Sift confectioners' sugar into a medium bowl.
Add lemon juice, milk, and vanilla.
Whisk, adding more milk if needed, until smooth and thick.
Spread glaze on cooled shortbread.
Sprinkle with dried lavender and orange zest.

Let rest at least 30 minutes before slicing into wedges.

17

———

ook Club falls on the third Thursday of every month, and it was rarely held in the same place twice in a row, whether we met at a member's home or the library. That month, it was the library.

I got there and didn't see anyone else I knew until I walked in and saw Peggy sitting behind the desk. She was laughing and chatting with a patron, but when I took a closer look, I saw who it was. Caleb, Paige's writing mentor. He surprised all of us when he showed up to Paige's retreat ribbon cutting with Peggy, but it made sense when I thought about it. He usually mentored people at the library, and they both had long, silver hair. So right there, tons in common.

I walked into the room where the book club was held and saw my friends gathered on comfortable, brown leather chairs. They were deep in conversation when I walked in, but clammed up when Elyse looked over and saw me. She elbowed Cat to her right, who then stopped speaking abruptly.

A few minutes later, everyone else took their seats, and Book Club began. As usual, it was a lively discussion with questions that no one would ever find in the back of the book. We always found we had a lot to talk about, and we all brought our own questions, which was my favorite part. Everyone always got so creative, and each one really made me think about what I had read in a new and different way. It often made me want to go back and read the book all over again.

As we walked out of the meeting room later, I turned and asked the group, "Is anyone in a hurry tonight, or do we have some time to talk?" It was nice not having to rush home to get back to Craig. They all said they had some time to kill before they needed to get home, so we walked down the block and piled into my apartment.

Everyone had seen the majority of the changes that I had made to the apartment, but most picked out one or two things that I had added since the last time they were all there. I took out a fresh batch of almond croissants and put them on a platter.

Once everyone was settled in the living room and around the kitchen table, Sarah started speaking. "I wanted to talk to you all about that young woman who reached out to me at school this week. I told her to come in and see me, and maybe we could come up with some ideas that could help her get started toward becoming a grief counselor. But I thought I would run it past you all to see if you had any resources for her. She obviously has limited income, and I'm sure there are grants out there for her to continue her education, but I don't know. What do you all think?"

Paige was the first to speak up. "I actually have a great resource for her. Peggy down at the library is part of a local organization that holds fundraisers to provide scholarships to women who are looking to re-enter the workforce or go back to school. Maybe that would be an option for her. I can ask if you'd like."

Cat's head popped up from scribbling in a small notebook. "What are we talking about?" she asked. Sarah reiterated what she had told us about Allison. "Oh. Were you talking about the New Beginnings grant?" asked Cat.

"Yes," replied Paige. "I had heard from Peggy at the library that they have a scholarship program for women just like Allison. I thought maybe Peggy could point her in the right direction or advise her on next steps."

"I'm actually one of the founding members," said Cat.

"Why does that not surprise me?" asked Grace under her breath.

Cat looked bashful as she continued. "It just seemed to go hand in hand with what I've been doing at the café, and we've seen a lot of women benefit from the grants. Why don't you have Allison stop by, and I can talk to her? If she's looking to go back to school, she would be the perfect candidate. We are choosing our recipients in the next few weeks, so this is perfect timing."

"This is great," said Sarah, clapping her hands lightly. "I'm so glad I said something. I will call her and tell her all of this. You women are amazing and I'm so happy and proud to call you my friends. Cat, you're an enigma."

"So what else do you all have going on?" asked Cat, diverting the attention from herself.

"Well, ladies," began Grace. "Don't forget, I have my book launch party coming up for book seven. And I'm expecting to see all your beautiful faces there."

"I'll have to check my schedule, Mom," Sarah deadpanned.

"Very funny, young lady. Just remember, Santa knows everything, and Christmas is coming."

"I'm just kidding. We'll all be there with bells on, as usual. How long we stay does depend on the food, however," Sarah said with a wink.

"Good news there. We have dessert covered," said Grace.

Everyone turned to look at me. Until then, I had managed to remain mostly silent. But once the attention was on me, I had to speak up. "Yes, Grace tried the lavender cupcakes I brought to Paige's retreat, and I'll be making ten dozen of those for her book launch."

"Holy mackerel," said Paige.

"I can't wait to try them," said Sarah. "Will you be making them again before the book launch?"

"I will probably do another test run. I'll let you all know when, and I'll bring them into the café so you can try them out ahead of time."

"I think we should make them wait," said Grace, "just to make sure they show up on the big night."

"You know we're going to be there," Sarah said. "So you can save the dramatics for your next book."

Grace laughed.

"What are you doing over there?" Cat asked Elyse, who had been mostly silent throughout our conversation, busily tapping away on her phone for most of it. "Are you with us?"

Elyse seemed to be deep in concentration and didn't hear Cat's question. Cat nudged her with her foot, and Elyse looked up from her phone. "What? What did I miss?"

"Pretty much everything," said Cat.

"Oh, sorry," said Elyse, setting her phone face down on the table. "I had someone texting me about a book they had on order."

"Oh, interesting. So, customers just text you at eight p.m. to ask about book orders. Sounds believable."

Elyse shot her a look, and Cat rolled her eyes back at her.

Paige cleared her throat to dispel the tension in the room. "I've been waiting for the right moment to tell you all," she began. We all scooted forward in our seats.

"Yes?" implored Grace.

"I've been waiting to tell you...," she repeated, then paused for dramatic effect, as Paige tended to do. "I have completed the first draft of my manuscript." Excitement erupted around my tiny table.

Paige had been working on one book or another for a few years, and, after having moved from Madison to the Clearwater area, had connected with Caleb, who had worked with her dad at the University of Wisconsin. He had gotten her started with a few tools that he used successfully. And in turn, Paige had apparently capitalized on his advice.

"That is such great news!" I exclaimed.

"I can't wait to hear more about it. Are you going to let us read it?" asked Elyse.

"I knew you could do it. I'm so proud of you, Paige," said Sarah.

Cat punched her playfully on the shoulder. "You must be incredibly proud of yourself."

"I am," she said, "and as for letting all of you read it, I think I would prefer to wait until it's a little further along. This is just the first draft, and it's pretty rough, but it's a start."

"Completing your first draft is an incredible accomplishment," said Grace. She stood up, walked over to Paige, and wrapped her arms around her. "I knew you could do it. I can't wait to see your book on the shelf."

"I happen to know the procurement manager at Back in the Day Books," joked Elyse. "So, get your signing pen ready."

"I have a long way to go," said Paige. "But, I couldn't wait to tell you all. This is the farthest I've ever gotten, and I have you all to thank for it. You've all had so much faith in me over the last few months that it helped me believe in myself as well."

"We're incredibly proud of you," said Sarah. "And, if you're looking for some beta readers when you *are* ready, I read for my mom all the time. I just close my eyes through the kissing scenes."

"She is *quite* liberal with a red pen," joked Grace.

"So now that we have all shared our news," said Sarah, "it's your turn, Jenna," she said, and five heads swiveled to me.

"Well, what I'm mostly focused on is next week. Craig's case is going to trial."

Cat sat forward. "How are you feeling about it?"

"If I'm being honest, I'm a little nervous. I have no idea how this is going to play out. I'm just getting settled and standing on my own, and I feel like a big part of that is knowing he is in there. But I have to keep the faith that the judge will see how Craig's behavior has escalated and maybe force his hand to get the help he obviously needs. I'm praying that he gets at least six months in jail to give him some time."

"And *you* some time," said Grace.

"And me some time," I agreed, "but there's no guarantee."

"Well, if the judge looks at the pictures you provided from all the damage he did inside my house, he will hopefully see that Craig does need a lot of help and hopefully will mandate him to some kind of treatment program."

"From your lips to God's ear," I agreed. "And there's more," I said, taking a chapter from Paige's book and pausing for dramatic effect. "I have decided to explore my options with the bakery."

"Are you *serious*?" asked Cat. "This is awesome! I'm so happy for you."

"This is the best news I've heard all day," said Grace. She looked to her right. "Sorry, Paige. No offense."

"None taken," said Paige. "I'm thrilled for you, Jenna. And you have five of your best customers right here in this room. As you know, this group is nothing if not persistent in getting their way. But I have to ask, is this something *you* want, right? Not just something that we've forced on you?"

"Oh no," I said, "the more I've thought about it, the more I feel like this could be feasible. It's always been a dream of mine, but not one that I ever felt was possible. But you all make me feel like it *is* feasible, and I'm excited to get started."

"What's your first step?" asked Elyse.

"Well, I'm going to go down to the bank next Tuesday to see if I can get a business loan. I'm hoping between my income and the annuity that my grandmother left me, I will get approved, but...," I looked at Cat, then continued. "I need help putting together a business plan."

"Well, you've certainly come to the right place for that," said Sarah. "Cat runs the café like a well-oiled machine."

"Well, I don't know about that," said Cat, "but I have put together a few business plans for myself, Paige's Uncle Mike, and some of the women who have worked for me." She looked at me. "Much like you, Jenna. And I'm happy to help you with yours."

"I really appreciate that," I said with tears in my eyes.

"Let's get together tomorrow to go over some numbers so you're ready on Tuesday."

"I would love that," I said. My head swiveled to take in the women who had wrapped me in their love. "I can't thank you enough for bringing this opportunity to me. I know it seems silly, but I've always considered this a far-fetched dream, and not something I could ever pursue in reality. So this all feels a bit surreal to me."

"I know a little bit about that," said Paige. "And if you start feeling overwhelmed throughout the process, you know that you can always come to me."

"I do know that," I said to her with a smile.

Sarah stood from the table. "Ladies, it's getting late, and it *is* a school night. But I want to say, Paige and Jenna, I'm so proud of you both." She hugged Paige and then walked over to me. I stood so she could wrap her arms around me, and I hugged her back. After stepping back, she picked up her tote bag next to the coffee table and looped it over her shoulder. "Cat, I'm going to send Allison to the café, so keep an eye out for her and her son, Noah. He's a real cutie pie."

"I can't wait to meet her," said Cat. "I'm sure we can find a way to help her." She yawned, then stood. "I'm going to take off as well." After hugging each of us, she made her way over to where Sarah was standing by the door. "Jenna, I will see you in the morning. Do you have time to stay after we close to start going over your plan?"

"I do," I said.

"Okay, I'll see you when I get in." One by one, the women all left, and I was there, considering all the news that everyone had shared. I didn't know how I had gotten so lucky to meet these women who had become my family. When I looked to the future for the first time in my life, I saw something bright. I saw something that looked closer to the hopes and dreams I had had as a kid.

ALMOND CROISSANTS

8 medium/large croissants, left out uncovered overnight
3 Tbsp sliced almonds
Powdered sugar

Syrup

2 Tbsp sugar
1 tsp vanilla extract
1 cup water

Almond Cream

½ cup granulated sugar
1 cup almond meal/almond flour
⅛ tsp of salt
1 stick unsalted room temperature butter, sliced

2 large eggs

Make the Syrup

In a small saucepan, combine 1 cup water, 2 Tbsp sugar and vanilla.

Bring to a simmer for a minute and stir until the sugar dissolves.

Remove from heat and let cool to room temperature.

Make the Almond Filling

In the bowl of a stand mixer fitted with the whisk attachment, combine ½ cup sugar, 1 cup almond meal and ⅛ tsp salt.

Mix until well incorporated, then blend in the butter.

Add the eggs 1 at a time and mix on med/high speed until the whole mixture is creamy and fluffy.

Assemble

Preheat the oven to 350°F.

Line a cookie sheet with parchment paper.

Slice each croissant horizontally like you would for a sandwich.

Work with each croissant one by one: dip it into the syrup, coating both sides and the ends well. The croissant should be moist, but not soaked. (Dip it once on each side.)

Arrange the croissants on a baking dish, cut side up. Spread about 2 Tbsp of almond filling on the bottom half of each croissant.

Place the top halves on and spread about 1 Tbsp of almond filling over the top. Sprinkle with sliced almonds.

Bake on the center rack for 15 to 18 minutes or until the cream is golden. Transfer to a wire rack and cool to room temperature or just warm.

Dust with powdered sugar before serving.

Best served the same day they are made.

18

On Friday, I got out a little early, so Paige and I took her golden retriever, Roxy, for a field trip to the Honeymoon Beach dog park. At four years old, Roxy was out of the puppy phase, but still a little wild. So we kept an eye on her as she chased the seagulls around and tried unsuccessfully to make friends with a Great Dane. I threw a frisbee for her at least a hundred times as we walked down the beach, and Roxy, being true to her heritage, brought it back every time. Getting it out of her mouth was a bit more of a struggle.

Every five throws, I looked down at my watch. We were anxiously awaiting word from Ben, who had been the responding police officer when Craig had broken into Paige's home. He was at court to report back on the meeting between Craig's public defender and the county prosecutor. I could have gone, but I just couldn't bring myself to look at him yet. Ben had offered to be there, and I was relatively certain his offer was inspired by a request from Paige. I was once again grateful for her friendship.

When it reached one o'clock, I couldn't take it anymore. I had to ask. "So, have you heard anything?"

Paige took her phone from her back pocket and checked her text messages. "Nothing. But he knows that we're waiting to hear something, so I'm sure he will call or text me as soon as he knows anything."

"Okay," I said. My hands started to tingle, and I shook them out. "I am really anxious about this."

Paige put her arm around my waist as we walked. "I know you are, honey. But no matter what happens between the attorneys today, we have to trust that the judge will look at all the evidence and the letters we wrote and do what's right. But let's talk about something else to take your mind off this till he calls," said Paige. "So, tell me how things went with Cat today. Did you work on your business plan?"

"Tomorrow," I said. "We were going to, but she had to help Sam with something today. Until then, with my limited knowledge of the expenses, it all seems pretty scary. I'll feel a little better once I have all the information in front of me."

"I can definitely see that," said Paige. "When we were all working on the retreat together, everything that I didn't know was what scared me the most. But once we started pulling all the information together, it got a little easier to wrap my mind around. It's definitely a positive that all the equipment that you need is already there. It sounds like you won't have to buy or rent anything."

That's true. It seems like it'll just be a matter of getting people through the door."

"Well, that should be less of a concern," said Paige, "because you have more and more business coming your way every day, and that's only going to increase."

I didn't have a response, so we walked for a while in silence. Roxy's panting every time she finally dropped the frisbee was the only sound that could be heard above the waves lapping the sand around our feet. We were both lost in thought and comfortable enough around each other to marinate in our own worlds as we walked. It gave me time to consider her words. Business *had* recently picked up, and most of that additional foot traffic was coming straight to the bakery case. I'd come in earlier three days a week for the last two months, and we were selling out nearly every day.

Paige took a turn throwing the frisbee for Roxy (who had clearly eaten her Wheaties that morning). "Do you think you'll have time for me if I start doing the retreats more often?" she asked as she reached to wrestle the frisbee away. "I thought you were supposed to be a soft-mouthed dog, Rox."

I chuckled. "I think she might be mixed with a velociraptor. But, yes! Of course. As long as you give me some warning before you change it to every week."

"No, no," she said with a laugh. "I don't think I could handle having people around every weekend. But I can't believe I've already gotten to the point where there is a waitlist through March."

"I can. You've created something incredible, and I'm *so* proud of you."

Paige looked down at the sand in front of us as we walked. She kicked a rock as we passed, and it rolled along the sand until it came to rest against one of the stakes cordoning off a large circle around a sea turtle nest. "I'm pretty proud of myself, too, but you guys have a lot to do with that success. And Raina has been doing a remarkable job with the marketing. I'm pretty sure she could do the same for you."

"I hope so. Cat mentioned setting up a meeting with her, but I just want to get through some of these other steps first. Once I hear back about the loan, I'll feel better about moving forward with the rest of Sarah's list."

"That's understandable," said Paige.

"I'm so scared of failing," I admitted. "I haven't done

anything like this before. I feel like I climbed to the top of a ladder and jumped feet first into big girl pants."

"Everything in your life is new, Jenna, and that is a feeling that I'm completely familiar with. But the good news is that you have all of us to support you through every step. You're not alone. We're all holding your big girl pants up with you." She grew quiet, then stopped walking. I paused next to her and turned to see why we'd stopped. She reached out and put her hand on my forearm. Her favorite form of connection when she had something important to say. "But, Jenna, you need to let us know if your big girl pants get too crowded."

I laughed at the mental image of all six of us crammed into the same pair of pants. "I appreciate that, Paige. And I know if anyone understands this, it's you. Having you by my side has done me the world of good. I'm just so grateful for your friend-ship. And when I admitted to you it was Craig who had destroyed your house, you were so kind and understanding toward me when anyone else may have lumped me in with him and turned their back on both of us."

"Not a chance," said Paige. "I never would turn my back on you."

Just as I threw the frisbee, Paige's phone rang.

"It's Ben," she said, looking at the screen. She quickly pressed the accept button. "Hello... Okay, do you mind if I put you on speakerphone?"

Paige held her phone out and pressed the speakerphone icon. Ben's voice came across. "Hi Jenna," he said, "how are you?"

"I'm— I'm— I'm not sure, Ben," I said. "I think that will be determined by what you say next."

"Well," said Ben, in a tone I was not familiar with. It didn't sound like the upbeat, chipper Ben I knew. "I just walked out of the courthouse back to my car and wanted to call you right away."

"Just spit it out, Ben," said Paige. "You're killing us here."

He sighed. "Well, it didn't go as we had hoped," he said. "The prosecution offered Craig a deal, which he accepted."

My throat felt like it was going to close up on its own. I managed to strangle out, "A deal? What does that mean? Will he not have to stay in jail?"

"Unfortunately, that's up to the judge next Wednesday. But the deal included two hundred hours of community service, credit for time served, mandated anger management, a hefty fine, and... orders of protection to keep him away from you and Paige."

My mouth hung open in shock. I looked at Paige whose face must have mirrored my own. "Credit for time served. What does that mean?" I asked.

"That means that if the judge accepts the deal at the next court date, Craig will go free."

"How can this be?" said Paige, indignant. "He's obviously deranged. They're just going to let him back out to keep terrorizing people?"

"I'm not sure, Paige," he said. "But it's ultimately in the judge's hands now. Just because the prosecution offers the deal and Craig accepts it, it doesn't mean that the judge will go along with it. So we still need to wait for the actual court date on Wednesday."

We heard some shuffling and the sound of an engine starting. "I need to run back to the police station and take care of some of the paperwork I put off earlier today. But I'll call you later, Paige. Jenna, I don't want you to worry about this. No matter what happens, we will be there to protect you."

Paige said goodbye to Ben and slipped the phone back into her pocket. "I'm a little concerned that Craig is going to come out hot and want revenge. I have cameras up at the house, but what does Cat have around the café?"

I thought about it for a moment, and other than the

cameras right outside the front door and inside the café, I didn't think there were any others. "I'm not sure," I said, "but I will ask Cat. If he does get out, you can bet Ben will be camped outside your house, Paige."

"I guarantee Adam will make sure you've got cameras up and protection for yourself as well. But hopefully, the judge will be reasonable and keep Craig where he belongs."

We spent the rest of our walk in quiet reflection, and by the time we returned to the parking lot with Roxy, I was feeling worse than I had in a while.

"I can see the worry written on your face," said Paige, "and I don't want you to be concerned about this right now. We have a few days to get everything lined up. I'm going to call Cat on the way home and ask her about cameras around the café, then I will get everybody up to speed on what Ben just told us. I'm sure we can all put a plan together to keep you safe if he does get out, Jenna."

"Okay," I said. I didn't really know what else to say.

We hugged goodbye, then I gave Roxy a few scratches behind her ears and got in my car. Paige's arm waved from the window of her bright yellow Jeep as she pulled out of the parking lot, and a moment later, I was alone with my thoughts.

I sat for a few minutes to try to still my shaking hands. I had been assuming this whole time that I had at least six months before Craig got out, and that I could use that time to continue my therapy and start feeling a little more confident. But it's hard to build confidence while looking over your shoulder.

19

———————

After the café closed on Saturday, Cat and I sat at our booth to work on my business plan. It seemed pretty straightforward from what I could tell, but I didn't have a lot of experience with the process of starting a business (or much else, if I'm being honest), so I was following Cat's lead on the information that was needed.

"Ok, I spoke to Raina yesterday, and we have secured her to do your marketing," Cat began, checking that off her list that went on for pages. "We have line items like the marketing budget that we need to include, and we can ask Paige about what she's paid Raina. I'm sure she'd share that information with you."

I nodded my head, unsure of what to say. We had all the expenses laid out, including the rent amount we'd gotten from Elizabeth, and the utilities Cat had estimated based on her own.

"Why don't you just use my Wi-Fi login for the first few months, or until you get your feet under you? The signal should make it just fine over there."

"That's very generous of you, but I don't want to take advantage of your kindness."

"It's not taking advantage of me if I offer it, silly," she said.

We got through the rest of the list of expenses pretty easily, all thanks to Cat having much of the information ahead of time. I wondered how long she had spent assembling it all. It was a lot.

"Now we get to the income part, which gets a little tricky because neither of us have a crystal ball. But we can go off of your sales for bakery items here at the café."

"But you will still be providing bakery items here, right?"

"I'm thinking about creating more 'take home' meals to put in the case, but I will still sell some bakery items. We will work out a fair price for everything, but I'm going to be your first official customer. We'll make Paige second," she said with a laugh. "Just don't tell her, okay?"

"Your secret is safe with me," I said. The support I was already getting from my friends made me feel hopeful.

"Great. We have your first line item for income: Cat's Bites." The figure she wrote beside her name nearly took my breath away. "Cat, that's—that's more than the amount spent in the café every month."

"That's less than the amount spent in the café every month. I took a little bit off so I can make a tiny bit of profit. But for the most part, Jenna, that's all you."

I swallowed my shock as Cat tapped her pen on the paper. "Let's keep going. What are you getting paid from Paige's retreats?"

I picked up my pen, which I had yet to use, and wrote the figure from Paige's first retreat.

"Okay, well, right there, you're halfway to your monthly rent. And if she's adding more retreats to the calendar, you're even closer."

I looked from the paper to Cat's face and back again. My mouth hung open. "I'm that close?"

"You are, and with all the people who have expressed interest in supporting you, Jenna, I honestly don't think you're going to have any trouble making the bakery profitable in the next couple months. As long as you have enough to live on until that point, I think you're going to be in pretty good shape, don't you?"

I studied the paper, searching for some mathematical error that would steal my hope away. "It certainly looks like it to me, but I know from working here that any number of things could go wrong at any time. The mixer could break, the place could flood, and I could have my doors closed for an extended period of time with no way to make money."

"Well, then you'll just bake over here, silly," she assured me. "It's going to be okay. Try to think about this in terms of ways that it could go right. It's not going to be easy, and it's never a bad idea to consider what could go wrong, but from what I'm looking at, Jenna," she circled the number at the bottom of the list, "this is going to go right, and you are going to be the architect of your success. How does that feel?"

After all my sessions with the therapist, I was used to being asked how something made me feel, but in this case, I didn't really have words. I never thought I would be able to create something for myself that could support me long-term.

"I'm starting to feel excited," I admitted. "However, while on paper, it looks like it will work, I'm still nervous about what could go wrong."

"It's good to be cautious, Jenna. But being too cautious is going to cause you to limit yourself and you'll be unable to do what you want to do, and if that happens, you will never grow. We grow when we push through the pain of change and uncertainty. In the same way that you have faith that you will go to heaven when you die, it's okay to have faith that this is going to work out. You've been working with me long enough that I already know you're going to kick ass."

I lowered my head, my short brown bob falling forward, and felt the first tear slide down my face. I watched as it hit the table in front of me.

Cat's gaze landed on the splashed tear, and she quickly scooted closer to me. "Oh, Jenna. I know this is scary, but I'm going to be here to help you while you get your feet under you," she said as she rubbed my back in circles.

I looked up at her and wiped my tears with the back of my hand. "It's not so much that I'm scared. I'm happy. I wasn't sure until this moment that I believed this was even a possibility. I guess I've been holding my breath until everything was on paper. I just don't want to fail."

"I can't say for sure that you won't, Jenna. But what I can say for sure is that you have a really good chance of succeeding based on all of this," she set her hand on the paper, "and based on this." She put her hand over my heart. "You have the biggest heart of anyone I know, and you deserve this. I think you're ready for Tuesday," she said, putting her pen down on the paper. "I feel confident that the bank will take a good look at you and decide that you're worth the risk."

As we gathered up the piles of invoices, receipts, and paid bills, there was a knock at the door. Cat and I looked over, and when I looked back at Cat, I'm sure she could read the confusion on my face. It was Adam.

"What's he doing here?" I asked. "Is he picking up an order?"

"No, I—," Cat said, then cleared her throat and began again. "After getting the call from Paige yesterday, I could tell..." she paused, and I knew she was talking about Craig's possible plea deal. "Well, I called Adam just to make sure we have enough cameras around so we can see what's going on outside the café and the entrance to your apartment," she said as she walked to the door and unlocked it.

Adam stepped in with his tool bag in one hand and two boxes under his other arm. He walked to the counter and set them down, then turned to us and smiled.

"Good afternoon, ladies," he said cheerfully. "What are we up to today?" He peered at all the papers on the table.

Cat looked at me. "Go on, Jenna. This is your news to share, not mine."

"Cat is helping me work on the business plan for the bakery."

"That's great news, Jenna! I'm so happy to hear that's moving forward. Have you gone to see the bank yet?"

"I go on Tuesday," I said, swallowing the bubble of anxiety that I had been pushing down since Cat and I had sat at the booth. Cat must have sensed it because she reached out and squeezed my hand.

"From what it looks like," she told Adam, "it's going to be a huge success. And we would appreciate it if you could spread the word a little bit once she's up and running."

"You *know* I will," Adam said, looking at me earnestly, "and I'm going to be your best customer. Your blueberry-lemon sweet rolls are out of this world. Well, I'll leave you to it and get these cameras installed. I am upgrading the one over the front door here," he pointed toward the door to the café, "and one is going over the stairway door that will record anyone walking up and stopping. I have a new-ish buzzer here with a camera that I had at the shop. I kept it after swapping it out for one that better matched a customer's decor," he said, rolling his eyes and smiling at me. "So this one works perfectly fine. And it's only a couple of years old. I'll need to run upstairs and install the second part of it in your apartment, Jenna. Is that okay?"

"Absolutely. I'll let you up there whenever you need me to."

With that, Adam took one of the boxes off the counter and walked back outside.

Cat stretched her legs and put them on the booth across

from us. "While we wait for him to finish, there is something else I wanted to talk to you about. Remember that woman that Sarah had mentioned, her previous student who had reached out about going back to school?"

"Allison," I said. "Yes. And her little boy is Noah?"

"I believe so," said Cat. "I'm going to have her come in so I can talk to her about the scholarship program. From what Sarah has told me, she sounds like a really nice woman who just needs someone to help her get a fresh start in life." She looked at me pointedly. "Something you might know a lot about. Perhaps you can be here tomorrow when she comes in. You're almost the same age. She's a little bit younger than you, but who knows? Maybe it'll spark a friendship. And I would really appreciate getting your take on her."

"I'd be happy to," I said.

We spent the rest of the time chatting about the retreat, Grace's upcoming book launch party, and Sarah's kids, who had both won a swim meet recently. When I brought up Elyse and her recent strange behavior, Cat got uncharacteristically silent.

"I don't even know what to say about that," she said, then clammed up. I could tell the conversation was over before it began, so I dropped it. But my curiosity was piqued. I had never been one to pry into other people's business, but I could definitely sense some tension between the two of them, and most of it seemed to revolve around Elyse's distracted behavior and tardiness with our group. She was constantly on her phone or arriving late. Well, later than usual. Elyse wasn't really known for her timeliness.

"Well, I hope that whatever is going on with her gets resolved," I said, to which Cat grunted and swept the papers into a giant pile. Moments later, Adam walked back in. "Are you ready to head upstairs for the second part of the installation,

Jenna? I don't want to interrupt you if you're still working. If you are, I can do a couple of other things."

"Oh no, we're done here," I said, then looked at Cat. "Right? Did we cover everything?"

Cat put her hands on the table and pushed herself to a standing position while sliding out of the booth. "I think you're in good shape, Jenna. Go ahead and let Adam upstairs to get that camera buzzer installed. I'm going to get this typed up for you and print it out so you're ready on Tuesday. Allison will be in tomorrow, so I'll have you read it over while you're here and let me know if you agree with everything or if there's anything that I missed."

"Okay, sounds good."

With that, Adam and I left.

BLUEBERRY-LEMON SWEET ROLLS

Dough
6 Tbsp. unsalted butter, cut into small pieces, at room temp
1 ¼ oz. pkg. (2 ¼ tsp) active dry yeast (not rapid-rise)
⅓ cup granulated sugar
¾ cup whole milk, at room temp
2 large eggs, divided
3 ½ cups all-purpose flour, divided, plus more for surface
1 tsp. poppy seeds
1 tsp. kosher salt
¼ tsp. baking soda
Filling
4 Tbsp. unsalted butter, at room temp
½ cup packed light brown sugar
2 tsp. ground cinnamon
2 cups fresh blueberries

Frosting
4 oz. cream cheese, at room temp
1 cup confectioners' sugar
½ tsp. pure vanilla extract
1 tsp. finely grated lemon zest, plus 1 Tbsp juice

Dough
In a large bowl, place butter, yeast, granulated sugar, milk, and 1 egg.

Add 3 ¼ cups flour, poppy seeds, salt, and baking soda.

Combine ingredients together to form cohesive dough.

Sprinkle some of the remaining ¼ cup flour on the work surface and knead dough until soft but not sticky, adding a little extra flour if necessary.

Transfer to a clean bowl, cover tightly with plastic wrap and refrigerate 2–12 hours.

Filling
Combine butter, brown sugar, and cinnamon.

Frosting
Drop the cream cheese into a bowl and sift confectioners' sugar over the top.

Add vanilla, lemon zest, and lemon juice and mix to combine.

Leave at room temp up to 3 hours or refrigerate up to 12.

Assemble
Lightly dust the work surface with flour.
Roll dough into 12- by 16-in. rectangle.

Spread with cinnamon mixture and scatter blue-berries on top.

Starting from the long end, roll dough into a tight log.

Cut log into 8 pieces and transfer to 9- by 13-in. baking dish

Let rise at room temperature until the rolls touch and are puffed and no longer cool to the touch, about 90 minutes.

Bake
Preheat the oven to 375°F.

Lightly beat the remaining egg and gently brush all over the tops and sides of the rolls.

Bake until rolls are light golden brown inside (30 to 35 minutes), covering with foil if outer parts begin to brown too quickly.

Transfer to a wire rack.

Spread with cream cheese frosting.

20

The café was as busy as usual on Sunday. We sold out of everything in the bakery case, and I was defrosting the backups I had set aside the last time I over-baked.

Cat came out at one point, saw the empty case, and raised her eyebrows at me as if to say, "Do you see what I mean?" I did. And it made me feel... hopeful.

After the lunch rush was over and Cat locked the front door, we began cleaning up. This was my second favorite part of the day outside of baking in the morning. It was quiet and helped me unwind after a hectic shift. I loved the process of putting everything back the way that it had been when the day began; like a reset button, but with Windex.

Cat was in the back wiping down the last counter, and I was just finishing up cleaning the glass on the bakery case, when there was a knock on the door. I turned around to see a slight, young woman with nearly white hair down to her waist. Next to her stood a little boy who was about four and completely adorable. He had curly brown hair and dark eyes. He stood almost in stark contrast to his mother's fair skin and light blue eyes that blinked at me through the glass.

As I swung the door open, she said, "Hi, I'm Allison," and stuck out her hand as she guided the little boy through. "And this is Noah." I shook her outstretched hand, then squatted down and put my hand out for Noah to shake. He looked at me through his eyelashes and gifted me with a lopsided, bashful smile. He grabbed my hand and pumped it up and down with aplomb.

When he let go, I pretended to grip my hand as if it were crushed. "Well, aren't you strong? And charming!"

Allison beamed with pride. "He loves meeting new people and has been working on his manners."

With that, Cat popped her head up from the back. "Hi, Allison. I'm just finishing up, but you and Noah go ahead and look around. I'll be out soon."

"This artwork is incredible," said Allison.

"Yes, Cat does a good bit of traveling and always brings back at least one piece of art from everywhere she visits. She calls this," I swung my arm in an arc across one wall, "her travel anthology. A lot of what she offers on the menu is inspired by her travels as well."

"Well, from what I have seen here, it's very well received. This place is always super busy."

"Have you been here before?" I asked, trying to place her.

"A few times, but I'm usually meeting someone here for lunch and then leaving. I waitress at a restaurant nearby, and I'm with Noah the rest of the time. I don't get a whole lot of time to socialize, but I do try. Anyway, the food here is amazing."

I nodded my head. "Cat's definitely a talented chef. So you're meeting her about the scholarship opportunity?" I said, trying to fill some time until Cat was finished in the back. I never was good at small talk, but if I was going to be running a bakery, I knew I needed to get used to initiating conversations and chatting with Allison would be good practice.

"Yes, my husband died a year ago, and I've been waitressing to help make ends meet. But I know it's time for me to go back to school so I can do something with my life and set a good example for little Noah." She looked down at him standing next to her with a toy car clutched in his hands and ruffled his hair. His big brown eyes stared up at me as she continued. "Cat is going to walk me through the application process."

With that, Cat walked through the swinging doors and into the café. "Allison, it's lovely to meet you," she said as she pumped Allison's hand up and down in greeting. She crouched down and greeted Noah as well, then rose and headed toward the round booth in the back. "Let's sit over here. Jenna, come sit with us."

Noah sat and played with his car nearby while we slid into the booth.

"I wanted to walk you through the application process, but first, let's talk about you a little bit. You definitely look familiar; I've seen you in here before."

"Yes, as I was telling Jenna, I don't have a whole lot of time for anything other than work and taking care of Noah, but I have been in here a few times for lunch with some friends from high school." She swallowed and looked down at the table, and I could tell there was something there. I wondered if it bothered her that her friends from high school had lives that had gone so differently from hers. She was so young and had to deal with so much alone.

As if she had read my thoughts, Cat asked about her support system.

"Well, my parents have moved out of state," she said. "But my late husband's parents were devastated, obviously, by the loss of their son, and have been more than willing to help out with Noah whenever necessary. They've been providing free childcare while I'm at work."

"That's wonderful," said Cat. "That has to be an enormous weight lifted."

"It is," she said, and paused. "It's definitely a blessing to get free childcare, but with anything else, it has its drawbacks. They can be a little... judgmental about my parenting decisions." She shrugged her shoulders. "It's free childcare, and we need to eat," she said. "So I do the best I can to get along with them, but to be honest, my relationship with them is a big reason why I want to go back to school. I don't want to be dependent on them forever. I need to support my little family on my own, and continuing my education is a good way to ensure that I can provide Noah with a good life."

I tried to keep my jaw from hanging open as Allison spoke. She couldn't be much older than 22, but she spoke as if she had decades of life experience as an adult. I supposed that losing your spouse so young and having to raise a child on their own would cause someone to grow up pretty quickly. I looked at Noah and realized his part in this equation. He had lost his dad and must be confused and suffering as well. It made my heart squeeze to think about him losing a parent. I knew it wasn't the same, but I could identify in a small way with how I felt about losing my grandmother, who had been more like a mother to me than the one who actually held the title.

"Anyway," Allison continued, "we're currently living with his parents, and it's less than ideal, but we're making it work." She paused again, and her face turned bright red. "I can't believe I'm telling you all of this. I don't normally go on and on about my personal life, but I guess I just want you to understand why going back to school is so important to me. Not only do I want to provide a good life for Noah," she said, looking over at him as he raced his toy cars around on the hardwood floor, "but I also want to set a good example for him. It doesn't do much good for me to tell him when he grows up that his education is important, when I barely made it out of high school myself. I want him to see that he's not alone. I want him to hear my words and see that I've followed through on them myself."

I listened to her talk about her son and the life she wanted for him and my heart filled with affection for this little family. She seemed so sweet and maybe a little overburdened by the hand life had dealt her. I hoped that Cat could get the scholarship for her; she seemed like someone who needed it.

"What is it that you would like to go to school for?" asked Cat, taking notes on the legal pad in front of her.

"I would really love to be a grief counselor. My own therapist has been invaluable over the last year. Helping Noah through his grief while I'm grieving myself has been one of the most challenging parts of all this. I would love to help other families in my position and support them while they navigate their grief journey. So much of what we read in books and online talks about the grief process and the steps we go through, but no one really talks about the fact that you can retrace the same steps over and over again. People end up getting stuck in the same place and don't know how to move on so they can reach the point of acceptance. They feel like something is wrong with them. I know I did until we had a breakthrough in therapy."

She paused and looked over at Noah, genuine affection shining in her eyes. "I would love to do that for someone else, many someones," she said, her tinkling laughter breaking up some of the heaviness in the room and causing Noah to look up from where he was playing.

"I think you would be a perfect candidate for the scholarship, Allison," said Cat, setting her pen down on the paper.

"Please call me Allie. At this point, you know so much about my life, you might as well. It's what my friends call me."

"Okay, Allie." She moved her pen onto the table and pulled a packet from behind the last page of her legal pad. Sliding it across the table, she said, "I'm going to give you this application form. The deadline to turn these in is coming up. Do you think you can have this back to me in the next couple of days? In fact..." she looked at me and smiled, then back across the table. I wondered what she had up her sleeve. "...are you free on Wednesday night?"

"Most likely. I typically have Mondays and Wednesdays off." She dug her phone out of her purse and checked her calendar. "I'm free on Wednesday night. Do you need help with something? You've been so incredibly kind to me by offering me this opportunity. I'd be happy to help."

"No, no," said Cat with a laugh, covering Allie's hand with her own.

"Our friend Grace is having her book launch party on Wednesday. You should come and meet the rest of our friends. Bring Noah. It's pretty informal, and it's just a couple doors down at the bookstore. Do you think you can make it?"

"I definitely can. If your friends are anything like the two of you, it'd be my pleasure. Thank you for inviting me!"

"Well, we're all pretty different, but our hearts are all the same."

"Noah and I will be there. I can't wait," she said. She flipped her phone over again to look at the time. "I'd better be going. I have a shift tonight, and it starts in an hour. I need to get Noah back home and get ready, but this has been incredible. I can't thank you enough for considering me." She looked at Noah, and added, "Us."

We stood and walked toward the door. "It was great to meet you, Allie," said Cat.

"Likewise. This has been wonderful. I don't get the chance to meet a lot of new people, so I appreciate you inviting me."

Cat smiled and took her hand in her own. "It's my pleasure. It doesn't hurt to have more people in your corner. Bring the application with you on Wednesday, and I'll make sure it makes it in on time."

Allie shook our hands, and I crouched down to give Noah a high five, which he provided with a flourish. "That is a strong arm you've got there," I said to him. "Do you play baseball?"

He giggled. "No, but I'm going to be a soccer player."

"Oh boy. Next time I see you, you'll have to show me your biggest kick," I said, and Noah's face shone with pride.

A moment later, they were gone.

Cat locked the door and turned to me. "So, what do you think?"

"I think I love her," I said.

Cat laughed, her green eyes sparkling. "Me too. She seems pretty grounded and has her head screwed on straight. And that little Noah, what a cutie patootie." She looked at me, knowing how great my desire to have my own family was. "Perhaps the two of you will become friends," she said. "But I had another thought while she was talking. Not if, but *when* you open your bakery, we're going to need a replacement for you."

I looked through the glass of the door to where Allie was strapping Noah into his car seat. "She'd be perfect," I breathed.

"I think so, too."

21

———————

When Cat got back from Ladies' League on Tuesday morning, I was pacing the café. By the time she made it past the hostess stand, I had grabbed my tote bag with my application and business plan inside and was halfway to the door.

"It's slowed down," I said, trailing off, my eyes on the sidewalk outside the door.

"Jenna. Look at me."

I turned my head, and Cat's green eyes swept over my face. "You're going to do just fine," she said, squeezing my shoulder and then pulling me in for a hug. I was feeling pretty anxious about how the process would go, and I wanted to just crawl under a rock and avoid the whole thing, but I knew that trip to the bank would be the first step in realizing the life I had dreamt for myself. I needed to be brave.

Once I was at the bank and seated in a chair in front of the loan officer's desk, I learned that the application process itself was pretty straightforward and not as scary as I had built it up to be. Kyle, as he had introduced himself, entered all the information into his computer as I recited it off, and when he asked for my business plan, he seemed pleased as he looked it over.

"This is very thorough," he said, holding the top sheet back to review the next page. He nodded his head once and set the papers down on his desk. "While I can't guarantee anything," he said, looking back up at me, "having a business plan this comprehensive definitely helps your file. I will let you know as soon as I get an answer from the underwriters."

"How long does that usually take?" I asked. I hated how anxious my voice sounded.

"It could be a couple days, or it could be a couple of weeks. It all depends on how busy they are right now. I've pushed a couple of these through in the last ten days. One came back the next day, and one came back five days later."

I fiddled with the zipper pull on my tote bag. "And were they approved?"

"One was approved. That was the five-day wait. The one that came back the next day was not approved."

"So it's safe to assume that the longer it takes, the better my chances are, correct?"

"Correct. They can usually look over a loan, do a few calculations, and know that it's not right for the bank's portfolio or is too great a risk. If they take longer, it means they are strongly considering and doing all the calculations."

"Okay, then I won't worry too much if it goes past a couple of days."

"Don't worry at all, Mrs. Mitchell. You have done all that you can do, and you've prepared as much as you can. Everything else is out of your hands. All you can do now is wait. But between you and me," he put his elbows on the desk and tented his hands in front of him, "I hope it gets approved. It's a great idea, and you're so well prepared. I think you have a very strong chance of getting this approved, but I obviously can't say for sure."

"Well, I appreciate hearing that," I said.

"I'll let you know as soon as I hear something," he said, and stood behind his desk, prompting me to rise from my chair. We shook hands, and after promising again to call as soon as he heard something, he walked me to the front door.

When I walked back into Cat's Bites a few minutes later, I could see Cat talking on the phone in the back of the kitchen, but I couldn't identify the look on her face. It looked like a mix of concern and sadness, and I immediately felt panic rising in my chest.

The second she hung up, I rushed back to where she stood just outside her office. "What is it?" I asked. "Did something happen?"

"Let's talk in my office."

By the time we stepped in and Cat closed the door behind us, I was practically hyperventilating.

"Please, just tell me what happened, Cat. Is everyone okay?"

"Yes! Oh gosh, yes, it's nothing like that," said Cat. "But, well, I'll just come out and tell you. Elizabeth Wells stopped in while you were gone. She was with a couple who were touring the space next door."

My throat closed up, and I felt cold all over. I couldn't believe the timing.

"They want to open up an Italian restaurant," Cat continued. "I don't want you to lose this opportunity, especially now that you've made the decision and started hoping and planning. I know that hasn't always been your mindset, and I hate for the rug to get ripped out from under you at this point. That's all."

My stomach dropped as I stood silently listening to Cat. Just as I had started believing that this could work, it looked like I might never get the opportunity. The ladies' belief in me had been contagious and I had just started to get a glimmer of confidence that I could make this a success.

Cat reached out and put her hand on my arm. "But there's

more. I pulled Elizabeth aside and asked her to please hold out on any lease offers until you hear back from the bank. I gave her a little bit of background. Nothing too personal, I promise. But enough that she understood how important this is to you, and she agreed to pause any more tours. I told her we would probably hear back in the next few days to a week."

"That's reassuring," I said, my lips forming the briefest of smiles.

"All we can do is have faith that it's all going to work out the way it's meant to, Jenna. And at least we have Elizabeth on our side now. I'm just choosing to think positively, which brings me back to what we talked about yesterday. I'd like to get to know Allie better. I hope she comes to Grace's book launch party because I want to get everyone else's opinion on her as well. Even when she's in school, I think we can make it work and be flexible with her sched-ule. Even if you decide not to open the bakery, we could use her help. And if you're baking for me from your own place, that leaves us with a lot of flexibility as far as the kind of help that we would need from her. But I want to make sure I'm not seeing her through rose-colored glasses because I feel bad for her and her situation."

"But feeling bad for people's situation is kind of how you operate, Cat."

She chuckled. "That's true," she said, "but I still have to get a feel for people before I know for sure, and I'm pretty certain with Allie, but I'd really like the rest of the group to get to know her a little."

She trailed off, then fell quiet for a moment as she stared blankly into the bakery case. She shook her head as if to clear whatever thought had been floating there. "So, back to Grace's book launch party. What are you bringing?"

We talked for a little while longer about the baking that I had been experimenting with and the lavender cupcakes I was making for Grace. As we closed up the café for the day, Cat stopped outside before I unlocked the door to the stairs that go up to my apartment.

"I believe in you, Jenna. You did a very brave thing today and I'm sorry that you came back to a feeling of uncertainty, but I think that tells us how much you actually *do* want this. If you were doing this just because we were pushing you toward it, then it wouldn't work. You have to want it, and I know that you do, but now I know how much. I really hope the bank comes back with good news."

I looked at her and I'm sure she could see the concern all over my face. She stepped into the space in front of me and squeezed my shoulder. "And if the bank calls with bad news, then we figure out what's next. But let's just wait and see what they say." She leaned forward and gave me a hug. As I returned it, I felt her arms squeezing tightly around me. I didn't want to cry. I felt like I had spent the last month doing nothing but crying when I thought about what had become of the life that I had wanted for myself, and here I was, finally at a point where I could see a different path, and one that looked much like the dreams I had always had.

I was afraid that it would slip away before I could get my arms around it.

"It's going to be okay, Jenna. No matter what. There will always be another opportunity, and even if it's not that location, we will find a way to make it work if this is what you really want."

I nodded my head, and Cat knew me well enough to know that I didn't trust my voice enough to speak. She looked me in the eye. "Try to take your mind off this and just relax tonight. Okay? We have a big day tomorrow, and you'll need to get your rest because you have a lot of cupcakes to make in the morning."

I finally laughed. "Have a good night, Cat," I said as I

unlocked the door. I looked over my shoulder at her as she smiled encouragingly.

"Have a good night, Jenna. I'll see you in the morning."

I was thinking about the potato gnocchi I was making for dinner as I headed up the stairs, but before I had my key in my apartment door, I remembered seeing an email that the book I'd ordered from Back in the Day Books had arrived, so I headed there instead.

POTATO GNOCCHI

1 pound mashed potatoes (Yukon gold or russet are best)
1 cup flour
½ teaspoon salt
1 medium egg (room temperature)

Mix together the flour and salt, place on a flat surface, make a well in the middle and add the potatoes and egg, mix together with your fingers to form a soft dough, it should not stick to your fingers.

On a lightly floured surface, cut small amounts of dough to form ropes and cut into ¾ inch (2 cm) pieces, then slide each piece on a fork and squeeze a little (but not too hard).

Sprinkle with a little bit of flour and toss, so they don't stick together. Let the gnocchi rest for 20 minutes before cooking.

Place in boiling water. Gnocchi is finished cooking when it floats.

Place in boiling water. Gnocchi is finished cooking when it floats.

22

———

I'd been waiting for the latest in the small-town romance series I was reading. I was a sucker for a good lumberjack love story set in rural areas; there's something about a man in overalls chopping down trees to provide warmth for the woman he loves. Swoon...

I walked into the bookstore and stood in front of the counter. Elyse was in one of the aisles tapping out something on her phone and didn't notice me, so I busied myself by flipping through the bookmarks on the wooden display by the counter. I noticed they were out of order and reorganized them, then looked over to see if Elyse was done yet. She wasn't. Out of the corner of my eye, I noticed a Christmas tree in the corner that hadn't been there before, so I spun around to see what else had been added.

A pre-lit garland was draped across the tops of the dark wood bookshelves, and at the end of each of the three rows were clues to Christmas-themed books. I stepped over to the first row and was delighted to find a teal suitcase on a low table. A tan fedora was balanced on the handle, and a tattered stuffed bunny rabbit lay on its side in front of it. A jar filled with scraps of paper sat in the center of the table, accompanied by a pen and a small pad of paper. I knew the book immediately and wrote, *The Deal of a Lifetime* and my name on a slip of paper and stuffed it into the jar.

Moving on to the next row, I found an identical table draped in a soft, cozy blanket, covered in small holiday-themed throw pillows and another jar. The end of the bookshelf had the words "Hope" and "Joy" cut out of red and green construction paper.

"Hmmm...," I hummed under my breath. Deep in thought, I tapped the pen on my chin and scrolled through my mental list of books. "Genius," I whispered, and wrote down, *Comfort and Joy*, then slipped the paper into the near-empty jar.

Historically, the clues grew more difficult by the time you arrived at the third and final shelf, but remembering books I'd read was my superpower, so I crossed over and stood in front of the table, noting the jar was completely empty.

Challenge accepted.

The table held an enormous envelope carried by a tiny stuffed mouse with a red scarf. Stumped for the time being, I took a step back to my left to check if Elyse was finished on her phone, but her back was to me, and she still seemed completely oblivious to my presence.

"Does anyone work here?" I jokingly asked in a tone I had heard from some of the curmudgeons that frequented the café. It reminded me of Craig, and I shivered.

Elyse startled. Her phone bounced off her sandaled foot, clattered to the wood floor, and skittered away under the shelf. "Ouch! Oh, hey, Jenna," she said, and then, as she bent down to retrieve her phone, "How long have you been standing there?"

"I got here about ten minutes ago, but you looked busy." I glanced at the phone she'd picked up and was currently inspecting. "Everything ok?"

She turned it over in her hand. "Looks to be intact." Around this time she must have realized I was there for a reason because she fumbled her phone into her pocket and closed the distance between us with her arms out. I returned her embrace, then stepped back toward the front of the store.

"I love the tables this year. I admit you've got me stumped on the third one, but I'll figure it out. Don't tell me."

"I would never. You know I don't give out hints. It takes all the fun out of it. So, are you just stopping in to say hi, or...," she trailed off.

"I got a message from you yesterday. My book is in?"

She lightly slapped her palm against her forehead. "Of course. Follow me."

We walked toward the counter, and Elyse disappeared through the office door, returning moments later with a red paper bag. "This was a popular one," she said. "Lumberjacks are hot right now."

"Lumberjacks are hot all the time," I said. "I think it's all the flannel." Elyse laughed, and I felt the heat rising on my face. "Temperature-wise, of course," I said, trying to cover for my embarrassing admission.

"Good to know. Jenna likes burly men in flannels. What about tall, skinny guys in baseball caps and t-shirts?" she asked with a wink.

I changed the subject, diverting the attention back to her.

"Hey, I've been wanting to talk to you, anyway. Are you ok? You've seemed so distracted lately..." Unsure if I should bring up the obvious friction between her and Cat, I left the rest unsaid, certain she would pick up on my meaning.

She pretended not to.

"Yes, I'm fine! Just a lot going on at the moment." As if on cue, her phone buzzed from her back pocket, and her facial expression went from feigned curiosity to masked anxiety, her eyebrows knit together over a stiff, painted-on smile.

"You've been spending a lot of time on your phone when

we're together. I'm not one to pry, but I just wanted to make sure you're ok. Everything's good with you and Drew?"

"Yes. Why wouldn't it be?" she asked, irritation creeping into her voice.

What in the wide world of sports was going on? Elyse was never short with me. Something is definitely off.

I decided to drop the whole subject and tried to get our conversation back on track. "So, have you had a lot of orders for this book?" I took a bookmark out of the display and set it on the counter, then spun it around by the tassel with my finger.

"I guess," she replied as she scanned the barcode on the back of the book. "Do you want this bookmark?"

"Sure," I said, then I stood there frozen for a moment, unsure of how to continue. There was clearly something wrong, but as soon as I'd asked, Elyse had erected a barbed-covered wall and locked me on the other side. I didn't feel I had the right to pry, so I decided to take a different tactic.

Fake cheerfulness.

"Your decorations look great! Did Drew help you put them up?"

"Did Drew...?" She gave me a look I'd never seen before, and I was instantly sorry I'd asked. "No, Drew did not help me, Jenna. I'm more than capable of doing things on my own." She gave me my total and then, under her breath, whispered, "I wish everyone would just leave me alone."

With shaking hands, I dug a twenty-dollar bill out of my wallet and set it on the counter. "I'm— I'm— I'm sorry, Elyse. I've obviously upset you, which was not my intention. I came in to pick up my book and was just making sure you're ok. That's all. Forget I said anything."

"I will. And for the record, everything is fine. I'm fine, and I don't need everyone telling me how to live my life. Don't project your trust issues on me, Jenna." She thrust the bag in my direction and dropped it onto the counter.

In my mind, my mouth dropped open, but I managed to still my face to not provoke Elyse any further. I picked up the bag and backed away from the counter. After a few steps, I turned around and headed toward the door.

Neither of us spoke a word as I walked out.

AFTER LEAVING THE BOOKSTORE, I turned left to head toward the park and bandshell so I could take a few minutes to ruminate on what had just happened. I'd never had as much as a disagreement with the other women and the experience unnerved me. I shook my hands out in an attempt to alleviate some of the tension I was squeezing into the center of my palm.

It wasn't until I passed what I called the wall of a thousand dogs—one of a few murals featuring local pets and their owners—that I was able to creak out a smile. I'd never owned a pet of my own, but I'd wanted to since I was a child, and always said I would as soon as I had the opportunity. Pets rarely, if ever, disappoint us.

By the time I'd reached the Dunedin Visitor Center, the holiday decorations had helped lift my mood. Each lamppost was wrapped in garland and twinkled with glitter-soaked ornaments of every shape, and every storefront was seemingly in the throes of a friendly competition being decided by their window display alone. It was enough to remind me that I needed to step up our game. Plastic maple leaves and flamingos in Santa hats were simply not going to cut it that year.

By the time I made it to the concrete steps of the library, I had mostly shaken off Elyse's words, but her tone had settled in the pit of my stomach like a week-old loaf of sourdough.

What had I done to upset her?

I crossed the street and wound my way through the park. Parents crowded onto benches, watching over children whose pastel-streaked hands grasped sugar cones that leaked ice cream down their forearms. It dripped from their elbows and fell to the ground, leaving a sticky, technicolor trail everywhere they went.

Do I have trust issues? Will I ever trust someone enough to get my happily ever after? Will this ever be me?

I passed the creamery, and before long, I was standing in front of Uncle Mike and Chris' haberdashery. Their window display consistently reflected characters straight from the event calendar at Ruth Eckerd Hall. That week's display featured a dapper Ebeneezer Scrooge in bespoke couture, pointing a dismissive index finger at a more modestly dressed, yet still fashionable Bob Cratchit huddled by a fireplace for warmth. Each month's display was its own art exhibit — one that clearly demonstrated that A Dash of Flair could dress a man of virtually any means.

A window display to my right caught my eye, and I knew right away that Uncle Mike was lending his creative genius to his neighbors at the local dress shop. Mrs. Cratchit was tying one of the shoulder straps on the dress of her daughter, Martha. Both of their styles were modern but modest, and their bonnets were replaced by elaborate braided updos. Genius.

Martha's dress, in particular, caught my eye, and I took a few steps to the right to get a better look. It was long enough to leave something to the imagination, as did the gathered fabric at the bust. Wide straps tied at the shoulders. It looked so comfortable. I was just stepping back onto my left foot to examine the rest of the dress when I noticed two eyes staring at me through the window. I forgot I was in mid-step and nearly reached my tipping point, but recovered at the last second.

What the...?

A moment later, the top half of a woman appeared around the doorway, and I recognized her immediately. It was Sharon, one of our regulars at the café and the owner of Neat and

Repeat, the dress shop I was standing in front of. Five days out of the week, it operated as a dress shop with more than enough choices for any taste or budget (even mine). But on the sixth day, typically Thursdays, she was only open to women on a very limited budget who needed a dress for a special event or something to wear to an interview. She took donations throughout the week, had them professionally cleaned, and displayed them throughout the store on Thursday mornings. She rolled the rest of the racks to the back room so the women who shopped that day knew that anything they found and liked would be free. They never had to ask. They brought their choices to the counter where Sharon oooohed and ahhhhed and made them feel fabulous about what they'd picked out. She then zipped everything into the same gorgeous burgundy satin garment bag she provided for *all* her customers and sent them on their way, taking some luck and a piece of her heart with them.

Sharon was an enigma. She was older than her clothes suggested, but it worked. Her smooth, tanned skin contradicted itself, and she was stunning without a drop of makeup. She had dark brown hair she had been growing since Woodstock, which she rarely had cut and yet somehow, it grew uniformly straight across the bottom and without a gray in sight.

Despite all of this, everybody loved her.

"I've been standing there wondering when you were going to give in and try it on."

My face burned. "I was just—"

"You were just about to come in here and see it for yourself. That dress was made for you. Let's go, Jenna. Chop chop."

I couldn't believe I'd just been 'chop chopped' as a twenty-eight-year-old woman. By Sharon. What choice did I have?

Twenty minutes later, I was standing in front of the mirror, turning this way and that to take it all in. I'd never been one to derive pride from my clothing, but Sharon was right. The dress was made for me. As were the six dresses I'd tried on before it. Sharon had wanted to 'save the best for last'. I was grateful she had.

The warm light pouring over me from the brass satellite fixture above cast a glow over my skin, creating the illusion of someone who spent more than fifteen seconds a day outside. It worked. The dresses were flattering and stylish and sweet... and I had to have them.

I'd already been adding up how much they would cost when Sharon came around the front of me to tie the second strap. "We will get these exactly right before you leave so you can pull it on over your head when you wear it."

"That sounds great." I paused as I continued to take it in. "I've got some decisions to make, but I definitely want this one."

"Lucky for you, we are having a sale: Buy six dresses and get the seventh one free. And since these dresses are all from last season, they're twenty percent off. It's practically a steal."

I did some quick math and found that I could afford them with those discounts. "Sold. I'll take them all," I said in my ten seconds of bravery, a trick I'd learned watching one of my favorite Matt Damon movies.

"Great! You get changed, and I'll start wrapping these up. Unless... you want to wear that one home?"

"Oh no, I'll change back into the clothes I came in, but thank you. I'll be out in a minute."

"I'll meet you up front." She picked up my bag from the bookstore, took the six dresses from the rack outside my curtain, and headed toward the register.

I stepped into the red cedar plank changing room and through the evergreen velvet curtain heard an odd, shrill squeaking noise. It sounded a lot like a magic marker. When I reached the back of the store where Sharon was wrapping a dress in tissue paper, an odd smell hung in the air. It smelled a lot like a magic marker. "Do you smell that?" I asked.

"Smell what?"

A fibber.

"So the deal you mentioned — buy six dresses, get the seventh for free — when did that start? I didn't see a sign for it on my way in."

"It's pretty recent. Here's the sign for it right here." She tapped a piece of notebook paper with hastily scrawled (black magic marker) letters hung cattywampus by a single piece of crooked tape, inches above a small Christmas tree at the end of the counter.

I played along. "Oh, interesting. How did I miss that?"

"You must have been distracted by that fabulous dress. Now hand it over, and I'll wrap it right up for you. I've got your total here."

I looked at the suspiciously low sum on the screen and nearly gasped. It was a fraction of what it should have been. A low fraction. "Is this correct?"

"Yes, yes, of course. You got lucky today because when I was ringing you up, I noticed one of the dresses had a small pull in it, so I discounted that one."

I could tell she wasn't going to be swayed, so I continued to humor her, but I was extremely grateful, nonetheless. "Thank you so much. I've never worn anything like them, and I was having so much trouble deciding after I put each one on."

"You look fabulous in anything you wear, Jenna, but I have to say, those dresses brought you straight to a twelve."

"A twelve?"

"Out of ten." Her laughter rang out through the small boutique, and quickly latched on to me. Perhaps it was embarrassment, but I hadn't laughed like that in weeks.

"Oh! Before I forget." Sharon bent over and started rifling around under the counter, popping up a moment later with an index card. "I have something I want to give you. It's my mother's Listie recipe that she brought here from Germany. It's a family recipe, so I want you to have it."

I was momentarily speechless as my brain flipped through a useless list of lame professions of gratitude. The old standby would have to do.

"Thank you, Sharon," I said, taking the recipe and scanning it quickly. "I bet these are great. Not too sweet."

"Exactly. I hope you try them out. Anyway, off you go," she said, hefting a long garment bag over the counter. "I can't wait to see you around in these."

I took the burgundy bag and thanked her, heading straight home with my purchase.

After hanging the dresses in my closet, I took the one from the window display out again and held it in front of me. I spun on my toes and looked in the mirror behind my bedroom door. The woman in the reflection stared back with confidence.

Who was that woman becoming?

ELSIE'S LISTIE

½ lb butter
½ cup sour cream
2 egg yolks
1 tsp. vanilla
2 cups flour
Powdered sugar

Combine butter, sour cream, egg yolks, and vanilla.
Slowly mix in flour.
Cover and refrigerate for 2 hours.
Flour a flat surface and roll out dough to ¼" thick.
Cut into 4" squares.
Lay squares onto an ungreased cookie sheet.
Bake 10-12 minutes (or until edges are lightly browned)
Once cooled, sprinkle with powdered sugar.

23

On the day of Grace's book launch party, I woke up early to get the baking done for the café and the event. I had so much to do, but I felt distracted; all night long, I had dreamt of Craig, and none of them were good. In the last one, I had opened my door to find him standing there in a tan jumpsuit, a sneer on his face and our divorce papers in his hand. I had woken up just as he stuck his foot in the opening so I couldn't close the door, and I hadn't been able to shake the feeling of unease that had followed me around all morning.

The day had come when we would finally learn the judge's decision.

I felt a little more comfortable knowing I had a camera set up outside now. I could see who was at the door before I let anyone up, but the dream had felt so real.

Once at the café, I was distracted as I went through the motions of preparing everything I needed for the day. When I got to Grace's cupcakes, I was still under the cloud the last dream had left behind, and the first batch burnt. Their sad, charred ghosts followed me around the kitchen the rest of the morning.

I need to slow down.

I got myself a glass of ice water, took a lap around the kitchen, and started over. I shook the tension from my hands while repeating my therapist's mantra for moments like those.

All I can control is what's in front of me right now.

After a few deep breaths, I started over and finished the rest of the baking without incident. I was piping purple frosting onto the last batch when Cat walked in, and before I knew it, we were open for the day.

There was a buzz of excitement around the café. Many of our regulars knew Grace well, and everyone was looking forward to her event. Earlier in the week, Grace had posted an event reminder on Facebook and had mentioned that I would be providing a surprise treat at her party, and people had been stopping by the counter all morning to congratulate me and tell me they were excited to see what I was bringing.

I wasn't used to so much focus being on me and all the extra attention felt strange. I'd been practicing taking compliments in therapy, but I didn't know how long it would take before it felt even semi-normal.

The day sped by, and after we finished cleaning up, I ran upstairs to get ready. Grace's event was being held in the afternoon, because, as she said, she's "not a teenager anymore, for Pete's sake," so I didn't have a whole lot of time to shower, get dressed and slip into the event before the rest of the guests arrived.

I was still anxiously awaiting to hear from Ben about whether the judge had made a decision on Craig's plea deal. He was at the police station, and Paige had reassured me that he was standing by waiting to hear from his contact at the courthouse.

I opened my music app and scrolled to Taylor Swift's Evermore album, shuffling the songs. The first few haunting notes of "Happiness" floated through the tiny bathroom as I stepped into the shower to quickly rinse off a full day of flour, butter, and hollandaise sauce with the promise of a long, hot bath later.

After drying off, I put my hair in a French braid and stood wrapped in my favorite fluffy yellow towel, admiring my new dress. It had been hanging from a hook on the back of my bedroom door, and I smiled when I saw it. The cheerful tea roses against the white reminded me of my grandmother's favorite blouse, and that little detail gave me the courage I needed to step out of my comfort zone and into something different.

I took the dress down, gently slid the straps off the hanger, and pulled it over my head, letting the towel pool at my feet. After taking my grandma's brooch from the jewelry box and affixing it over my heart, I turned slowly in front of the mirror on the back of the door and took in all that was different in its reflection. The dress, certainly, but there was something new that shone from my eyes. Confidence was brewing there.

I locked the apartment door, and by the time I got to the bottom of the stairs, I could hear the excited chatter of people nearby. A line had already formed outside the bookstore. I had attended a couple of Grace's book launch events since I'd known her, and each crowd was bigger than the last. I was glad that Grace's team had already picked up the cupcakes because there was no way I would have made it through the throngs of people with multiple trays.

I walked past the line and saw Elyse standing outside the bookstore, waiting to direct foot traffic. "Jenna!" she exclaimed as she turned and saw me. "That dress! You look gorgeous!"

I saw the exact moment when our conversation from the previous day crashed back into her consciousness. "Oh, God, Jenna. I've been wanting to text you all day, but I wanted to say this in person. Come over here with me. Please." Her eyes searched mine, her discomfort evident in the furrow of her brow. She placed her hands on my elbows and walked backward, away from the crowd, pulling me with her.

"I am so sorry for the way I spoke to you yesterday. You were trying to be a good friend, and I let my emotions take over my brain. You didn't deserve that, and I am so incredibly sorry." She ground the toe of her right Chuck Taylor into the sidewalk, one of her many nervous tics.

Having made more than my fair share of mistakes in my lifetime, I let her off the hook immediately. "You're forgiven. I can tell something is bothering you, but I'll just say I'm here when you're ready to share the load." I stepped forward and embraced her, and we stood there like that for a few moments, rocking back and forth while the crowd grew around us.

"Come in, come in," she said as she stepped back. I pretended to rummage around in my bag while she wiped away a stray tear. We returned to the bookstore entrance, and she unhooked the red velvet rope. "Coming through," she said to the people standing just outside the door. They turned to look at me as I walked past them, and I recognized a few of the attendees standing at the front of the line. Regulars at the café, they were used to seeing me in long skirts and an apron, and the nods, smiles, and thumbs up gave me a boost of confidence as I stepped through the door.

I saw—and heard—Grace as soon as I walked in. She stood at the front of rows and rows of brown wooden folding chairs, one foot propped on the bottom rung of a tall, white director's chair with her name stitched in hot pink across the white canvas back. Elyse had given it to her before the last book signing event, and it fit Grace's personality to a tee. She was waving her arms around, and I could hear her gravelly voice from the front door, even over all the noise that was coming from outside. I made my way over to where she stood, talking to Sarah and Cat, who had somehow beaten me there.

Grace's eyes widened when she saw me, prompting those around her to turn in unison. Sarah's jaw fell open before she snapped it shut. "Jenna! That dress is... it's... wow. You look incredible!"

Cat winked at me. "I don't think I've ever seen your knees, Jenna," she joked, even though she'd seen me in a bathing suit at Paige's several times.

Grace put her arm out to invite me closer, then folded me into her side. "Jenna," she said, "those cupcakes are absolutely divine. I just don't know how you do it."

"I'm glad that they're working out," I said. "I'm really grateful you chose me to make them."

"There is no one else's cupcakes I would rather have at my event, Jenna. You're the best in town. You're probably the best in several towns. But aside from that, you're my friend, and I'm *always* going to choose you."

I swallowed the emotions that threatened to spill over. "Thank you," I said once I felt I could control my voice. A moment later, I felt a tap on my shoulder and turned to see Adam. He was dressed in his usual blue jeans, but he had on a nice button-down shirt (tucked in!) and no baseball cap.

"Where's your hat?"

"My mother taught me never to wear a hat to special events; especially one like this. My rule is that if I'm wearing a shirt with buttons, I leave the hat at home."

I laughed. "That's a good rule," I said. "And it sounds like your mother is a smart woman."

In a rare moment of unease, he looked down at his brown slip-on loafers, but quickly recovered. "How is the camera buzzer working out?" he asked as he looked back up at me.

"So far, so good," I said. "Paige stopped by the other day, and I was able to see the top of her head perfectly."

"Hey," came from behind me in Paige's voice. "Don't disparage my stature. This is just the way God made me." She came around the side of me, put her arm around my shoulder, and squeezed. "The cupcakes look amazing," she said, gesturing toward the table covered end to end in a sea of lavender. "I've been waiting to eat these again for a week. Grace, are they fair game, or are you going to make me wait?"

"You can wait with the rest of us," said Grace.

"Oh, then here, let me help you with this," said Paige. She grabbed a napkin and wiped purple frosting off Grace's top lip.

"I tripped and fell into a cupcake," Grace said.

"Likely story," said Paige, her tone dripping with playful sarcasm.

A few minutes later, Elyse began letting people through the door, and Grace climbed into her chair as they all scrambled to find the best seats. After dropping into the chair reserved for me at the front, I looked around and saw that there was only standing room left, and not a lot of it.

"I'm going to have to consider another venue for her next book launch," said Elyse, leaning against a bookshelf to my right. "Her popularity has definitely grown since the last one."

"I'm so happy for her," I said. "I know how hard she works."

"Yeah, but she somehow makes it look easy," said Elyse.

Those who could had taken their seats, and I looked down the front row to see Peggy and Caleb sitting front and center in their own reserved seats. Peggy was a great ally for the local writing community and always put Grace's books in a prominent location on the local author shelf and on various displays throughout the library. She had definitely had a hand in Grace's growing popularity with local readers.

The little curly-haired boy sitting on his mother's lap in the last row caught my eye. I could recognize the mom's nearly white hair anywhere and was so happy that Allie had decided to come.

After Grace had finished her reading, she made her way over to the signing table, and I tracked down Allie and Noah.

"Well, how are you doing, young man?" I said, crouching down to hold my hand out for him. He slapped my palm and fist-bumped me, and I felt my heart swell. I stood and started talking to Allie. After discussing how our weeks had gone, I asked, "Did you bring your application?"

"I gave it to Cat already. She said it could take a little time."

"I'm waiting to hear some news myself," I admitted. "I applied for a business loan to open my own bakery."

"Are you serious?" she said. "That's incredible. Are these your beautiful cupcakes?" she asked, sweeping her arm toward the table where the sea of purple was quickly receding.

"Yes, those are mine. Have you tried them?"

"They're incredible," she said. "Who would ever think that lavender belonged in a cupcake? But now I can't imagine eating a cupcake without it. You're going to have a lot of people relaxing in those chairs before long," she said with a laugh.

As any four-year-old child would tend to do at a book launch party, Noah started getting antsy, so I pulled up a music app, handed him my phone, and showed him how to use it. "Here you go, little buddy. If you push these buttons right here, you can make a song."

"Cool," he said, his brown eyes growing larger as he saw what the app could do.

I turned my attention back to Allie. "Yes, I filled out the loan application a few days ago, and he said it would take a few days if it was bad news and longer if it was good. So I'm kind of hoping that I don't hear anything for a while."

"That makes sense," said Allie. "I'll keep my fingers crossed for you."

We continued talking, and our conversation soon grew to other topics. Allie shared with me an opportunity she had to enroll Noah at a nearby preschool, but admitted that she was concerned that her in-laws would be upset about Noah not staying with them during the day.

"I really want him to have a head start when he gets to kindergarten. He's very smart, and I don't want to squander *any* opportunity with him." She looked down to where he squatted by her feet, tapping away at the music notes as they popped up on the screen. "I know he'll have plenty of time in school, so I don't necessarily want to rush things, but I don't know... I'm really considering the program they have at this preschool. It's a tough application process there, and they don't take many kids, but I'm weighing my options. I may give it a shot for Noah's sake and deal with the fallout from his grandparents later."

I looked down to Noah, who had navigated around my phone and was playing a word find game I used to keep my mind busy when anxiety tried to overtake me.

"I can see your point," I said, pointing at my phone.

"Noah," admonished Allie as she crouched next to her son, "you can't be clicking around on other people's phones." She looked up at me in embarrassment. "I'm sorry," she said.

"No, it's quite alright. I know the risk I'm taking when I hand a four-year-old child my phone. There's nothing in there that could get him in trouble. Or me," I added with a laugh. "It's mostly pictures of the things I've baked, screenshots of recipes that I want to try, and a few apps to keep my mind occupied when I'm trying to fall asleep."

Allie stood, and we continued talking, eventually landing on the topic that had brought her into our lives in the first place —her journey to becoming a grief counselor. She spoke of her late husband with such pride and love, coloring each word as she recounted their last Christmas together. It was Noah's first that he had been truly excited about, and it struck me that rather than focusing on it being their last, Allie was grateful that they had all been together for it. I wondered if I'd reach that point in my own grief for my failed marriage, to be grateful, at the very least, for what it had taught me.

I fought the adrenaline that suddenly flooded my body at the thought of my ex-husband, and, smoothing my dress, I waited for Noah to finish pulling a toy racecar out of his tiny pocket and held my hand out for a high five. "See you soon, little dude. Take care of your mom." My mind was racing and distracted as I hugged Allie goodbye and excused myself. "Let's get together when we have more time to talk," I said, looking around.

Grace's line had dwindled, and she was standing in the corner of the room with the rest of our friends, away from the guests who remained. I caught Cat glancing over at me, but she turned her head away quickly when she saw me looking back.

I can only imagine what that's about.

"I'd like that," I heard Allie say. I looked back at her and smiled, but my mind was ten steps ahead as I squeezed her arm, then walked toward my friends.

"Have you heard anything yet?" I asked Paige as they widened their circle.

She pulled her phone out of her pocket and checked it. "Nothing yet," she said, "but he is going to let us know right away."

"Are you okay, Jenna?" said Grace, rubbing my arm.

"I'm not feeling well," I admitted. "I think I'm going to head out early. I'm sorry, Grace."

"You probably woke the early birds this morning, Jenna. Please don't apologize. I'm so happy that you came, and I can't tell you how many people have asked me about those cupcakes. I wonder if your ears were ringing all night long."

"They were. But I thought it was just from all the sugar I've consumed today. I may have eaten a few of the cupcakes that didn't work out."

Grace threw her head back and her laugh rumbled through

the room. "Go ahead and get some rest, Sugar," she said as she wrapped me in her familiar embrace. "Thank you for everything. I will talk to you in the morning."

"Let me walk you to the door," said Paige.

I said my goodbyes to everyone I knew along our way out, including Allie leaning against a round table, her eyes scanning the back of one of Grace's books.

"It was great chatting with you," I said to her, feeling guilty about how I'd run off on her a few minutes earlier. "Hopefully, I will see you soon. Will you come in and give me an update when you hear back from the committee?"

"I definitely will. And I'm going to check in with you to see if you've heard back from the bank. I'm rooting for you," she said. "And right now, it looks like you have a room full of potential customers."

"From your lips to God's ear," I said, putting my hand out for another fist bump from Noah. I ruffled his curls and then turned and walked toward the exit with Paige.

"I just want to make sure you're doing okay," she said under her breath as we approached the door. "I can't imagine how you're feeling right now, and I just want you to know that I'm here for you. We all are. I will call you as soon as I hear from Ben. I promise."

"Thank you." I swallowed the lump that had been fighting for purchase all day. "I just have to hope that the judge can see through whatever he said to get this deal in the first place. I haven't felt this safe in years, and I'm terrified that it's going to go away just as I start to get my feet under me."

We stepped out into the fading evening sun. "I understand," said Paige as the door closed behind us. "And no matter what, we've all got you. We're not going to let him near you, and from what Ben said, there will be an order of protection in place." She reached out and grabbed the pinky of one of my hands and swayed it back and forth. I hadn't realized how much tension I'd been holding in them until it was suddenly released, and I wondered how Paige always knew exactly what to do to get me out of my head. "Which means that if he does decide to come near you, he's going right back to jail."

I rolled my shoulders and exhaled. "Okay. That makes me feel a little better. I just need to try to relax a little bit before I go to bed. I'm going to take a bath, put my pajamas on, and maybe order a pizza."

"That sounds like a great idea. I'm going to check on you in a little bit."

I was so distracted that I barely noticed her step in for a hug, but I quickly recovered and gave her a half-hearted squeeze.

"I'm sorry," I said, "I just— I'm going to go." I could feel the overwhelm building and really just needed to be on my own. My hands were cold and tingly and my chest was growing tighter by the minute, making it hard to take a full breath. The ones I did manage left on a shaky exhale.

Paige gave me a knowing look and a side hug before walking back inside.

I ran across the street to the pizza place that had moved next to *A Dash of Flair* and ordered a plain cheese to be delivered. I walked back and unlocked the front door that led up to my apartment. After walking through it, I double-checked it was secure before walking up the stairs. I normally made it to the top without getting winded, but by the time I reached my apartment door, my heart was beating wildly against my ribcage. I needed to center myself, and decided that I'd skip a bath. A long, hot shower was the fastest way to get there.

I turned the water on, and while I waited for it to heat up, I stood in front of the mirror again. Anxiety had eaten away at my confidence, but I was still glad I had worn the dress. I needed to learn how to stretch past my boundaries and sit in the discomfort, and my rose-covered rebellion had done the trick that day.

Minutes later, I was standing under the spray of the shower, the words to a new song rippling through my mind as the water rinsed my tension down the drain.

I was just finishing up rinsing my hair when the buzzer sounded. I'd just heard the rumble of my stomach over the running water.

Perfect timing.

As I rushed through the last few steps before I could get out, I took a quick inventory of all the shows I needed to catch up on and chose the one I knew would distract me the most. The buzzer sounded again. I hurried out of the shower and threw on the first pair of sweats I could find and a t-shirt that had seen better days. It would have to do.

The buzzer sounded one more time as I arrived at it, and when I looked at the screen to see who was there, it was black. I made a mental note to mention it to Adam. He had told me it was a second-hand unit, and I didn't expect it to be perfect. I figured it was Paige coming to check on me again.

I pushed the button and said, "I know you're just here for the pizza," hoping a joke with some levity would help dispel the rest of my tension.

A muffled voice came back through the buzzer, "I'm here with your pizza, ma'am. Should I leave it outside the door?"

That was quick.

I buzzed them up and ran back to throw my bathrobe over my clothes. I pulled a $5 bill out of the antique flour jar I kept on the counter. I thought to myself how nice it was to have a place to put mad money from any tips I received at the café. I never would have been able to do so when I lived with Craig. I had tried a few times, but the money I added disappeared before it ever amounted to anything.

Returning to the door, I swung it open.

It was Craig.

24

———

He pushed his way past me and into the apartment. He had a stack of papers in his hand, and he was white hot with rage. His dirty brown hair was in desperate need of a cut and stuck up at every angle as if he'd been dragging a hand through it for hours. He was wearing the same clothes he'd had on when he was arrested. He smelled like an ashtray that had been doused in vinegar and smothered in raw onions and for the briefest of moments I imagined it permeating the fabric of my perfectly appointed couch. My throw pillows. My peace.

His eyes were wild with anger, his face contorted.

I turned and looked for my phone on the kitchen counter, where I always plugged it in when I came home. Not there.

I backed up into the apartment and grabbed my purse hanging on the back of a kitchen chair. "You need to leave, Craig," I said, holding my bag against my chest as I raked my hand through the contents, feeling blindly for my phone.

"What the hell is this, Jenna?" Craig screamed. "This whole thing was supposed to have been cancelled weeks ago and today I get papers that everything is *final* already? Without *my* approval?

My hand continued rummaging around inside, searching desperately as I backed up into the kitchen with every step he took forward. My phone wasn't there.

Craig shook the papers, his clawed hand crumpling the sheets it held. "You think this is the answer? So you can go and do whatever you want with whomever you want? I bet you already have a boyfriend. Is that why you're leaving me? Who is he?"

"I don't have a boyfriend, Craig," I said, my voice shaking, "but I can no longer live with this version of you. You're not the man I married, and even he wasn't right. Things between us have never been healthy. And this is what I need to do. For myself." I knew my words were falling on deaf ears, but I needed to say something to still my racing mind. I needed to work out a way through the situation I had found myself in.

"All you're thinking about is yourself right now, Jenna."

I continued backing up as he grew closer and closer to me. I attempted to put some distance between us by walking backward around to the other side of the small rolling island in the kitchen.

As I reached the other side, he moved quickly toward me, and I turned to search for something to protect myself with. My eyes landed on the knife block in the corner next to the oven, but I knew it was useless. There was no way that I was going to be able to use a weapon on anyone, even if my life depended on it.

I had never been so terrified. My legs felt like jelly, and my breath came in short hitches. My chest seemed unable to allow much more than tiny sips of air. "Craig, you need to leave. You're not supposed to be here," I said, hoping that I could use reason to turn things around.

"*I'm* not supposed to be here?" he said. "*You're* not supposed to be here." He lunged for me, catching the arm closest to him in his grasp. I yanked it away at the same time I tripped over the throw rug and we tumbled to the ground between the sink and the tiny island.

This is it. This is how it ends.

I could hear my pulse pounding in my ears as I squeezed my eyes shut. The pressure of his body crushed me, and then suddenly... the pressure was gone.

My eyes were still squeezed shut, but even as the noise in the room intensified, the pounding ended and was replaced by low grunts and loud shuffling. As I opened my eyes, I was shocked by the sight that greeted me — Craig moving backward through the air, and as his face receded, the faces of all my friends came into view.

Within seconds, Ben had Craig face down on the floor by my feet with a knee in his back as Craig continued screaming obscenities about me and my friends. "You stole my wife! You poisoned her mind and twisted my words. You will all pay for this!"

"The only one who's going to be paying today is you. You *know* you're not supposed to be here, and yet you couldn't help yourself. Now you're going back where you belong, and maybe, just maybe, you can figure out where you messed up and get the help you need." Ben held Craig's hands behind his back with one hand while reaching around to grab his handcuffs. Once he secured Craig's hands, he dragged him up to his feet and spun him around so he was facing away from me, but not before I saw the sneer spread across his face. His mouth opened, and I braced myself for another verbal attack, but the sound of sirens approaching cut him off before he could begin. His mouth snapped shut, and his eyes looked around wildly as the reality of his situation hit home.

Ben dragged a suddenly deflated Craig toward the door. "Time to go, loser," he said as they disappeared through the opening. It didn't sound like he was being very careful about ensuring Craig made every step on the way down. Adam stood holding the camera button down, and from my vantage point, I could see flashing lights on the screen, then several bodies rushing toward the building.

A moment later, Adam released the button and turned to face us. "He's gone."

My friends all moved toward me at the same time, crouching around me in a semicircle, everyone talking at once.

"Jenna. Oh my God. Are you okay? Let me look at you. Did he hurt you? Are you bleeding?" I was still sitting on the floor, with my head in my hands, shaking from head to toe. I couldn't seem to form words.

"Someone grab that blanket," said Sarah. A moment later, warmth enveloped me, and Sarah's face slid into view. "It's okay, Jenna. We're here. He's gone. He's not coming back for a long time. You're safe now," she said. "Take some deep breaths."

I looked up at her; her eyes were wide with fear, but her voice was calm. Cat, Elyse, Paige, and Grace were at eye-level, still as statues other than mouths opening and closing like a fish that can't believe its bad luck.

Adam stood from his squatting position. "Let's get you off the floor and onto the couch." Strong arms lifted me a moment later and led me to the living room. I sank onto the couch cushions that had become a familiar haven and was grateful for their softness.

Grace and Cat dropped down onto the couch on either side of me. "When you're ready, you can tell us what happened, but there's no rush. We just want to make sure you're okay. Did you hit your head?" I didn't think so. I shook my head and realized my neck was a little sore from when he tackled me to the ground. I still could not stop shaking, nor could I speak. It was like my vocal cords were completely seized up.

"Jenna, I'm so sorry," said Paige. "It was my responsibility to keep an eye on news from Ben, and I dropped the ball." She choked out. "I'm so, so sorry." She knelt down in front of me, and tears spilled down her cheeks. Her hands rested on my knees, and I put one of my hands over hers. It was all I could manage to do to comfort her.

Elyse paced back and forth across the living room. "When I heard his voice, I just wanted to—"

"Not now, Elyse," said Cat, cutting her off. "We can talk about all that later. But we need to get Jenna calmed down a little."

"You're right," said Elyse, and immediately stopped pacing. But I could still feel the energy radiating off of her in waves. "I just—"

"We know," said Grace, "we all feel the exact same way."

Cat walked over to the buzzer and pushed the button. We could hear the buzzer sound from outside. She pushed the video button, and the view from the street popped into view. A few moments after she sat back down, the buzzer sounded again, and I jumped, every muscle in my body seizing up with tension.

"I've got it," said Paige, walking over to the buzzer with Cat by her side. "I don't understand how he got in," said Cat. "Is this thing not working?" Cat pushed the camera button again, and the Pizza by the Palms logo came into view.

"I'll just run down and grab that," said Paige, digging her wallet out of her purse. A moment later, she went downstairs, followed by Adam. Cat pushed the button to activate the camera view downstairs several times, and each time, it worked.

"I don't understand this," she said. Adam came into view on the camera just as Paige was taking the pizza from the delivery person. I heard him say, "Is it not working? It was working when I installed it. I tested it myself, to be sure."

"I don't know. It was working a moment ago," said Paige.

"But if he put his finger over this camera, she wouldn't have been able to see him." Adam's finger entered the field of view, and the screen went black.

"Mystery solved," said Grace.

Paige and Adam returned to the apartment, and Paige set the box on the counter. The smell of the pizza I'd looked forward to filled the room, but I had no desire to eat. I had completely lost my appetite and knew my nerves wouldn't allow me to keep food down anyway. I looked at my friends and waved my hand toward it as if to say, help yourself. But they all shook their heads.

"I'm good," said Sarah.

"I can't believe this," said Cat. "It feels so surreal."

Finally, my vocal cords relaxed enough to squeak out, "I can believe it. He always finds a way to ruin a good day. How did you know?" Having spent the rest of my energy on those three short sentences, I leaned forward and put my head in my hands, willing the rest of the world to disappear.

Elyse walked over from the buzzer where she and Adam had been trying to figure out how to keep something like that from happening again. "Ben rushed into the event and told Paige that Craig had been released without his knowledge." I looked up and caught Paige's gaze in my own and saw raw pain there. "Apparently, there had been an escape attempt at the courthouse," she said. "His contact had been pulled away and wasn't able to give me a heads-up until thirty minutes ago. He had been trying to call us all the way here." Tears spilled over, and she swiped them away with the hand that wasn't holding mine. "My phone was on silent in my purse. I must have absentmindedly flicked the switch while we were talking before you left. I feel terrible."

Sarah sat on the other side of me and rubbed my back. "Ben came straight to Grace's event, hoping to find you there. When

Paige told him you had gone home, we quickly gathered the rest of the group."

Adam was having trouble reigning in his anger and pacing across the apartment, but spun around at that point. "I pulled up the feed and saw Craig walking into the building minutes before. We ran all the way here." His voice hitched. "We found the door at the bottom of the stairs unlocked and heard Craig yelling." He trailed off as his eyes slid to the open door.

"We heard a crash as we ran up the stairs," said Cat from the other side of the kitchen counter. She was filling up a glass with water. "I've never been so scared in all my life."

With shaking hands, I took the glass she handed me and tried to swallow enough of it to clear the dust from my mouth.

The ladies all stayed with me for the next hour until I could form words again. When Paige offered to stay with me, I gratefully accepted.

"What about Roxy?" I asked. "You can't leave her alone all night."

"I'll run over to the house right now and pick her up and bring her home with me," said Elyse.

Paige handed Elyse her keys and rattled off her alarm code. "Just be sure to reset it when you leave."

"Of course," said Elyse. "I'll leave now and go pick her up. Anything you need, Jenna, just give me a call."

"We still haven't found her phone, have we?" asked Grace.

Cat had turned my purse inside out, taken all the bedding off my bed, and searched everywhere. We couldn't find it.

"Just call my phone if you need anything," said Paige, "and I'll keep you updated until we find Jenna's phone."

One by one, the women left, leaving me and Paige alone.

"I know you're not okay, and I'm not going to ask, but is there anything that you need from me?"

I shook my head, but I was still not quite able to put cohesive thoughts together. "I really just need to go to bed," I said. "I'm sorry."

"Please don't be sorry, Jenna. You do what you need to do. I will grab a sheet and blanket and be right here on the couch."

I hugged her tightly as she rubbed my back up and down in the same way that my grandmother used to do to soothe me when I would arrive at her house after a particularly bad day with my parents. I wished Gigi was there with me now, but I was grateful for Paige, nonetheless.

"I'll be here for the rest of the night, so don't panic if you hear me moving around when you wake up," she said. "Try to get some rest."

I left her in the living room, putting sheets on the couch. I crawled into my bed, exhausted from the adrenaline coursing through my body for over an hour. My shaking had finally stopped, and although my anxiety was high, I was exhausted and fell asleep within minutes.

25

I slept fitfully all night. The dreams that I had been having of Craig showing up at my door had come true, which only made the dreams even more realistic. After tossing and turning all night, I did manage to get a few solid hours after the break of dawn.

When I woke up, the sun was streaming through the window next to my bed, and I could hear Paige talking in the living room.

"I think she's still asleep," I heard her say. "Oh, are you kidding? Well, that explains it. Okay, alright, yeah, I'll run down right now. I'll see you in a minute."

Curiosity got the best of me. I was suddenly worried that somehow Craig had gotten out of jail, but I couldn't figure out why Paige would be going downstairs. I rolled out of bed and wandered into the living room, slipping my arms into my robe as I walked. Paige had all her bedding folded up in a corner of the couch and was just standing from her chair at the kitchen table.

"How did you sleep?" she asked.

"Meh. Not too bad," I lied, and she allowed it. "What about you?"

"I happen to be exactly the right height to fit perfectly on your couch. So, I slept like a baby," she lied back, and I allowed it.

I wanted to ask who was on the phone, but didn't want to seem nosy. Luckily, she didn't leave me wondering for long.

"So, Cat just called. Allie came by the café this morning."

"Oh, really?"

"Really. She found your phone. In her purse."

"Oh, that makes sense," I said.

"How did it end up in her purse?"

"Noah was playing with it at the book signing, and he must have slipped it in there. And I wasn't thinking straight when I left, so I didn't look for it. I ordered the pizza in person, or I would have realized sooner."

"Well, Cat's got it downstairs, so I'm going to run down and grab it, and I'll be right back."

After Paige left, I took the opportunity to brush my teeth and put some clothes on. I was fully dressed by the time she came back in.

Out of breath at the top of the stairs, as usual, she paused and leaned over, but held her hand out with my phone. "It was ringing on my way here," she said. "I ran as fast as I could. I didn't want to answer it."

I was so grateful to finally have my phone back. I instantly tapped the screen to see who had called, and when I saw the caller ID, my heart pounded inside my chest.

"It was the bank," I said. My eyes were practically bugging out of my head as I looked at Paige. I felt nauseated and sweaty.

"I saw the number," she said. "I didn't want to say anything, but that's why I ran so fast. Well? Go ahead and call them back. I'll wait right here."

"Are you sure you don't have to be anywhere?"

"Nowhere that's as important as this right here."

"Okay," I took a deep breath and let it out slowly, my stomach tied in anxious knots. "Well, here goes," I said.

Paige was perched on the edge of the couch, her hands clasped between her knees, looking up at me. I felt almost like I was back at the talent show at school, my grandma staring up at me from the front row, beaming with pride as I butchered *Stairway to Heaven* on her guitar.

I brought up the last number and pressed the 'Call' button. Kyle picked up on the second ring.

"Hi, Kyle. I believe I just missed a call from you," I said after swallowing what felt like cotton balls that had sprouted from nowhere.

"Hi, Jenna. How are you?" Kyle replied.

"You tell me. I'm a little nervous. It's only been a few days, and you said the longer I had to wait, the better."

Kyle sighed. "I did say that. Well, unfortunately, Jenna, I don't have good news for you today."

My heart sank. "Okay."

Paige was watching my face and could probably see the disappointment written all over it. She got to her feet and stood next to me, rubbing my arm. I was grateful she was there, but I would rather have taken that news alone.

"Did they say why?"

"It's nothing that you've done or haven't done, Jenna, other than you don't have the credit history and your business is unproven. So it's just too great a risk for them. That being said, if this is something that you really want to do, there are other avenues for you. Sometimes, the government provides small business loans, and you would be a great candidate for many of the available grants.

"You seem passionate about the bakery, so I hate for one setback to be the end of your dream. I believe you have a successful idea, but it's hard to convince an underwriter of that when you don't have the history to back you up, or any assets to secure your debt."

"I understand that."

Paige was wandering around the kitchen, straightening things that didn't need straightening, and I knew that I was going to have to tell her everything Kyle said as soon as I hung up, when really I just wanted to crawl back in bed and forget that this week had ever happened.

"Alright, Kyle, well, thank you for calling, and I appreciate your faith in me."

"I'll be keeping an eye on you, Jenna, and I hope you find a way to make this happen. And when you do, I will be first in line. I've heard your cupcakes and croissants mentioned more than once around the bank. I know your bakery would be very popular, but unfortunately, underwriters don't operate on local chatter. They need actual facts and figures." He trailed off, obviously unsure of what else to say. I appreciated his kindness, but at that point, I just wanted to be off the phone.

"It's okay, Kyle. I appreciate you trying. And I will talk to you later."

"Take care, Jenna. Try to have a good day," he said.

As soon as I hung up, Paige ran over to me and wrapped her arms around my waist.

"Oh, Jenna," she said. "I'm so sorry. Talk about kicking you when you're down. Murphy's Law really sucks sometimes."

"It's okay," I said lying to her for the second time that morning, "but I actually would like to just forget about that call for right now. I just don't have the mental capacity to deal with any of this."

"I'm going to text Cat. When I was downstairs, she told me to tell you that she has your shift covered today. She's already pulled some of your backups out of the freezer to put in the bakery case."

When I didn't reply, she set her purse back down on the couch. "Are you sure you don't want me to stay?" she asked.

"No, I just want to be alone. I'm going to go back to bed."

"I can understand that," said Paige. "Well, text me if you need anything. I'm just a phone call away."

"Thank you," I said again. "I appreciate you staying here with me last night and for running down to grab my phone from Cat." I walked her to the door, and as she stood at the top of the stairs in the hallway I could tell she was close to tears.

"I'm fine, Paige, or I will be anyway. I just need a little bit of time to get my mind around everything that's happened in the last eighteen hours."

"Understood," she said. She gave me one more hug and then walked slowly down the stairs, looking over her shoulder at me a few times as she went. When she reached the bottom, she turned and waved with a solemn look on her face.

"Bye, Jenna," she said.

"Bye, Paige. Have a good day."

"You too," she said, and then realized her error. "Er, you know…"

With that, Paige walked outside and closed the door behind her. I went down and locked it then went back up and crawled into bed.

I spent the rest of the day doing exactly what I told Paige I was going to do: wallow in bed. I didn't often spend this much time feeling sorry for myself, but after the events of the night before and the crushing disappointment of that morning, I didn't feel like I had much of a choice. It was time to wallow.

For the most part, I ignored my phone. But I did see some text messages coming in from our group chat:

Grace: Just checking in on you, Jenna. We're here for you.

Elyse: Everything will work out, Jenna.

Cat: Take the next couple days off, Jenna. We're fine here, and you need your rest. You've had a tough week. We're all thinking about you.

Sarah: I know that things look bleak right now, Jenna. But you are so strong. You're one of the strongest people I know. And if anyone deserves good things, it's you. Don't give up on your dreams because of one setback. There are many other ways to fulfill your dreams. And that was just one.

Obviously, Paige had gone down to the café and told Cat about the phone call I had received from the bank, which was fine. I expected it. To be honest, I'd rather she told them than me. I just didn't have much to say to all their positivity. I was feeling pretty negative, and I just wanted to sit in it for a bit.

I didn't know what tomorrow would look like, but I gave myself the day to figure out what was next. Other than the scattering of text messages, my friends mostly left me be. I didn't even get any collect calls from the jail. I wondered if they were blocking him from calling me somehow because of the order of protection. Maybe this would be the last time I needed to deal with being afraid of Craig.

I laid in bed and stared at the ceiling until dinnertime, then got up for a little bit to make myself a batch of pineapple bread pudding because I was feeling a little shaky but wanted something sweet.

By the time the sun rose the next morning, I was dressed and ready to face the day. Nothing made me feel closer to my grandma than baking, so I figured I might as well just go into the café.

PINEAPPLE BREAD PUDDING

10 slices white sandwich bread
½ cup salted butter, melted
5 large eggs
20 ounce can crushed pineapple, drained
1 cup granulated sugar
1 ½ teaspoons vanilla extract

Preheat the oven to 350 degrees.

In a large mixing bowl, whisk together the eggs, sugar, pineapple, vanilla and melted butter.

Tear the bread into chunks and add to the liquid mixture.

Stir gently until fully blended.

Pour the mix into a lightly greased 9x13-inch baking dish.

Bake for 30-35 minutes until the top is golden and the pudding is set (not jiggly).

Remove from the oven and let cool slightly before serving.

26

Friday at the café was a pretty average day. Busy breakfast, busy lunchtime, and then things slowed down around two o'clock. As I started cleaning up the bakery case, which had emptied out again, I heard Cat washing pots and pans in the back.

"There's hollandaise sauce everywhere," she yelled from the kitchen.

"That's a sign of a good day," I said, trying to muster up some enthusiasm. I decided to leave the chairs down for a bit just in case we had some last-minute diners, but it had been pretty slow for the last hour or so. About thirty minutes before closing, I heard the bell ring and turned from where I was wiping down the front of the bakery case to see Adam standing there.

"Hey Jenna," he said.

"Hey, Adam, are you here for lunch?"

"Oh, I just stopped in to see Cat about something. She needed to switch out one of her displays."

"Oh, I didn't know she was having trouble with them again. Go on in the back. She's just getting cleaned up."

"Alright, thanks, Jenna." He walked through the swinging doors behind my counter.

Ten minutes later, the bell rang again, and Grace, Paige, Sarah, and Elyse walked through the door.

"Are you all here for lunch?" I said. "I think she's cleaning up, but I'm sure she'll still make you whatever you want. Go ahead and grab the booth." They walked over and gave me a hug, then headed to the back of the café. They didn't normally hug me before eating lunch, but I supposed that with all other things that had happened that week, they were probably feeling sorry for me. I was fine. Perfectly fine. Everything was fine.

Ten minutes after they walked in, Ben Alcott and Peggy ambled in.

What is Peggy doing here with Ben?

I turned and waved at them, and they smiled and waved in my direction. Ben's head swiveled over to the booth in the back where the rest of my friends were seated, their chatter probably drawing his attention.

Five minutes after they walked in, a red-headed bombshell walked through the door. When her honey-colored eyes swept over me, I wanted to hide under the counter. It was Elizabeth Wells.

"Is Cat here?" she asked, swinging her soft-sided briefcase over her shoulder.

"She's in the back."

"Hey, Elizabeth," I heard Cat yell. "Come on back. I just finished cleaning up."

At three, when we normally close, Cat, Adam, and Elizabeth were still in the back when Uncle Mike and Chris walked through the door. Uncle Mike flashed a smile and a thumbs up at me, put his hand up to his head like a phone, and mouthed, "Call me." I had no idea what was even happening. They ambled over to where the group had gathered around those sitting in the booth.

Moments later, a flash of black hosiery and red heels crossed from the edge of my field of vision. Elizabeth walked past the counter, followed by Adam and Cat. I was starting to put the chairs up on the tables furthest away from the occupied booth.

"Jenna, could you come over here for a minute?" Cat asked.

I turned around and saw all my friends standing in front of the counter. Out of the corner of my eye, I saw Allie and Noah walking up to the door, and for a moment I was sad. We were going to have to disappoint her because Cat was done cleaning in the kitchen. I quickly ran through a list of things I had already baked and set aside for the next day, wondering if any of them would appease little Noah. My sadness turned to confusion when she walked straight over to Cat and smiled.

"I have to say, you've got my curiosity going," I heard her say.

"Alright, what is going on?" I asked, finally putting the pieces together and realizing they didn't match up. I stood frozen in one spot, trying to work out what was happening. Grace, Paige, Sarah, and Elyse had walked over and were standing behind Cat. Uncle Mike and Chris were standing off to the side of them with big smiles on their faces. When I got within a few feet of Cat, Elizabeth stepped forward and handed me a piece of paper.

"Congratulations, Ms. Martinez. I have your lease agreement here for you to sign."

The shock of hearing my maiden name again wore off as the meaning of her words hit home. I was so embarrassed that I prayed for the floor to open up and swallow me whole. "Clearly, there's been some miscommunication," I stumbled. "Unfortunately, my loan was not approved. I'm sorry, I haven't had the heart to tell you yet."

Elizabeth laughed gently and looked at Cat before continuing. "Well, those underwriters are fools, because as it turns out, they just made the biggest mistake of their careers. All it takes is a single flame to spark someone's confidence. And you, Jenna, have enough of those flames to light up the whole block."

I could feel my mouth hanging open, but I couldn't seem to find the physical coordination to close it. I'd never felt so confused in my life. And that was saying a lot. Elizabeth had pulled me closer to the center of the café where everyone was standing. She handed the paper to Cat and said, "Maybe it's best if you're the one to explain it to her."

Cat stood in front of me holding the leasing agreement, and said, "It takes a certain type of person to succeed, Jenna. It takes guts, grit, determination, and heart. I'm sure Elyse has a giant thesaurus at the bookstore to give me more words, but what it mostly comes down to is heart. Every single person standing in this room," she swept her arm around, "have seen your heart, Jenna. We've seen your grit and determination, and guts, and we believe in you. I don't know that I've ever been more heartbroken than I was when Paige told us about the phone call from the bank. No one deserves to feel like that, least of all you.

"I called everyone together, and after a quick phone call to the rest of the board, it was unanimously decided that you would be one of two recipients for our grant next year. I called Elizabeth and told her you'd be signing a lease today, and Grace set up the rest. Peggy got the official paperwork pushed through this morning, and Elizabeth has worked with the landlord to delay the security deposit until January first, when the grant will pay out."

Elizabeth stepped forward and put her hand on my arm. "You have until January first to get the storefront ready for opening day."

"I don't know what to say," I told them as I looked around at the group, whose eyes were waiting expectantly for my reaction. I reached down and drew enough energy to smile at each of them, but I couldn't find the words to accurately convey how I felt. For the second time in a week, I was in shock. But this was the type of shock that tingles with joy instead of paralyzing with fear. The shock you get when everything you've always wanted is right in front of you, waiting for you to say yes. If only I could find the words.

"This is something you still want to do, right?" asked Elizabeth.

"I know this is a surprise," said Cat, "and if you still want to think about it—"

"No," I managed to spit out. "I don't need to think about it. I just don't understand how this all came about."

"There are many people who deserve a second chance at a new beginning, Jenna, and of all the women I've had the pleasure of awarding this grant to, you're one of the most deserving. I want to see you spread your wings and soar. I want to be at your side when you see what all your hard work can do. I want to see you have agency in your future, and that's exactly why this grant exists."

Little Noah began to clap and jump up and down onto his tippy toes. He wasn't sure what he was clapping for, but his enthusiasm was contagious. After a moment, everyone around me was clapping as well.

I could feel my face getting hotter and hotter from all the attention pointed at me, but it was starting to sink in. They were clapping for me. Me. They were clapping for my future. And all of these people, this family who found their way into my life, one by one, were going to be a part of it. They believed in me so much that I had no choice but to believe in myself as well.

"Yes," I said finally. "I want this, and I'm so grateful. I don't really know what to say. Hopefully, I can find the words at some point, but for now, all I can say is thank you," I looked at Cat, "and thank you for believing in me."

"Now we need to find your replacement," said Cat, winking at me and nodding her head to the right, toward where Allie and Noah stood. Allie was busy opening a granola bar for Noah, and when she looked up, all eyes were on her.

"What? Is this okay? If he doesn't get a snack, he gets hangry."

"Oh no, it's fine," said Cat with a laugh. "But I did want to talk to you."

Peggy stepped forward. "And I wanted to talk to you as well."

"You go first, Peggy," said Cat. "You've got the floor."

Peggy turned to Allie. "You have been a member of this community since you were born, and many of us have watched you grow and have been cheering for you from the sidelines for a long time. We see your dedication to your son and commitment to bringing him up in a loving environment, and we know that you want to give him the best life possible."

"Yes," she said, "but what—"

"We give out two grants every year, and I'm honored to be the one to tell you that our committee has chosen you to be the other recipient for next year."

Allie dropped her bag to the floor, and Noah crouched, taking the opportunity to dig for a second snack. Allie looked just as shocked as I had felt a moment before.

"Are you kidding?" she asked. "This is— I—"

"I'm so happy for you," I said, walking over and wrapping my arms around her.

"I don't know what I'm going to tell the restaurant where I work. School is going to take up so much of my time."

"That's where we come in," said Cat. "If they give you any trouble, you can always work here. It'd actually work out great because we're going to need someone to replace Jenna."

"And that lovely preschool you've been looking at is right down the street," I added.

Allie wiped a tear the moment before it dripped from her chin. "This is incredible," she said. "And overwhelming."

"If you need a few days to think about it, take all the time you need. We won't start looking for anyone until we hear from you."

"Yes," she said. "Yes, I would love to work here. All of you are so amazing. I'm just dumbfounded right now. I don't know what to say."

"Just say you'll be here in two weeks to start your training," said Cat. "Jenna will get you up and running before she opens her bakery."

Allie looked at me, her clear eyes brimming with unshed tears. "I can't wait to get started."

"You're in for a wild ride," I said, thinking of all the ways my life had changed for the better since walking through those doors.

"I'll bring a helmet," she said.

OPENING DAY

Six weeks of preparation at the bakery, training Allie at the café, and baking up a storm at home to calm my nerves — and it all came down to one event. Opening night.

The final hours before I needed to be downstairs had slowly ticked down, and it was time to get ready. I'd already showered to wash off the light dusting of flour I always wore home from the bakery, so all that was left to do was get dressed.

I had agonized over which of my new dresses to wear and had finally settled on a knee-length lavender sundress with straps tied at the back of my neck. It gathered at the bust like the one I'd worn to Grace's event, and the high-waisted a-line cut was flattering, especially for someone who enjoyed eating carbs (and lots of them). I slid the dress over my head and turned left, then right to take in the unfamiliar reflection. The tans and whites and browns I'd worn for so long to avoid standing out had been replaced by a sea of colors and patterns. Just seeing them lined up in my closet — ginghams and florals, stripes and polka dots—was a visual reminder of how far I'd come in such a short time.

After slipping on a pair of white sandals and pulling a comb through my dark brown bob, I swiped a pink gloss over my lips and called it good enough. Maybe someday I'd delve into the world of mascaras and eye shadows, but the dress and lip gloss felt like big enough changes for the time being. I still wanted to feel like myself.

My phone dinged with a text message as I swung my tote bag over my shoulder. I reached into my bag to pull it out, and it dinged again before I could swipe it open. I saw the next three messages come in live as I clicked on the Sensational Six group text.

Grace: One hour until your grand opening! You did it!

Cat: It's the first day of the rest of your life, Jenna. I'm so incredibly proud of you. Is it ok if I take all the credit?

That made me laugh because it was the antithesis of Cat's personality to take any credit at all, especially when she deserved it.

Elyse: I hope you made croissants. Also, break a leg and I'll see you soon.

Cat: Please don't break a leg. I can't run the café and your bakery at the same time. I would if I had to, but please try not to break anything.

Paige: Sounds like your next right step needs to be a cautious one. Lol By the way, have you been on Facebook today? A ton of people have marked "Going" on your event tonight!

Sarah: I'm getting home a little late, but I should still be there on time. I will have the kids in tow, so it looks like I'll be putting two sugared-up maniacs to bed later. Any sugar-free options?

I held my phone against my chest and smiled. I had no idea what I had done to deserve this group of women as friends, but somehow, I had found my way into their lives... and stuck.

I reread their messages again, then typed out my reply.

Me: Grace, I can't believe it's only an hour away! I'm headed down now.

Me: Cat, I will happily give you all the credit, especially after I fall down the stairs now that Elyse jinxed me.

Me: Elyse, I made extra croissants just for you.

Me: Paige, I've been too afraid to look. I guess I'll be surprised!

Sarah: Sadly, no sugar-free options, but Auntie Jenna will only slip them three or four fruit tarts on the sly. No worries.

I slipped my phone back into my bag and a nervous giggle bubbled up as I heard the dings of their replies. I'd have to read them later; it was time to go.

I MADE it down the stairs (intact) and out the door, and was greeted by an intense feeling of déjà vu when I saw the line of people waiting on the sidewalk. It looked a lot like Grace's line for her book launch party, except this line was for *my bakery*. If this was what owning a business was going to be like, I was going to have to admit to my friends that they'd been right.

Elyse is going to absolutely eat this up. There's nothing she loves more than being right.

I wound my way through the line, greeting people I knew from the café and book club, and smiling at those I hadn't met yet. There were so many, and the idea that they were lined up to come into my bakery was surreal. As promised, Kyle from the bank was front and center with a smile plastered on his face.

I unlocked the door and went inside, promising they wouldn't have long to wait before closing the door behind me. I was going to have to move up the timeline if any more people arrived. I didn't want my first day in business to result in angry neighbors.

After turning on the lights, I took a moment to soak in everything we had accomplished in such a short amount of time. In six weeks, we had transformed the space from a dark and dreary pizza place into a bright and airy patisserie, complete with white café tables and chairs, yellow and white striped curtains, lavender counters, and of course, exposed and lightly whitewashed brick walls. Uncle Mike had truly lived up to his word. He worked tirelessly on the design until he had it exactly how I wanted it, bringing it flawlessly into existence. The bakery case sparkled. The black and white checkerboard floor was scrubbed and buffed within an inch of its life. The lavender quartz countertops blinked at me, their sparkly bits reflecting the light from the round, yellow and lavender daisy-shaped fixtures that hung from the white beams along the ceiling. They, of course, matched the vinyl window decorations that had been installed the day before.

It was more than I ever dreamt it would be. It was, in a word, breathtaking.

The bell by the front door dinged as I stepped out of the cooler with the first tray of croissants.

"Hello? Jenna?" It was Grace. No one else had a voice like hers.

I popped out of the kitchen as she was stuffing her huge purse behind the counter. "Hi there. I'm just filling the case now. Can you believe that line? I'm going to have to start letting people in early!"

"Let me help you get set up. What else goes in the case? Point me in the right direction and we'll have you open for business in no time." Grace pushed up the sleeves of her lemon-yellow cardigan and led the way into the back.

By the time we carried out the last two trays, Elyse, Cat, Paige, and Sarah were already sitting around one of the café tables polishing silverware.

"Nice touch with these," said Sarah, holding up one of the floral-embossed metal forks.

"Uncle Mike insisted on the real thing," I explained. "He said that even if people ended up throwing out a few here and there, having real silverware would elevate the 'feel' of the bakery. He found those on a restaurant supply site and said he got them for a steal, so he gifted them to me."

Paige laughed and shook her head. "Why am I not surprised? He gifted me a Nespresso machine and about a thousand pods for the retreat."

"Is he looking for any more nieces?" asked Grace. "My coffee pot is on its last legs, and my grandkids have thrown out all but five of my forks."

"I told you to give them plastic utensils, Mom. We are down to using salad forks for every meal at our house as well," said Sarah as she slid the last fork out of her towel and into the tray.

"Well, then what would I complain about?" quipped Grace.

We all turned when the bell rang, and Uncle Mike stepped through the door with Chris. "Hello, hello!" he said as they walked over to the table where we were gathered. "Looking good, Jenna. Did my friends at the boutique set you up or what?"

"They sure did." A week after I bought the first dresses, Sharon stopped at the café to let me know they had picked out 'a few things' for me. When I stopped by after work, they had an entire rack of dresses ready for me to try on, and I left with... several more. "Hopefully, you make a commission over there," I said with a laugh.

Chris pulled out a chair at a neighboring table and began folding the linen napkins stacked on it. "We take care of each other when we can. They've sent quite a bit of business our way."

"This town definitely takes care of its own," said Elyse. Everyone nodded in agreement.

Sarah looked outside and chuckled. "Seems like the line is proving your point."

"Should we let them in soon?" asked Paige, her eyebrows raised in concern.

Uncle Mike looked at me. "Jenna, this is your moment. What do you think? Are you ready?"

"More than ready."

My friends walked me to the door. Uncle Mike held it open as I walked through it, and the rest of the Sensational Six filed out after. I looked out onto the line of people squeezing in to hear what I had to say.

This is a first.

I cleared my throat and reminded myself that I was strong, even when my hands shook. I searched the crowd for a familiar face and found Adam, front and center. "First, I want to thank you all for coming to my grand opening," I began, focusing my attention on him to help quell my anxiety. "This dream has been a long time coming, but, thanks to my friends, a short time in the making. When I began baking with my Grandma Gigi as a young child, I would pretend I was in my own shop, creating one masterpiece after another for my own customers. I would put on my tiny baker's cap and apron and be transported in my imagination to a French patisserie where I baked almond croissants and fruit tarts and spent my life covered in flour.

"Never in my wildest imagination did I believe it would ever come to fruition. I know now that this day was always going to happen. I just needed to believe in my dream," I turned to look at my friends standing behind me in a semicircle, "and have people around me that believed even more than I did."

I reached out and grabbed the satin cord that held the fabric cover over my sign. "Today, I want to thank the people who believed in my dream so hard, that they made me believe in it, too. If it wasn't for everyone standing behind me and all of you coming into the café asking when I was opening my own bakery, I wouldn't be standing here today, thanking you for your part in my dream come true. With that said, I'd like to welcome you all to The Flour Shoppe." I pulled the cord and revealed the beautiful sign my friends had helped me design. It was absolutely gorgeous; even better than the mock-up I'd seen on paper. The Os matched the purple and yellow daisies on the windows and light fixtures, and "Shoppe" was in a lovely script that ended in an e curled around a cupcake. It was divine.

Everyone standing around me broke into applause, and I felt the heat rising from my neck. I fiddled with one of my straps and scanned the crowd again. I saw a curly-headed little boy on top of his mom's shoulders, and he was clapping hard enough for the both of them as Allie held his legs firmly in place. I smiled at her, and when the applause died down, she lifted one hand to accompany her smile with a thumbs up.

I led them all into the bakery, where croissants and fruit tarts, cupcakes and profiteroles waited to be sampled. Elyse stepped behind the register as Grace and Sarah walked the room with trays of pastries followed by Cat and Paige with cups of coffee served in china with daisies that perfectly matched the decor. Uncle Mike had them custom-made in record time. "What good are all these contacts I've made if I can't help my family?" he'd said when he dropped by the bakery the week before. At the time, I'd been dumbfounded by his thoughtfulness, and when I offered to pay him back, he'd laughed. "Consider them an oven-warming gift," he'd quipped once he caught his breath. No one found Uncle Mike more amusing than Uncle Mike.

The rest of the evening was a blur of faces, both familiar and new. Caleb and Peggy came in and cleared out a good portion of the croissants and lavender cupcakes. "For the ladies at the library," she said with a wink.

Caleb bumped her shoulder with his own. "And for the lady at home?"

Peggy looked up at him and pushed a lock of silver hair behind her ear. "Watch it, or I might drop all these cupcakes off there on the way home."

"You wouldn't!" Caleb said in mock horror.

"Try me," Peggy teased.

"These are all for the ladies at the library," Caleb said to me with a twinkle in his eye. "We're so happy for you, Jenna."

Peggy nodded her head as she bit into a croissant. "And us."

Out of the corner of my eye, I saw Adam making his way around the room, chatting with people we'd known our whole lives. Teachers I hadn't seen since elementary school, regulars at the café, friends from book club, and familiar faces I couldn't place came up, offered their congratulations, and promised to stop in with orders for this event or another.

One of the women from Paige's retreat came up and shook my hand, but looked like a fish out of water in the huge crowd. "I'm Diana," she said in a near whisper. She looked to be about my age and could have been Allie's sister with her fine, cornsilk hair, and light blue eyes. "I saw the event on Facebook and had to come and show you my support. I haven't stopped thinking about the breakfasts at the retreat and I've been waiting patiently for you to open." She held up a craft paper bag with my logo across the front. "And now I've got a date with a fruit tart. I just wanted to tell you before I leave how happy I am for you."

I had a feeling that crowds weren't her scene, and I quickly thanked her for coming and gave her a hug. "I'd love to hear about what you're writing."

"Oh, I don't know..." she said, trailing off.

"Or we can just chat about whatever. I'll be here every day but Monday, so just stop in whenever you feel like it, ok?"

She nodded and looked at the bag in her hand, then back to me. "Congratulations again. I'll see you soon then?"

"Looking forward to it."

After Diana walked off, Ben and Paige made their way over. "Coffee? Tea?" she asked, holding up her tray with a smile.

"I think I have enough adrenaline coursing through me to last a lifetime. I may never drink coffee again."

"Trust me, I know exactly what you mean."

Ben laughed and threw his arm over Paige's shoulders. "This one shook like a leaf all night at her ribbon cutting. You'd think she was headed for the gulag."

"Alright, alright," she said, reaching up to weave her fingers through his. "I was taking a *huge* leap of faith. Just like you are right now, Jenna. It's ok to be nervous, but remember who you've got by your side."

"The Sensational Six will not let you fail," said Sarah as she walked up and stood next to Ben.

Cat saw us gathering, walked over, and slipped her arm around my waist. "I'm going to miss you at the café, but I'm so happy you'll be right next door. Where I can keep an eye on you."

"Yet another Cat St. James success story," said Grace, bumping Cat's hip with her own.

"Pssshhh," scoffed Cat. "She's her own success story. I just gave her a push in the right direction."

I heard Elyse's laughter before I saw her come around from behind me, drying her hands on a paper towel from the bathroom. "I think this would classify as a shove, but who am I to judge?"

"Watch it, or you might be next," said Cat with a laugh. Elyse balled up her paper towel and threw it at Cat, hitting her square in the face.

"Two points," she said before bending over to pick it up.

"All in all, a successful event," said Grace, looking around at the people still milling around chatting and lounging at the tables.

I followed her gaze and saw Uncle Mike pointing at the

light fixtures and gesturing toward the walls with a gleam in his eye as he talked to some regulars from the café. Chris stood beside him, beaming with pride. Caleb and Peggy stood by the front door talking to Adam, who must have caught them on the way out.

It was better than I ever could have imagined, and I wished Gigi could have been there to witness my dream coming to fruition. I touched the brooch and felt her standing there with me.

"It's a good life if you don't weaken," I said, echoing my grandma's favorite aphorism.

"Here here," said Paige, raising her cup of coffee, prompting others to raise whatever drinks they held in their hands.

"To Jenna," they said in unison. "...and the Flour Shoppe," added Elyse.

I cringed inwardly at all the direct attention pointed at me, but my gratitude for the people standing in front of me won out. "I wouldn't be here without all of your support," I said as I looked at each of them.

"Hogwash," said Grace. "You were always going to be here. We just helped you get here quicker."

GRADUALLY, the crowd dispersed, and after helping me clean and get set up for the next day, most of the Sensational Six headed home. Everyone but Elyse. She sat at one of the café tables, tapping away on her phone. I dried my hands on my apron, then hung it on a hook next to the kitchen door and headed out to sit with her.

"What's up?" I asked her as I dropped into the chair across from her. Startled, she looked up from her phone, then set it face down on the table in front of her.

"Nothing much," she replied, but her gaze wandered off. Clearly, 'nothing' was something.

I bent my head to try to catch her eye, and she finally made eye contact with me.

"Nothing much, huh?" I waited to see if I could draw her out with silence.

"I just..." she trailed off.

I waited some more.

"...Life doesn't always turn out like we plan, does it?"

Looking around at the evidence of that sentiment, I chuckled. "No, it would seem it's just one surprise after another until we die."

"That's what I'm afraid of."

This was troubling. No one in our circle had a more positive, sunny disposition than Elyse, snarkiness notwithstanding, and her words—and tone—were completely out of character.

"You know you can talk to me," I said. "You know every skeleton in my closet. It's ok to introduce me to a few of your own. I can handle it."

She spun the phone on the table with one finger and leaned back in her chair.

"Drew is traveling so much for work. Sometimes, I can go with him, but I'm needed at the bookstore and can't always drop everything in the blink of an eye."

She paused. I waited.

"I'm bored. I'm lonely. I'm feeling unfulfilled." She sighed. "I know from the outside it looks like I've got it all together..." This brought out a chuckle from both of us. "...but I feel like I'm wilting inside."

"Oh, Elyse. I'm so sorry! I had no idea that's how you've been feeling! Is there anything I can do?"

She stopped spinning her phone and reached across the table to cover my hand with hers. "Having you as a friend has been such a joy. You have the purest heart of anyone I know. No, there's nothing you can do outside of this."

She leaned back again. "I've got a little side hustle going, and Drew found out about it and isn't happy with me. He told Cat, and now I've got two people harping on me about my safety, and I just don't want to hear it anymore."

"Your safety?" I asked, alarmed. "What exactly is this side hustle? Are you moonlighting as a bouncer? Taking up mixed martial arts? What could possibly have them so concerned?"

Elyse sighed again. One more and I was going to have to get her a paper bag to breathe into. "I'll share in time, but for now, I'm trying to figure out what I want to do. I need to fill my time, and I've found a way to do that while doing some good in our community. I'm trying to protect the people who have been wronged."

"Like a vigilante?" I asked, warning bells ringing in my head.

"Not exactly, but close. Anyway, that's all that's going on. Just me filling time and helping out in the community."

I could tell the closet door wasn't going to open any further, so I decided not to push the issue. It was clear she was expecting the same reaction she'd gotten from her husband and best friend.

"I understand. And I'm here if you want to talk about any of this."

"I appreciate that, Jenna. I really do." She stood from the table and picked up her phone, tossing it into her orange backpack, which she then slung over her shoulder. "I'm going to head out. Tonight was a huge success and I'm so incredibly proud of you." She was standing next to me, so I rose to say goodbye. She wrapped me in a bear hug, and as we stood there, swaying back and forth, she whispered, "I'm so grateful to have met you. You're one of the best people I know." Her voice caught at the end, and she quickly dropped her arms and read-justed her bag as she wiped her eyes with the back of her other hand.

We walked to the door together, and as I locked the door behind us, I watched her walk toward her Audi parked outside the bookstore. Her shoulders were slumped, and her feet barely left the ground with each step.

That wasn't the Elyse that I knew, and my stomach squeezed at the thought of my friend suffering in silence and possibly putting herself in danger.

KEEP CHEERING **for Jenna and her friends...**
Find out what Elyse is up to that has Drew and Cat so bent out of shape in book three of Clearwater Dreams.
Pre-order "Not Another Beach Read"!

JOIN THE BOOKS & Buddies reader group on Facebook!

Sign up for Jess Ames' newsletter and get updates when new books and exclusive bonus chapters are released at **JessAmes Author.com**, and be sure to follow @jessamesauthor on Facebook, Instagram, and TikTok!

ABOUT THE AUTHOR

Jess Ames is "Mama" to nine, "Mimi" to four, "friend" to all, and an adequate wife. When she's not writing or editing a book, you can find her hanging out with her husband and kids in "Farmburbia", cooking, golfing, traveling, and of course... reading.

She's knocking on the door of fifty, but has the sense of humor of a twelve year old and the body of a fifty-four-year-old (according to her fitness app).

Jess is living the dream of the little girl who wanted to be a writer when she grew up. They are both still waiting for that moment, so she's writing in the meantime.

ACKNOWLEDGMENTS

First, I need to thank all the wonderful readers who have picked up "Everything You've Ever Known", read it, and asked for more. Your love and encouragement have kept me going through many a 4:00 a.m. editing session, and I wouldn't be here, publishing another book, without your support.

To my kids who all purchased book one, showed up to book signings, told everyone they know to support my career as an author, and continue to support and encourage me every single day. You make me so damn proud!

To G, who gives me the time, space, and peace I need to do what I love. I've never eaten so much pasta in my life, and I appreciate you more than I can ever express. You're my ride or bye until The End. I adore you.

To my parents who read everything first and provide the feedback that helps me improve, I wouldn't be here without your encouragement and love.

To my Grandma and Grandpa Schell who have embodied the spirit of true family and unconditional love. Thank you for every single thing you've done for me, and for pointing out the hard truths, even when I wasn't ready to see them.

To my editor, Amy Scott, who deletes my exclamation points without complaint and never judges me for all my extra "that"s. I appreciate your insight and attention to detail. I'm so lucky to have you on my team!

To my cover designer, Ashley Santoro, who takes my ramblings and turns them into beautiful works of art. As my readers' first impression of my books, your talent is responsible for a good portion of my success.

To all the members of the Women's Fiction Writers Association (WFWA), thank you for answering my dozens of questions with each book. I appreciate the time all of you put into advancing the careers of every member.

To author and eternal writing bestie, Deonna Kay, you've made writing these books so much easier and *way more fun!* I am so grateful for your companionship on this journey.